MURDERS AND METAPHORS

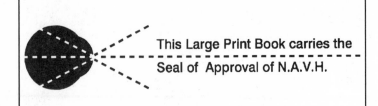

This Large Print Book carries the
Seal of Approval of N.A.V.H.

A MAGICAL BOOKSHOP MYSTERY

MURDERS AND METAPHORS

AMANDA FLOWER

WHEELER PUBLISHING
A part of Gale, a Cengage Company

Farmington Hills, Mich • San Francisco • New York • Waterville, Maine
Meriden, Conn • Mason, Ohio • Chicago

Copyright © 2019 by Amanda Flower.
Wheeler Publishing, a part of Gale, a Cengage Company.

LIBRARY OF CONGRESS CIP DATA ON FILE.
CATALOGUING IN PUBLICATION FOR THIS BOOK
IS AVAILABLE FROM THE LIBRARY OF CONGRESS

ISBN-13: 978-1-4328-6521-4 (softcover alk. paper)

Published in 2019 by arrangement with The Quick Brown Fox & Company LLC

Printed in the United States of America
1 2 3 4 5 6 7 23 22 21 20 19

For My Dear Readers
you brought Violet and
Charming Books back to life

Some people seemed to get all sunshine, and some all shadow . . .

— Louisa May Alcott, *Little Women*

Chapter One

The cold wind bit into my bare cheeks and the tip of my nose as I ran down the snow-covered path like I was being pursued by a pack of wolves. Above my head, the woods' bare tree branches reached toward me like wrinkled arms and were only made eerier by the cold clear sky and the bright white moon. No snow fell tonight; it was far too cold. On my back, I felt the judgmental yellow eyes of hundreds of woodland creatures. As I ran faster, the trees' thin branches tore at the sleeves of my winter coat like bony fingers, imploring me back into the woods. I ran on but couldn't push them away because my glove-covered hands were too busy protecting the precious cargo that I needed to deliver safely home.

There were no wolves chasing me. We didn't have wolves in Cascade Springs, New York, and hadn't in a hundred years. I was being pursued by time itself because, like the white rabbit in *Alice in Wonderland,* I was late, so very late.

As I slipped, tripped, and stumbled through the woods, I took care not to let a single drop of the precious spring water in my watering can escape. I couldn't lose one drop of the water I had collected from the village's mystical springs from which the village had earned its name. I needed every last drop to water my magical birch tree that grew in the middle of Charming Books, the bookshop I ran with my Grandma Daisy.

Two parts of what I just shared would have seriously confused the people who knew me back in grad school: the fact that I was running and the mention of a magical tree. I wasn't athletic, and scholarly types didn't believe in magic outside books. Had they heard me say either statement, they would have immediately concluded that I was just another doctoral student who had succumbed to madness in the pursuit of her PhD. Sometimes I thought they weren't too far off the mark on that one.

The toe of my boot caught a tree root buried in the snow. I stumbled with a yelp but somehow remained upright, and more importantly, the water remained in the watering can. *Don't lose a drop,* I reminded myself. *Not one drop.* I had to go at night to collect the water to avoid the risk of being seen by tourists or villagers. My family had kept this secret about the magical spring waters for the last two hundred years for fear that we would be ridiculed for having magic or even chased from the village. No one knew about the magic other than the Caretakers themselves. I wasn't going to be the one who let it slip, even if that meant collecting water on such a cold night.

Finally, the backyard of the large periwinkle Victorian home that was Charming Books came into view as the path broke through the trees. I dared to increase my speed. I threw open the back gate, dashed up to the back door of the house, and stumbled into a dark mudroom next to the servants' stairs leading to the second floor. A narrow archway in front of me opened into the large kitchen.

"Violet Waverly," Grandma Daisy shouted as I skidded on the soles of my winter boots, which were so encrusted with snow and ice that they had lost their tread. With a yelp, I continued to glide along the kitchen's polished pine floors. "You are late!"

And she was right. I was late, and I had no one to blame but myself. I had been the Caretaker of the shop for six months, and still I seemed to forget my most important responsibility that came with the job: watering the tree.

I ran by my grandmother, not bothering to stop and say hello or even wave. I ran through the kitchen and through the door that led to the main part of the shop.

The over-two-hundred-year-old birch tree grew in the middle of the large room, and even in the middle of winter was decorated with bright white, smooth bark and green leaves. Its trunk divided halfway up its length, and its branches reached for the skylight in the ceiling. A spiral staircase wove around the tree, leading to the children's fairy loft and my apartment on the second floor of the giant house.

Faulkner, the shop crow, perched on his favorite spot, the second branch from the very top, and stared down at me in his best judgy manner. "You're late, you're late for a very important date!"

Apparently I wasn't the only one who had *Alice in Wonderland* in mind on account of my latest scrape. Faulkner had come to my grandmother's back door as a young bird with a broken wing, and when she nursed him back to health, he had just decided to stay. He'd had the run of the shop until my cat and I moved in.

My black-and-white tuxedo cat, Emerson,

was strangely MIA. He was usually the first on the scene when there was any promise of commotion. Emerson loved commotion, loved being in the midst of it, and he certainly loved making it.

A ring of about six inches from the tree to the edge of the hardwood floor circled the birch. I sprinkled the precious water from the watering can into the dirt. When I shook the last drop from the can, I half expected something to happen. But, like always, nothing did. The tree only reacted when it wasn't watered on schedule. Then, it showed its age. The leaves began to brown, and bark began to peel. It seemed that the magical spring water was the only thing that had kept it alive and out of hibernation the last two centuries, and the water had to be straight from the spring. I couldn't collect it beforehand because it seemed to lose its magical properties. I had learned in the short time that I had been Caretaker of the tree and the shop that the magic didn't care what I thought. The magic was much subtler and came from the books themselves.

I gave a sigh of relief. My most important job was done. The tree wouldn't need water for another forty-eight hours. I promised myself and the tree I wouldn't forget again.

"Violet!" my grandmother called from the

kitchen.

I lowered my head like a young child who knew she was about to be scolded. Before I had been the Caretaker of the shop, it had been my grandmother's job after her mother had passed it on to her over fifty years ago. I would have been willing to bet that in all that time, she had never once forgotten to water the tree, and she certainly hadn't ever run through the woods like a crazy person.

"Violet!" my grandmother called again.

"Off with her head!" Faulkner cried from his perch.

I squinted up at the bird. "So not helping."

He fluffed his feathers to appear larger and walked up and down his favorite tree branch, bobbing his head. There's nothing quite as humiliating as a crow making fun of you, even if you are the only one to see it.

"Violet!" Grandma Daisy called a third time. Her tone was a tad more urgent than the last time.

I gave Faulkner one more withering glare, and then I headed to the kitchen. I pushed opened the kitchen door, but Grandma Daisy wasn't there. She was in the neighboring room. The office–slash–storage room had been the dining room back when the original house was built in 1813, just after the Battle of Lake Erie. When my great-grandmother had turned the house into a bookshop, the room had become the warehouse room where we received and sorted the books. I frowned as I saw that the room was in complete disarray again. Books, papers, and files were scattered across the computer desk and over the large dining table in the middle of the room that we used as our sorting station. The boxes that I had packed to ship out had been opened. I had spent most of the night before organizing the space, so it was more than a little heartbreaking to see the havoc my grandmother could wreak on a room in just a few hours' time.

I didn't even know why I bothered. Grandma Daisy and I would never see eye to eye on how things should be organized in the shop. I wanted everything in its place, but Grandma Daisy didn't see that as a need since the books in the shop literally picked their customers themselves.

My seventy-something grandmother paced around the room. Her sleek silver bob that fell just below her ears brushed the side of her face. She wasn't in her usual shop outfit: jeans and a Charming Books sweatshirt. Instead she wore a striking blue 1970s pantsuit complete with bell-bottoms that surely had come compliments of Sadie Cunningham, my friend and the owner of Midcentury Vintage, the local vintage clothing shop just across the street from our bookshop. Around her throat she wore a bedazzled white scarf with snowflakes all over it. Her cat-eye glasses completed her throwback outfit. If I'd tried to pull off that look, people would've thought it was Halloween. But on Grandma Daisy, the ensemble didn't look costume-ish in the least. She looked like a movie star and was ready to go to the book signing we were hosting at a local winery that night.

I decidedly was not ready. I glanced down at my black puffy coat, jeans, and snow boots. I resembled a marshmallow that had been left over the firepit for far too long.

"Did you see this?" Grandma Daisy waved a piece of paper in the air. The white page flapped back and forth. "Did you see it?"

I stood in the doorway. "See what?"

"This!" She shook the paper again. "This!"

"I can't really read it with you flapping it back and forth in front of my face like that."

She blew a wayward hair out of her face and walked over and handed it to me. It was a printout of an email. The subject was

BELINDA PERKINS BOOK SIGNING — REQUIREMENTS.

Dear Charming Books Proprietor: Please provide the following for Belinda's book signing. As you know, she is a *New York Times* bestselling author of six expert-level books about wine and is accustomed to a certain level of service at her events.

I read through the list of requirements. "A certain level of service," I muttered. "Belinda grew up in Cascade Springs. She knows what the village can provide, and this list should have been given to Morton Wineries, not us. I doubt she would even be interested in wine if she hadn't grown up here." There were several wineries in Cascade Springs and dozens in the Niagara region, but Morton Vineyards was one of the finest and had one of the best reputations for ice wine on either side of the American-Canadian border. I was certain that was why Belinda had picked that venue for the event.

I stared at the paper. "Some of these demands are ridiculous. 'Temperature of the room to be seventy-four degrees, not a degree warmer or cooler. This is the temperature at which Belinda is most comfortable and can best engage with her readers.' "

"And security guard," Grandma Daisy said.

"Security guard?"

She nodded. "At the bottom of the email. It says that Belinda would like a security guard present." She shook her head. "Too late for that. I can be security. I'm pretty tough." My grandmother showed me her bicep to prove it.

I looked heavenward. "Why would she need a security guard for a book signing in Cascade Springs? Doesn't that seem odd to you? Does she need protection from a wild fan? I didn't know sommeliers, or nonfiction writers, for that matter, had wild fans. They might be well known in the world of wine, but I doubt the general public cares all that much."

My grandmother shrugged. "I'm glad that we have the opportunity to host the signing, but working with both Belinda's publicist and Morton Vineyards has been a nightmare. I can't wait for this night to be over."

I couldn't have agreed more. The book signing idea had come from Belinda's book publicist. She had said that Belinda wanted to do a signing for her new book about wine tasting in her hometown. Grandma Daisy and I would have happily hosted the event in the shop, but that wasn't good enough.

The publicist had said Belinda wanted the signing at a vineyard, and since Morton Vineyards was the more prestigious in the village, it was a natural fit, and the signing fell at the perfect time for the most foot traffic. It would take place during the Mortons' annual ice wine harvesting party, when they, with the help of friends and other volunteers, harvested the frozen grapes left on the vines for ice wine. What neither the publicist nor Belinda had considered was that Morton Vineyards was just about the last place in the village, if not the planet, that I wanted to go.

I looked up from the paper. "Even if we wanted to, there are several items on here we can't control. Did the Mortons get a copy of this? It will be at their venue."

"I have no idea. Where on earth are we going to find free-trade white chocolate–covered cashews at this hour? Where does she think we live? NYC? We can't just walk to the closest specialty store."

"Yeah, the cashews are a bit of a challenge." I frowned. "I would think that she would have sent this list when the signing was set up."

Grandma Daisy pressed the back of her hand against her forehead like a 1940s movie siren. "We have to do it. We really can't have publishers thinking that we blow off their requests."

I arched an eyebrow. "Publishers can't really be too pushy with us either. They need us to promote their books." I looked at the email more closely. "Besides, I don't think this came from Belinda's publisher at all. The email address says sebastian@bpsommelier.com. I think this came from her assistant or a personal publicist. We'll do our best, but with the signing starting in less than an hour, that's all we can do."

"Touché, my dear granddaughter. I knew that you'd be the one that would talk me off the ledge. We will just do the best we can."

I nodded. "They can't expect anything more. Even if they had given us this list a week ago when we first heard about the signing, we might not have been able to accommodate them. Some of these things — Icelandic spring water — just aren't going to happen. Cascade Springs spring water is just as good if not better, but if we give it to her in a glass, she won't know the difference."

Grandma Daisy clapped her hands. "You are my granddaughter. We think on the same mischievous plane."

I wasn't sure if that was good or bad.

Grandma Daisy took the paper from my hand. "I'll go to the market now." She looked me up and down. "While you change. Then I will come back here to pick you up in my car."

"Why can't we take my car?" I couldn't hide the faint whine in my voice.

She arched a silver eyebrow at me. "Because the number of books that we have to take to the signing will never fit in your Mini Cooper."

"I'll pack up the rest of books while you're gone so we can shove everything into your ancient car when you get back." My grandmother's compact car was over thirty years old. Since she hardly ever drove the car, it was in good condition — if you didn't mind that the driver's side door didn't open and there was no power steering or power locks or windows. Other than that, it was great and had only a little over fifty thousand miles.

She shook her head. "The car isn't that bad."

"Tell that to my knees as I try to climb into the driver's seat from the passenger side door."

Grandma Daisy plucked her large parka

off the desk chair and put it on. "I'm off, my dear. Do not worry. All will be well. The tree is watered. That's the most important thing. The rest will fall into place."

Even before it was confirmed, I knew deep in my heart that she was wrong.

CHAPTER TWO

After my grandmother left, I carried the six cases of Belinda's books to the front door so we could put them in Grandma Daisy's car the moment she returned. Faulkner supervised my work from the tree. As I set the last heavy box on the pile, he bobbed his head. "Some people seemed to get all the sunshine, and some all shadow . . ."

I recognized the quote but couldn't place where I had read or heard it before. Knowing it would come back to me eventually, I shot the crow another irritated glance before running up the spiral staircase to the second floor of the shop. Each step groaned as my foot fell on it.

The house had been built just after the War of 1812 by my ancestress Rosalee Waverly. Rosalee had found herself a widow with a small daughter after the war. She left her hometown and came to Cascade Springs because she had heard of the mystical and healing springs of the Niagara region. Even back then, Cascade Springs was a place where weary travelers stopped to bathe in and drink from the healing waters. When she came upon the village, Rosalee found the birch tree growing, and she knew the spiritualism about birch trees in Native American culture. She built her home around the tree and watered it twice a week with the mystical spring water. The tree lived much longer than it should've — and continued to thrive — and stories of people coming to Rosalee for help and healing were passed down through the family.

The house had gone through a number of remodels in the last two hundred years. The most significant of those was in the 1890s, when the modest home was transformed into a sprawling Queen Anne Victorian. It was my great-grandmother who turned the house into a bookshop, and when she did, the magic evolved just like the house itself. The spring water's essence infused itself into the tree and by extension the books themselves, so that the essence of the water could communicate with the Caretaker of the tree and shop by sending her messages through the books. Yes, it was a lot to take in. I'd seen the evidence of the magic firsthand myself, several times, and I still wasn't entirely sure seeing was believing.

Ever since Rosalee's time, care for the tree had passed directly down a line of women until it landed squarely on my shoulders. Grandma Daisy had been the Caretaker just before me, but I was now the Caretaker of this place, and to be honest, the flying and magical books took some getting used to. At first, all I'd wanted to do was hightail it back to Chicago, the city I had run away to when I fled Cascade Springs just after high school graduation.

At the top of the staircase, I stepped into the fairy woodland–themed children's room. The seats in the space were in the shape of toadstools and overturned logs. Painted fairies peeked out around the sides of bookshelves crafted to appear like limbs of trees. It was my very favorite place in the bookshop, and the place where I had spent most of my time as a child when my mother was so ill. The Caretaker duties should have passed to her, but when she died when I was thirteen, they had skipped a generation and fallen to me. Of course, I'd known nothing of this until I returned to Cascade Springs last summer after twelve years away. The only reason I had come back was because my grandmother claimed to be dying, which was a lie. Grandma Daisy usually got her way, honestly or otherwise. Even with her tricks, I knew her heart was in the right place, and she had known it was time to pass the mantle of being the Caretaker over to me. It didn't matter if I was ready for it or not.

I unlocked the door to my apartment with my key and stepped inside. I glanced around and didn't see my cat Emerson anywhere. I really was starting to become suspicious. The feline was up to something; just what it was remained a mystery. I knew I wouldn't be too happy about it when I found out.

I needed to change before Grandma Daisy returned. The Mortons were fancy and their winery was fancy too. My jeans weren't going to cut it. I settled on black pants, a wine-colored blouse, and a velvet jacket from the 1940s that Sadie had talked me into buying from her shop. It wasn't really my style. Having been a graduate student most of my adult life, my clothing ranged from jeans to T-shirts, but the jacket seemed like the right thing to wear for an evening that would include both indoor and outdoor activities. I knew Sadie would much rather I wear one of the party dresses that she liked to foist on me, but at twenty below zero outside, it was far too cold for that.

I got dressed and wove my long,

strawberry-blonde hair into a loose braid that hung over my right shoulder. To complete the look, I added the black velvet beret that Sadie had also given me. I looked in the mirror feeling quite pleased with myself. The black of the hat and jacket made my eyes look even bluer. I thought Sadie would be pleased too. I just wished she had been going to be there to see my outfit.

Sadie wasn't going to the event at Morton Vineyards. She had recently broken off her engagement to the younger of the Morton sons, Grant, and had no intention of going to the vineyard ever again. Instead, she planned to drown her sorrows in Rocky Road ice cream and Nicholas Sparks movies all weekend.

I envied her plan, although I would be more inclined to watch documentaries about nineteenth-century authors than movies based on Mr. Sparks's novels, but the principle was the same. I'd had my own uncomfortable romantic entanglement with the Morton family that I would much rather forget. The eldest son in the family, Nathan, had been my high school sweetheart. There was a time I had thought we were so much in love that we were destined to be married and live happily ever after. That destiny fell apart when my best friend, Colleen, died our senior year, and to protect himself, Nathan implicated me in her death. Nothing kills a romance faster than accusing your love of murder. As it turned out, Colleen died in a sad accident that was no one's fault, and I forgave Nathan for what he did. I knew his parents had pressured him into putting the blame on me. As you can guess, the elder Mortons weren't my favorite people, and did I mention that Nathan was now the mayor of the village of Cascade Springs?

Despite my personal discomfort, this was a case where business had to come before creature comforts. There would be over three hundred people at the Mortons' party, and that translated into a lot of potential book sales that Charming Books couldn't afford to lose.

I hurried out of my apartment and down the spiral staircase that wrapped around the birch tree. I stopped short at the second step from the bottom. There was a book lying on the step. I knew that the book hadn't been there when I'd gone up the stairs. I bent at the waist. It was a copy of *Little Women.* The quote Faulkner had said earlier came to mind. "Some people seemed to get all sunshine, and some all shadow . . ." I turned to the crow. "Did you know this was going to happen?"

"Try to be good," was his only reply.

I didn't have much time, so I tucked the paperback of *Little Women* into my tote bag to take with me to the vineyard. From learned experience, I had a feeling the shop wanted me to take the book with me. I'd look it over when there was some downtime at the book signing. There must be a reason the shop's essence wanted me to read it. I bit the inside of my lip. I just hoped that it had a good reason and not a much more ominous one.

The ironic aspect of the book the shop was choosing to reveal to me was that I already knew it by heart. I was a PhD candidate at the University of Chicago and was writing my dissertation on the transcendentalists, include Emerson, Thoreau, and Louisa May Alcott's father, Bronson. Louisa was strongly influenced in how she viewed the world by her eccentric father, so I'd read *Little Women* many times before. I suspected I knew the March sisters better than they could even have known themselves had they been real.

Perhaps the shop's magical essence was just reminding me to return to my dissertation edits. I could only hope that it was something as simple as that, but I had learned not to ignore the magical essence when it suggested I read something. I had ignored it in the past, and that had not ended well for me or the shop.

There was a honk from outside Charming Books. Grandma Daisy was back from her scouting expedition to find the last-minute items on Belinda's rider.

I told Faulkner to behave and headed out the door with the first box of books. Faulkner cawed in return. As my grandmother and I loaded the car, I remained concerned that I hadn't seen Emerson in the last few hours, but I didn't have time to look for him now. We had to be at the vineyard in twenty minutes to start setting up for the signing. The Mortons would never forgive us if we were late.

Emerson could take care of himself. That much I knew. He was a resourceful cat, whom I had adopted after his owner suddenly passed away. His previous owner had been my grandmother's boyfriend Benedict Raisin. Benedict had been a village carriage driver and would take Emerson on all his rides. As a result, the tuxie hated to be cooped up in the bookshop. He was always sneaking away into the village. I guessed that's where he was now, although I hated the thought of him being out on such a cold night.

I climbed into the car through the passenger's seat, which was no easy feat in my winter coat. I winced, expecting to hear a tear in my clothes, but somehow I made it into the driver's seat in one piece. Grandma Daisy sat in the passenger's seat after I was settled.

"I think I got close enough to what she needed," my grandmother said unconcernedly.

I decided not to worry about what "close enough" meant. Sometimes being left in the dark was a blessing. "We'd better go. We have just enough time to get there before Mrs. Morton sends out a search party."

My grandmother shook her head. "I strongly doubt that. The search party has already been sent."

On that cheerful note, I stuck my key in the ignition, just as I felt something cold press against the back of my neck. "Ahh!" I screamed and dropped the keys on the floor of the car.

"Meow?" came the questioning response.

"Emerson!" I cried.

Grandma Daisy clicked her tongue. "I have been wondering where he's been hiding all day. Surely not in the cold car all this time."

I placed a hand on my heart, hoping to keep it from beating out of my chest. "I think my life was shortened by two years there."

"Pish," my grandmother said. "Maybe six months, but surely not two years."

The little tuxedo cat hopped over the car's front seat into Grandma Daisy's lap and cocked his head. The left side of his face was white, the right side black. I had always thought his coloring was meant to demonstrate the goodness and mischief sitting on his shoulders. Each side was whispering into his pointed ears. Nine times out of ten, mischief won.

My hand was still on my chest. "Emerson, you can't scare me like that. Do you want to give me a heart attack?"

He meowed in return and then turned to look out the front window of the car. He was ready to go.

That wasn't going to happen.

I shook my finger at him. "No way. You're not going to this event with us. It is completely out of the question."

He twitched his black ears, but that was it. He didn't make any other effort to move.

"Maybe we should just bring him with

us," Grandma Daisy said. "Clearly, he wants to go, and you know if we put him back in the shop, he will only find a way back into the car. I don't know how he does it, but the cat always gets his way."

"Maybe because we are both pushovers."

"Speak for yourself," Grandma Daisy said as if calling her a pushover was the greatest insult I could throw at her. "I'm not a pushover." She stroked the cat's black back as she said this, and he purred.

Uh-huh, I thought, but wisely held my tongue. "Emerson can't come to the winery. I'll take him into the house."

I leaned over my grandmother to open the passenger side door, and the cat jumped into the back. When I tried to reach him in the back of the car, he jumped to the front.

"Violet," my grandmother said. "This is a waste of time. We're going to be late. We can't be late for this signing. There are a lot of book sales on the line."

I groaned, unsure what to do. I didn't have time to take the cat back to the bookshop without being late to set up the signing, and I knew that the Mortons hated tardiness. And even if I took Emerson inside Charming Books, there would be no guarantee he'd stay there, but it was far too cold to leave him in my car while I was at the book signing. My only choice, it seemed, was to take him with me to the signing and hope he stayed out of sight.

"Fine. We will take him." I rubbed my head. "I can't believe I agreed to this." I shook my finger at the cat in Grandma Daisy's lap. "Just keep a low profile at the vineyard. Find a place to hide or something. Don't show yourself to Nathan's mom, okay?"

Emerson curled into a black-and-white ball with a slight smile on his face. I glanced at my grandmother, and she was smiling too. They'd got me, and they'd got me good. I scooped up the car keys and started the engine.

CHAPTER THREE

Emerson was perfectly relaxed during the short drive out of the village proper and into the wine country that surrounded Cascade Springs. This part of the village had some of the most beautiful pieces of land, and even though it was well after sunset, the large full moon gave off enough light for us to see the snow- and ice-laced grapes growing on trellises on either side of the road.

The winery had been in the family for five generations. When Nathan and I dated in high school, I had spent a good amount of time on the twenty-acre winery. It looked exactly the same. There was an expansive two-acre lawn that at the moment was covered with eight inches of snow. The lawn led up to the house, which was a large, white-frame affair built in the Georgian style. All the windows were lit, and the large home/business looked like a bright beacon on the cold, dark night.

A line of cars crawled through the winery's circular driveway into the parking lot on the east side of the house. The party and book signing were to begin in an hour, promptly at nine at night, and it seemed that everyone wanted to arrive early to make sure they had a chance for Belinda Perkins to sign their book. That was good for business. The fact that Grandma Daisy and I were late for the setup was not. Mrs. Morton would not be pleased, of that much I was sure.

At midnight, the signing and the party would end and the cutting of the frozen grapes would begin. The grapes for ice wine were cut late in the night at the coldest hour to ensure the grapes were completely frozen when pressed. The frozen grapes gave off the sweetest juice, which was why ice wine was one of the sweetest dessert wines available.

I knew all of this because I had so often heard Nathan's father drone on and on about the wine-making business when I was a teenager. There had been a time when I could spout off all the facts about making ice wine as well as any of the Mortons, but that time was long past.

I believed now that they had talked so much about it because it had always been their plan for the two boys to take over the family business. When we were young, it hadn't seemed like either Nathan or Grant was interested in doing that, but since then, both sons had fallen in line with their parents' wishes. Nathan had come to the wine business after being elected mayor of the village and Grant after a very public disgrace for committing fraud. If it hadn't been for his family's wealth and political connections, he would have been sitting in prison today instead of hosting this swanky party with his family.

After what seemed like forever, we finally reached the parking lot. "I think we're very late," Grandma Daisy said with Emerson in her arms as I ungracefully climbed out of the passenger side of the car. I wondered if my grandmother would let me pay for the driver's side door to be fixed. I doubted it. The only way to have it done would be in secret. I was seriously considering that as I tumbled out of the car.

I yanked the dolly from the back seat. "Mrs. Morton is not going to be happy." I rolled it to the trunk to stack books.

"It's not the only matter," she said as she hoisted two grocery bags out of the back seat with her free hand. "I got most of the items mentioned on Ms. Perkins' list and just wung it with the rest. It will be good enough."

Wung it, huh? I wasn't so sure about that. The thought of my grandmother winging anything was downright scary; add in the Mortons' involvement and I had a lot to be concerned about.

"What should we do with him?" My grandmother nodded down at the cat.

I wished she had thought about that before she talked me into bringing him with us.

"We can't leave him in the car," Grandma Daisy said. "It's far too cold. He'll freeze."

I held open my giant tote bag. "Put him in here. We'll get him inside and then figure out what to do. This is such a bad idea," I muttered.

My grandmother tucked the cat into my tote bag like he was a baby she was securing into a car seat. He didn't fight her at all, and finally, when he was settled to her satisfaction, she stepped back.

I loaded the last of the books on the dolly and followed Grandma Daisy up the walk toward the big house.

Lights lined the walkway, and a giant ice sculpture of a wine glass and grapes stood just outside the front door. An ice sculptor was in the middle of the yard working on another piece. A number of onlookers stood around him in their winter coats, holding wine glasses in gloved hands. The buzzing of the chainsaw hurt my ears, sounding much louder in the still evening air than it normally would have.

A man in a Morton Vineyards parka directed us toward the back of the house to what I assumed was the help's entrance. I paused in the middle of the walkway before we reached the back door.

The view of the frozen vineyard took my breath away. White twinkle lights lined the edges of the large glass greenhouse and also wrapped around the trees and arboretum that led into the vineyard itself. Battery-powered lanterns dotted the vineyard to guide those helping with the harvest later that night.

I bit the inside of my lip. I had loved helping with the midnight grape harvest. I had known Nathan my entire life, and we had been close friends since childhood. I had been a part of the harvest every year from the time my mother said I was old enough to stay up late to join the team collecting grapes. Nathan had been part of the event since he was able to talk.

When we were thirteen, Nathan took my hand and led me to a dimly lit corner of the vineyard. That's when he kissed me for the first time. It was a sweet and innocent kiss between two mere children, but I thought my feet would never hit the ground again. Two months later my mother died, and my world crashed to the ground. Nathan had been with me through that, my greatest heartache. I couldn't dismiss that.

My grandmother nudged me in the back. "Keep moving, Violet. Camille Morton must be ready to spit nails if we don't have everything set up and ready to go yet."

I grimaced as I thought of how angry Mrs. Morton was sure to be. "Right, right." I had to force myself to move forward. I wasn't ready to face the Morton family. But I straightened my shoulders; this was something I had to do. For my business and for myself.

A man in a dark suit opened the door for us, and he grinned from ear to ear. "Hello, beautiful ladies," he said smoothly. "If you hadn't arrived in the next ten seconds, I believe my mother was going to call your police chief, Violet, and ask him to arrest you for ruining her party."

Grant Morton, Nathan's younger brother by just one year, was as physically different from Nathan as he could be. While Nathan was tall, lean, and blond, Grant was short, with a squat muscular build and a thick mane of dark hair. Both brothers were handsome, but no one would have believed the two were related if they hadn't been told they were.

I ground my teeth. "Chief Rainwater is not *my* police chief."

His dark eyes sparkled. "That is the rumor in the village, but my brother will be very happy to hear that that's not true. The poor fool is still carrying a torch for you. It's tragic to watch." He turned to my grandmother. "It's lovely to see you, Grandma Daisy. My, don't you look sharp in those bell-bottoms. I suppose they were a gem that Sadie found for you. She does have a knack for clothes. I will give her that."

"How kind of you," my grandmother said coolly. Just like me, Grandma Daisy was less than pleased by how Grant had treated Sadie.

He placed his hand to his chest. "Grandma Daisy, please be kind. I would be heartbroken if I thought you were vexed with me."

"I'm sure you will survive, Grant. You have survived much worse," she said primly.

A cloud fell over Grant's eyes, but just as quickly as it came, it cleared. "We had better move you and those books inside before my mother has all our heads. You know how she gets before a big event."

Unfortunately, I knew exactly how Mrs. Camille Morton got before a big event. It wasn't pretty.

Grandma Daisy and I, and I suppose Emerson too, because he was inside my tote bag — being suspiciously well behaved, I might add — followed Grant into the house. We arrived in the wing of the building that housed the giant industrial kitchen and the servant pantries. To make a short-cut to the tasting room, the main room in the winery, Grant led us through the kitchen. The kitchen had all the stainless-steel appliances and amenities of a professional kitchen. The French country style that Mrs. Morton loved was evident in the blue-and-white toile wallpaper, white cabinets, and reclaimed wooden worktable that dominated the left side of the space.

Adrien Dupont was at the large island in the middle of the room using tweezers to add minuscule specks of cilantro to the caviar on spoon-shaped breadsticks. Sweat gathered on his brow, and his large biceps flexed under his chef's jacket while he worked. He set the last piece of cilantro delicately in place and stepped back. "Take them."

A waiter whisked the tray out of the

kitchen with a flourish.

"How are the ramekins of mousse coming?" Adrien asked the room.

"Good, Chef," a young woman said after peeking into the large oven on the wall.

"Bien," he said, and noticed Grandma Daisy and me for the first time. "Violet! Daisy!" he cried in his deep French Canadian voice. "It is so good to see you here."

"I didn't know that Le Crepe Jolie was the one catering the ice wine party," Grandma Daisy said. "But I am glad that you are. That guarantees that the food will be the very best."

"Oh." The large, muscular man blushed. "You are too kind, Daisy."

Le Crepe Jolie was the French café on the Riverwalk that Adrien owned with his wife, Lacey. Lacey and I had been friends in high school, and we had rekindled our friendship after I returned to the village as if I had never been gone.

"Is Lacey here?" I asked, searching the faces in the room. I was surprised not to see her. At times it seemed that she and Adrien were attached at the hip. It was rare to see one of the Duponts without the other. They were the most in-love married couple I had ever met and doted on each other's every whim. Their relationship would have been nauseating to watch if it weren't so genuinely sincere. I would have been lying if I'd said I didn't envy them.

A strange expression crossed the chef's face. "I don't know if she's coming."

I frowned. "That doesn't sound like Lacey. She's always up for a party, and I know she loves catering these big events with you. Is she sick?" I asked.

He shook his head.

"Grandma Daisy, Violet, you can continue this bit of village gossip later," Grant said with a condescending air. "But I really must guide you to the tasting room so that the book signing can begin. I'm sure you don't want to keep the famous author or my mother waiting."

I wrinkled my brow. I wanted to ask Adrien more about what was going on with Lacey. It just wasn't like her to miss a big event that the café was catering. She took pride in being at her husband's side in every aspect of the business. It was why they worked so well together.

"Ladies?" Grant nodded to the kitchen door.

"I'll try to stop by the kitchen later if I get a chance," I told Adrien.

He simply nodded and resumed calling out orders to his sous chefs.

When Grandma Daisy and I stepped out into the hallway, Grant said, "The tasting room is at the end of the hallway. That's where the signing will be. A table is already there waiting for you to set up." He held out his hands. "Please hand me your coats and bags, and I will check them for you."

Grandma Daisy and I struggled out of our heavy coats. Removing them, we both appeared to have instantly lost thirty pounds. Grant took the coats from our hands, and Grandma Daisy's purse. When he reached for my tote bag, I jerked it away from him, and Emerson hissed in protest.

Grant froze. "Did your bag just hiss at me?"

I blinked as innocently as I could. "What an odd question. That's not possible."

Grant looked like he wanted to say more, but I was quicker. "We have some items in her bag that we need for the signing. Pens and things like that. You can never have too many backup pens at a book signing."

He arched his eyebrow. "Last time I checked, pens didn't hiss."

"Come along, Violet," my grandmother said, coming to my aid. "We mustn't waste any more time."

"Right you are, Grandma Daisy." I walked around her and out into the tasting room with my head held high. It wasn't until I got halfway across the expansive room that I realized Emerson's thin black tail was poking out the top of my tote bag.

CHAPTER FOUR

"You're finally here!" Camille Morton said in a loud voice that did nothing to hide her displeasure.

As she spoke, I caught sight of Emerson's tail flicking back and forth out of the corner of my eye, and I quickly shoved it down into the bag. There was a soft hiss in reply that I alone could hear. There was going to be payback from the tuxie for that move. I just didn't know in which form it would come.

Mrs. Morton stood in the middle of the tasting room, which was subtly decorated to look like an ice-crystal wonderland with all the Morton Vineyards wines and merchandise displayed at their best advantage.

The winery's tasting room was expansive. It was at least thirty feet across and had a fourteen-foot ceiling supported by thick cedar beams. Two long bars with shelves of Morton Vineyards wine flanked the opposite wall. There were several large displays

47

throughout the space, but the ice wine display was front and center. Just like outside, ice sculptures made up a large part of the decor.

There were half a dozen people in the room, but certainly not enough to account for the full parking lot outside. I guessed that Mrs. Morton was waiting to let the general public inside the tasting room until everything was absolutely perfect. The only people holding up her perfection now were Grandma Daisy and me.

I scanned the large space to see where the signing would take place. I thought I could avoid Mrs. Morton's reprimands if I got right to the business of unpacking Belinda's books. I finally made out the spot across the room in front of one of the two giant Palladian windows that flanked the front door. But instead of springing into action when I saw the place, I froze, unable to move.

Just next to the table, a blond man in a perfectly cut dark suit stood talking to a familiar-looking woman standing near the front door of the winery. Even with his back to me, I knew who he was. I would have recognized that back anywhere. He tilted his head back as he laughed at whatever the pretty blonde woman had said. I bit the inside of my lip. Nathan Morton still had an effect on me, and I hated it.

Grandma Daisy linked her arm though mine. "Chin up, my girl. It won't be so bad." She made her way toward the table and Nathan, pulling me along with her.

When she reached the table, Grandma Daisy said, "Nathan, it's nice to see you."

"You as well, Grandma Daisy," Nathan said in his best mayoral voice. He nodded at me. "Hello, Violet. Haven't seen you in the bushes much lately."

"It's the time of year. I'd much rather be inside reading," I said, relieved that Nathan was teasing me. Last fall, to avoid seeing him, I had been guilty of hiding in the bushes around the village a time or two. I was glad we could joke about it now. Perhaps Nathan was starting to thaw toward me. I had been getting a chilly reception from him ever since I had begun spending more time with the police chief.

"What's this about bushes?" my grandmother asked.

"You will have to ask Violet about that," Nathan said with a smile. He changed the subject. "I'm very glad that Charming Books could come out and sell Belinda's book for us. It is one part of this evening that I didn't need to worry about because I knew that you would have us covered."

49

Mrs. Morton's heels clicked on the hard-wood floors. "Nathan," she said sharply. "This is not the time for chatter. The doors for the book signing are set to open in five minutes. Violet and Daisy have work to do. You know how important this event is to the winery."

Nathan opened his mouth as if he were going to argue with his mother, but then snapped it closed. He might be the mayor of the village, but it seemed to me that his mother was still very much his boss.

I plastered the friendliest smiled I could muster onto my face. "Hello, Mrs. Morton. Thank you for including Charming Books in this event."

"That was Nathan's doing, not mine," she said.

"Mother," Nathan said.

I took a step back from mother and son. "It will just take Grandma Daisy and me a few minutes to set up."

"And not a second more," she hissed. "There are a lot of people here eager to meet Belinda and have her sign their books."

"Nathan," the blonde I had noticed earlier said. "Are you going to introduce me to the booksellers? I always like to meet the good people who are selling my books."

That's when I recognized the reason the

woman had looked familiar to me. Hers was the face on the back of the book we were selling that night.

I held out my hand to her. "Violet Waverly, and this is my grandmother, Daisy."

"Oh, Daisy and Violet. Both flower names; how quaint is that? I really am back in the tiny village of Cascade Springs. Everything is so fascinating and sweet. It almost makes your teeth ache."

I wrinkled my brow. It was easy to forget that Belinda and Lacey were sisters. They were so different. Even so, it made it only that much stranger that Lacey wasn't at the event tonight.

"We're so pleased that we are your booksellers for tonight. We're expecting great sales."

"And so is my publisher," she said with a smile. She wore a burgundy dress with a train. Her long blonde hair fell down her back, and on her right wrist she wore the largest diamond bracelet I had ever seen. A giant sapphire stone was on the ring finger of her right hand. It caught the light, and the blue stone reflected off the opposite wall. It was clear that Belinda Perkins had done very well for herself since she'd left the village, very well indeed.

When I finally took my eyes off Nathan, I

noticed a slight man, handsome in a polished sort of way, hovering near Belinda. His dark hair was slicked back with product. He wore a suit that was clearly cut to his precise measurements. There was a blue pocket square in the breast pocket of his suit that was the same color blue as the gem on Belinda's hand.

"Belinda," Mrs. Morton cooed. "We can begin the signing in just a moment, just as soon as Charming Books finishes setting up." She shot me a withering glance.

"Everything looks lovely, Camille, just like I wanted it to be. I'm so glad that I am able to finally do a signing in my quaint little hometown. I've lived in New York City for so long and traveled so much. It's nice to come home."

As the two women spoke, Grandma Daisy and I made short work of unpacking the boxes of books. It took only a moment.

Belinda picked up a copy of her book and showed it to Mrs. Morton. "This is my fifth *New York Times* best-selling title, but seeing my book on display never grows old."

Grandma Daisy and I gave each other a look. I didn't think Belinda's comment could have come off as more insincere if she'd tried.

I placed three pens that were to Belinda's

direct specifications in front of where she would be sitting. "Everything is ready."

"Very good." Mrs. Morton checked the gold watch on her wrist. "Not a moment too soon, either." She turned to Nathan. "Can you let the guests inside?"

Nathan nodded before he headed to the large antique wooden door at the front of the room. He didn't even look in my direction. It took all my willpower not to roll my eyes. We weren't twelve anymore.

Belinda took her seat like a queen settling onto her throne. It might have been her dress's train that gave me that impression.

"I hope you were able to find everything on Belinda's list." The man next to me held out his hand to shake mine. "Sebastian Knight. I'm Belinda's fiancé and manager."

I shook his thin hand, which felt small and fragile in mine. "Violet and Daisy Waverly from Charming Books."

Grandma Daisy had a stack of sticky notes in her hand, ready to give them to Belinda's fans for the book signing so she could accurately inscribe their books. "Oh, we most certainly got everything that Belinda might need. You don't need to worry about that." She lifted her cloth bag, which had been hidden by the book table's linen tablecloth.

"White-chocolate cashews?" Sebastian asked.

"That's what I'm calling them," my grandmother replied, and tucked the bag back under the table. I knew that she did this so he wouldn't have the opportunity to double-check her work.

Sebastian scowled.

Belinda smiled at the table. "All those lovely copies of my book. It never gets old to see them. Even hitting the best-seller list is still a treat after all this time."

Right. She'd said something similar to Mrs. Morton only minutes before. The more often she said it, the less sincere it became. I held out my hand. "We're happy to be your bookseller for this event."

She studied me as she shook my hand. "You look familiar."

"You may not remember, but I'm an old friend of your sister Lacey."

She ripped her hand from my grasp. "I don't want Lacey to have anything to do with this event." Her voice was sharp as a knife.

Mrs. Morton bustled in between us. "Belinda, is everything all right? I hope Violet hasn't done something to offend you."

Belinda glared at Camille Morton. "I didn't know that there would be people associated with my sister here at the signing."

Mrs. Morton looked at me accusingly.

I held up my hands in innocence.

Grandma Daisy gave me a quizzical look, but before I could explain, Nathan opened the doors and the signing had begun.

CHAPTER FIVE

An hour into the event, wine and book lovers milled around the tasting room. Despite the grandeur of the winery, most were dressed for warmth, as they would be participating in the midnight grape cutting. No one was costumed as grandly as Belinda in her long gown.

Belinda smiled at the next person who came up to her, holding up a book to be signed. "Would you like me to sign it to you?" she asked.

Grandma Daisy sidled up to me. "It seems to me that Belinda has a little of Jekyll and Hyde in her, doesn't she? Why did she freak out at you just before the signing?" It was the first time my grandmother had had the chance to ask the question because we had been too busy with the long line of customers wanting to buy Belinda's book on wine. Sales had been strong, and I guessed that we had sold well into two hundred books so far.

"Something to do with Lacey," I said out the side of my mouth.

Grandma Daisy raised her brow.

Belinda smiled as she signed the woman's book with a flourish. After the woman walked away holding the book to her chest, Belinda turned to Sebastian. "Whoever purchased the items on my short list, the Icelandic water was especially delicious this time."

I shot my grandmother a look, but she smiled as sweetly as you please. "I told you Cascade Springs water was just as good as that Icelandic stuff," Grandma Daisy said in a low voice only I could hear.

"I believe that it was the bookshop keepers who attended to the list," Sebastian said.

Belinda smiled at Grandma Daisy and me like she hadn't freaked out at all when I'd said I was a friend of Lacey's. "Thank you so much, ladies. Sebastian takes such good care of me." She smiled up at him from her chair. "Don't you, my love?"

He smiled back, but the expression didn't quite meet his eyes.

"Sebastian is a sommelier in his own right. Isn't that true, my love?" she asked as another person stopped in front of her table to have his books signed.

"That must be enjoyable to be in the same business as your fiancée," Grandma Daisy said.

"It is. It is helpful to Belinda that I know the ins and outs of the business. It makes her life easier if I can concentrate on the business end and she can focus on her writing, both the books and the reviews for other publications." Sebastian pressed his lips into a thin smile. "I will never be the star of wine culture like Belinda is. Wineries and restaurants bend over backwards to earn her approval. You may have seen how the Mortons have treated her. There's a reason for that. Every winery in the country wants a favorable review from Belinda Perkins."

"Can you make the book out to Bone and Hearth Vineyards, the winery that you destroyed?"

My head snapped in the new speaker's direction.

A middle-aged man with salt-and-pepper hair stood in front of Belinda with a scowl on his face.

Belinda arched an eyebrow at him. "Are you sure that's what you want me to write?" she asked coolly.

"Yes," the man said. "I think it's best that you were honest for once in something that you write."

Belinda signed the book just like he'd asked her and gave it back to him. "I'm always honest."

He leaned over her. "Someday, your own words are going to come back to haunt you, and then you will be sorry."

Belinda still had the same pleasant smile on her face. "I doubt that."

"We will see about that," the man said, and stalked out of the winery.

"This is like watching a soap opera," Grandma Daisy said.

Sebastian shook his head. "Some people can't take any criticism. Belinda wrote a review about his winery a couple of months ago and just told the truth about their mediocre vintage. The joke's on him, since he bought the book, and she will receive the royalties on it."

At this point in the signing, there were only twenty people left in line waiting for their books to be signed. The very last person in line was a teenager dressed all in black. She had black hair that hung halfway down her back. She was hard to miss. There was something about the girl that was familiar to me. I guessed that she might have been a student at the community college where I was an adjunct professor. But I knew I had never had her in class. Perhaps I had seen her around the campus?

Knowing the end was near, my stomach grumbled in protest that I hadn't tasted any of the desserts or tapas that waiters were carrying around the room on trays. I was looking at the wine with interest too. I wasn't much of a drinker, but I could use a glass after the evening I'd had.

As I scanned the room, I noticed my friend Lacey Dupont standing opposite me holding a copy of Belinda's book to her chest. She stared at her sister with a look that was such a mix of fear and hope that it broke my heart. With no one at the sales table, I started toward her.

My movement must have caught Belinda's attention away from a man's long-winded story while she signed two copies of her book for him. She looked up and locked eyes with Lacey. "Sebastian!" she called.

Her fiancé was immediately at her side.

"Get her out of here," she hissed.

Sebastian started toward Lacey.

I stepped into his path. "What's going on? Is something wrong?"

Belinda jumped out of her seat. "Can't someone please remove that woman?" She waved her hand in Lacey's direction.

I turned. "Belinda, that's your sister."

"I know exactly who it is, and I want her gone," the wine expert snapped. She spun around and glared at Mrs. Morton. "Camille, I would have expected more of you, to follow all my rules to the T. Don't you know the power I have?"

Horror etched on Mrs. Morton's perfectly made-up face. The last thing on earth the refined woman would want was an embarrassing scene at one of her events.

Everyone in the room was staring now. Sebastian made a move to push me aside, but I jumped in his way again. "Belinda, this doesn't make any sense," I said in a low voice, hoping to bring some calm to the situation. "Why would you want your sister to leave?"

"She's no sister of mine," Belinda spat, twisting her pretty face into an ugly mask. "Sebastian, would you do something?"

In the time that we were speaking, Lacey crossed the large room still holding the book to her chest. "Hello, Belinda." Her voice shook. "Can you sign my book?"

Belinda glared at her. "No."

Lacey was crestfallen. "Please, I thought we might take the time to start over while you're here."

Belinda laughed. "Why would I do that? I have no use for you after what you did to our family. How dare you come here and try to ruin this event for me! I always knew that you were jealous of all my success."

Belinda seemed oblivious to the scene she was causing. Lacey looked around the room, and her face was bright red. "Belinda," she began.

"Leave," Belinda shouted back.

"But —"

Belinda pointed at her sister with her bejeweled hand. "You're the reason that I need security while in this village. They told me you wouldn't be here. They promised me you wouldn't be here, but I know how you really are. I knew you would find a way to ruin my life a second time."

"You're my sister, Belinda. I love you despite everything that has gone wrong in the past."

"It is easy for you to love me. I'm not the one who made the wrong choice, now, was I?"

Mrs. Morton and Nathan hurried over to the table.

Nathan took Lacey by the elbow. In a hushed voice, he said, "Lacey, if you and Belinda have some personal issues to settle, now is not the time nor the place."

With tears in her eyes, Lacey nodded and set a pink envelope on the corner of Belinda's table. "I hope you will read the letter."

"Get that away from me," Belinda said.

Nathan scooped up the envelope and shoved it back into Lacey's hand. "Lacey, please."

Lacey spun on her heel and fled from the room. I ran out of the signing after her and caught her in the hallway. "Lacey, wait!"

She turned, and tears ran down her round cheeks. The silver barrettes that she always wore in her light-brown hair hung limply from her head. "I'm fine, Violet. Go back into the party. You're here to work."

"You don't look fine to me. What happened back there? What going on with your sister?"

She removed a folded tissue from her pocket. "You heard her. She's not my sister. I have nothing to say about it."

I blinked. This was nothing like the cheerful and optimistic Lacey I had known all my life.

The kitchen door swung open, and Adrien came out. "Lacey, my love, what has happened? Why are you here? You said that you weren't coming."

She turned toward him and cried into his shoulder.

He lifted her chin. "I am proud of you for

trying. It was very brave of you, *ma chérie.*"

Tears ran down her face. "Just take me home, Adrien." She buried her face into her large husband's muscular shoulder again. "I just want to go home."

"I have to help clean the kitchen, my love, but with our staff, we will make short work of it. Then, yes, we will go home."

There was so much love and tenderness on Adrien's face and in his voice, I knew Lacey would be in the very best hands.

She straightened her shoulders. "I'll help clean up too. The work will do me good. I need something to do with my hands. It will give me time to clear my head. I always think better when my hands are moving." She gave me a watery smile. "Thanks for checking on me, Violet. You are such a good friend to me. I'm so grateful that you've moved back to the village. Stop by the café tomorrow and I will explain. I can't talk about it tonight."

"I will," I promised.

When I returned to the tasting room, Belinda's chair was empty. Sebastian was gone as well. The elder Mortons stood on one side of the room with deep frowns on their faces. They would be looking for someone to blame for the ruined event, and I had a sneaking suspicion that that person was going to be me.

My grandmother consoled the last few people in line who hadn't gotten their books signed by the author. "We're so sorry that the author had to leave early," Grandma Daisy said. "But we will certainly have her sign all of your books. Just leave your name and book with me, and we will take care of it."

My grandmother's speech seemed to appease the small group.

I noticed that the girl with the black hair was no longer in the room. With things back under control, I thought it was a good time to check on Emerson. I had left my tote bag under the signing table, praying that the tuxie would follow my orders and stay there, but when I opened the bag, I realized what a fool I had been. The cat was gone.

CHAPTER SIX

"What's wrong, Violet? How is Lacey?" Grandma Daisy asked.

I chewed on my lower lip. "She's with Adrien, but we have another problem now."

"What's that?" She adjusted her glasses on her nose.

"Emerson is missing." I couldn't keep the worry from my voice.

She wrinkled her nose. "You didn't really think that he would stay in that bag, did you?"

"No," I said, trying my best not to whine. "But I was hoping he would."

She arched an eyebrow at me.

"But what other choice did I have but to bring him inside the winery? I couldn't leave him in the car to freeze." I shook my head. "We should have spent the extra time to take him back to the bookshop."

"Don't worry." She touched my arm. "We will find him."

"We have to," I said.

"We will." She squeezed my arm one more time and then let go.

Nathan came into the room shaking his head and looking like he'd gone three rounds with the village's budget committee.

"Nathan," Mrs. Morton said. "One of the people leaving said they saw a cat run outside. How many times do I have to tell you boys not to let the barn cats into the house? You know how I feel about animals in the building."

My stomach dropped. That wasn't a barn cat. I knew it in my bones.

"What color was the cat?" I asked, inserting myself into their conversation.

She scowled at me. "I believe that he said it was a black-and-white cat. A tuxedo, he called it."

"And where did he see it?" I asked as disinterestedly as I could.

Her frown deepened. "Going out the back door."

Nathan watched me.

"I'll be right back to help pack up the books, Grandma Daisy." I hurried through the room and into the back hall. As I scurried beyond the kitchen, I caught a glimpse of Adrien through the open door, but there was no sign of Lacey.

I brushed past a man I didn't know. I was so focused on finding Emerson, I didn't even look at his face. All I saw were his shiny shoes. He made a faint noise as I forced my way by him.

I ran out the back door without my coat even though it was freezing. I didn't know where Grant had put it, and I didn't have time to look for it. The severe cold took my breath away. I almost went back into the building. I wouldn't do Emerson any good if I froze to death.

A bundled-up woman carrying a battery-powered lantern walked toward the winery. She looked like she was ready to take part in the grape cutting that was to start within the hour. I had to find Emerson before that. All the commotion in the vineyard might scare him away, and he could get lost.

"Did you see a black-and-white cat?" I asked breathlessly.

"Oh, yes," she said. "I tried to catch him, but he ran off into the vineyard. He'll surely freeze if he spends the night out here." She pointed. "He just went that way. Maybe if you hurry, you can catch him." She handed me her lantern.

Taking the lantern, I thanked the woman and ran into the endless rows of grapes.

The path was dark. The only light came

from the dimly lit lantern the woman had given me and the full moon. If it weren't for the bright moonlight, I wouldn't have been able to see but a few inches from the lantern. The grapes were frozen on the vines, glistening in the lantern light like tiny amethysts, and the remaining leaves on the vines were withered.

"Emerson!" I called.

There was no answer.

I began to shiver violently. There was cold and then there was *cold*. This was the real stuff, the kind where you feel like you will never be warm again. The chill seeped into my bones. I thought about Emerson out in this cold, and tears leaked out the corners of my eyes and promptly froze to my cheeks.

"Emerson! Emerson!" I called. Was he hurt? My heart clenched at the thought of losing the little cat. As frustrating as he could be, I loved him dearly and would be devastated if something happened to him.

I called his name again.

And faintly, not far off, a meow answered me.

I stood very still before I took off into the vineyard and held my lantern high. I called again.

A moment later the returning meow came. It was to my left, just down the second row of grapes. Up ahead I saw Emerson standing in the middle of the vineyard row. Relief washed over me. "Emerson, you gave me such a fright. You can't run off like that, especially not on a night like this." I stepped forward, and my relief was short-lived because the little tuxie took off down the row.

I ran after him, forgetting the cold. Thankfully, the moonlight was so bright that his white markings were clear to see.

The cold air burned the inside of my throat and chest as I ran down the long row of grapes. Emerson stood at the end of the row. I slowed my pace as I drew closer to him. I didn't want to give him another reason to take off again. I bent at the waist. "Good kitty, good Emerson."

He just stared at me with his big yellow-green eyes. He didn't move a muscle even when I stood next to him, but I wasn't going to risk letting him stand there any longer, or worse, dart off into the endless rows of grapes. I scooped up the cat. The pink pads of his paws were like ice. I opened my velvet jacket and tucked the little cat inside, close to my heart. I buttoned the jacket up the best I could. The thin garment wasn't warm enough for either of us in this weather. "We need to get you inside and warmed up. Mrs. Morton is going to lose it when she sees me walk into the winery with you, but that can't be helped. It doesn't matter anyway; she already believes that I single-handedly ruined her event." My teeth chattered.

Emerson nestled against me, and I braced my right arm under his body to keep him from falling out the bottom of my jacket. In my left hand, I held my lantern high. Somewhere in the vineyard, I could hear laughter that traveled far on the cold air. The guests were starting to come out into the vineyard to cut the frozen grapes from the vine. Perhaps I would be able to sneak back into the winery with the cat without being noticed. Wishful thinking, but at the moment, it was the best I had.

I turned in the direction of the brightly lit winery, and my foot caught on what I believed to be a vine root. I stumbled forward and wrapped both arms around Emerson to avoid losing the cat again. I dropped the lantern in the process. The glass shattered, but somehow the battery-operated bulb survived the fall. Its yellow light shone on an unmovable woman's face frozen to the ground.

CHAPTER SEVEN

"No, no, no, no. This is not happening. This can't be happening!" I shook my head in denial like a toddler refusing to follow his parent's instructions.

I stared at the face on the ground. Despite my best protests, this was happening, but I was a master of denial and didn't want to believe it. "Please don't be dead. Please don't be dead," I told the woman on the ground.

But my plea went unanswered as I knelt on the ground to take a better look at the woman. Belinda Perkins's unseeing eyes stared back to me in the lantern light. Her once perfectly styled blonde hair was buried in snow, and she was dead, very dead. No amount of asking her to stay alive was going to change that. My biggest indicator was the curved grape-cutting knife sticking out her back.

Her frozen face held a stricken look to it,

as if she couldn't believe that someone would stab her, stab her in the back. An unexpected betrayal.

I jumped to my feet. The soles of my boots slipped on the snow-covered ground that had a sheet of ice underneath. I supported Emerson with my arms, holding him like a baby under my jacket. I needed to call the police, which meant Chief David Rainwater would be there soon. Rainwater would take care of this.

I took two steps back, and my foot caught on something. I expected to hear the shatter of glass because glass from the lantern was everywhere, but it wasn't that. It was a bracelet. I stooped to pick up the piece of jewelry. It was the large diamond bracelet Belinda had been wearing on her right wrist throughout the signing. Was this bracelet the reason she had been killed? Perhaps her attacker had struck her with the intent to steal it. If that was the case, he hadn't done a very good job. I wondered if maybe he had been making his getaway from the murder and dropped the bracelet in the process. I glanced at her hand. The giant sapphire ring was still on her finger. When I looked closer, I saw something else under her hand. A pink envelope. I had missed it before because it blended into the snow.

Belinda's name in Lacey's curvy script was clearly written on it.

I tried to remember. Had Lacey left the letter with Belinda after all? After Belinda refused to take it? Or had Lacey tried to give her the letter again and stabbed her older sister when she didn't take it? No, that couldn't be. I shook my head even though there was no one there to see me do it. Lacey would never do that. Never. I couldn't believe it.

There were voices just a row away from me in the vineyard. I debated grabbing the letter and hiding it. I knew it would be evidence in the murder, but if I left it there, what would that mean for my friend? I was crouching to pick it up when I heard muffled footsteps coming toward me in the snow. I stood up straight and held Emerson closer to me.

Nathan appeared in the moonlight. "Vi, have you completely lost your mind? Why did you run out of the winery like that? And what are you doing out here without your coat? Do you want to freeze to death?"

"Not really." I was shivering so hard my teeth chattered.

Nathan removed his long wool overcoat and wrapped it around me. "Are you holding your cat? Why would you bring your cat to my family's vineyard?" These were all understandable questions, but he didn't give me time to reply.

"I don't know why you do what you do half the time. You can't just run out of my mother's party like that. Do you know how ridiculous you looked? Mother will never —"

"Nathan, just listen to me for a second," I cut him off, not caring what his mother thought of me. To be honest, I already had a good idea what it was.

He blinked at me.

I pointed to the ground.

"What is . . ." he trailed off. Even in the dim light, I could see his face pale. "Is that Belinda?" he whispered.

I nodded and burrowed into his coat. "I'm afraid so." I couldn't take my eyes off the knife sticking out her back. She had been stabbed in the back. Literally. It seemed like such a gruesome way to die. "We need to call Chief Rainwater," I said.

His eyes snapped in my direction. "Rainwater? Is he the one you call when you need rescued?"

I glared at him. "I don't need anyone to rescue me. I was doing just fine handling this until you showed up."

"You were doing a great job freezing to

death," he said.

"Violet! Violet!" my grandmother's voice called through the stillness.

"Over here!" I called.

She bustled down the row of grapes. "Violet! Did you find Emerson?"

"Grandma Daisy, thank goodness you're here!" I grabbed her hand and pulled her back toward the body on the ground.

Grandma Daisy pulled up short. "Oh my! Is that Belinda Perkins in the snow? And is that a knife sticking out of her back? Is she dead?"

"Very," Nathan said.

"We need to call the police," Grandma Daisy said.

"I was just going to go do that when Nathan showed up."

"I'll call then," Grandma Daisy said, starting back toward the winery.

"Wait!" Nathan shouted. "We can't make a scene. Just give me a few minutes to convince all the guests to leave, and then you can call the police. We can't have scandal where the winery is concerned."

"Nathan, that's not going to work," I said.

"Why? It has to work. After they leave, the police can have free rein of the place, but we can't lose our credibility as a safe place."

"A world-class sommelier was just murdered in your vineyard. People are going to know. You can't cover this up, and your parents can't cover this up either, no matter how much they will want to."

Nathan stared at me. I knew that we were both thinking about what had happened twelve years ago. When his parents had made up a lie about me to protect Nathan from getting in trouble with the police when Colleen died. That wasn't going to happen this time. I wouldn't allow it. I wasn't a scared seventeen-year-old girl anymore. They couldn't intimidate me.

"David Rainwater is on the way," Grandma Daisy said. "I just called him from my cell phone while the two of you were arguing. I spoke to him directly to make things go more quickly. He will call up the rest of his people."

Nathan turned and ran back toward the house to warn his parents, I was sure. For some reason, that broke my heart all over again, just like it had when we were seventeen.

"What should we do until he gets here?" I asked.

"What do you think?" my grandmother asked. "Look for clues. There might be something here that will point to her killer."

The pink envelope came to mind, but I

77

shook that thought away. Lacey would never hurt anyone. She could never hurt anyone.

I was about to tell my grandmother that if we searched the area for clues, our boots would leave tracks in the snow, something that Rainwater would most definitely not want. However, I was too late in saying it, as Grandma Daisy was already walking around the body bent at the waist. All she needed was a magnifying glass to complete the look.

"Are you going to help me or what?" my grandmother asked.

I sighed and stared at the snow-covered ground looking for clues too.

"Violet!" a deep male voice cried into the cold air. I immediately recognized Rainwater.

"Over here!" I called back.

The police chief made his way down the row of grapes. He held his flashlight at eye level, and the powerful beam fell directly on my eyes. I threw up my hand to block the glare.

"David, watch where you're pointing that thing. You're blinding both Violet and me. My eyesight isn't what it used to be. I want to keep what I have left." Grandma Daisy had her gloved hand over her cat-eye glasses.

"Sorry," Rainwater muttered as he lowered the light and pointed the beam on the ground.

I blinked away the spots in my eyes. When my vision cleared again, I realized that the police chief stood right in front of me. I blinked a few more times. "Hi" was the best I could say. Chief David Rainwater was a striking man. He was Native American, a member of one of the last tribes in western New York State. He had smooth tawny skin, sharp cheekbones, and a straight nose. His most striking feature, though, was his amber-colored eyes. Sometimes I wasn't convinced he was even a real person. He was too perfect to be a mere mortal.

Those amber eyes bore into me. "Hi? That's all you can say to me? Hi?" he asked.

I moved my gaze and stepped back. Sometimes looking into the police chief's eyes was like being pulled in with a tractor beam. With a dead body literally holding evidence that I knew would incriminate my friend in the murder a few feet behind me, I needed my wits about me. "You got here awfully quick."

"I was in the area doing patrols," he said.

"Grandma Daisy told you what we discovered."

Rainwater turned to my grandmother. "Part of me hoped this was just a ploy to make me come out here and see you. We all know that you can be sneaky when you want to be, Daisy."

Grandma Daisy put the hood up on her coat. She had been the smarter one of the two of us and had taken the time to find her coat, hat, and gloves before she ran outside. Even wearing Nathan's coat, I couldn't stop shivering.

"No prank this time, David. Violet really did find another dead body. She's almost like a bloodhound when it comes to these things."

"Thanks, Grandma," I muttered.

Rainwater looked me up and down. "What's wrong with your arm?"

"My arm?" I asked, fighting another shiver.

"Why are you cradling it like it's broken? Are you hurt? Did you fall?"

"Oh!" I said. "I'm not cradling my arm. That's Emerson."

As if on cue, the little cat poked his head out from the inside of Nathan's coat.

Rainwater looked at the clear night sky as if petitioning it for relief. "What's your cat doing here?" the police chief asked.

"Stowaway," Grandma Daisy said. "He is a tricky little rascal, our Emerson. When he wants to go places, he goes whether you want him to be there or not. If it weren't for him, we might not have found Belinda for hours. He led Violet right to him."

"Your cat has cadaver dog skills?" Rainwater asked.

Officer Clipton appeared behind the police chief. "Sir, what do you want us to do?"

Rainwater's officers had arrived. Clipton was a no-nonsense female officer who didn't know how to take a joke.

"Start securing the scene, and I will get Violet and Daisy's statements."

"What about the statement from the cat?" Clipton asked seriously. "If he's the one who found the body first?"

"I'll do my best," Rainwater replied. He turned back to my grandmother and me. "I do need an account from both of you as to what happened from the beginning."

"Can we talk where it's a little bit warmer?" My teeth chattered. "I'm freezing."

The police chief nodded. "You and Grandma Daisy go back inside the winery. I'll find you when I'm done consulting with my officers here. Do not leave until I have had a chance to talk to both of you."

Against my better judgment, I took one last glance at Belinda. It was a blessing that most of her body was now obscured by the police on the scene. All I could see was the toe of her high-heeled shoe, and the sight of it made me impossibly sad. "Poor Lacey," I murmured. I thought this not only because she'd just lost her older sister, but also because of the letter. I wished I'd had time to grab it and stash it away somewhere. It was far too late for that now.

Grandma Daisy clicked her tongue as we walked back to the winery. "Yes, poor Lacey. That sweet girl has been through enough in her life, and to have this happen after the scene inside the winery. She will be so torn up."

I bit the inside of my lip because I was afraid that scene inside the winery just might have promoted my friend to number-one suspect in her sister's murder.

CHAPTER EIGHT

Grandma Daisy and I entered through the back door of the winery, just as we had arrived hours ago before the signing. I wanted to go straight to the kitchen to talk to Adrien. A large part of me hoped he and Lacey had gone home. It would be even better if Lacey had left the winery before the murder.

My plans were foiled by Grant, who stood in the black-and-white-tiled entryway, effectively blocking my way into the kitchen. "What kind of trouble are you getting into now, Vi?"

"Grant Morton," Grandma Daisy said. "You always seem to be up to mischief, but this is neither the time nor the place. A woman has been killed in your backyard. I suggest that you wipe that smirk off your sanguine face and do some damage control."

Grant frowned. "I know all about that.

My family is having a council of war as we speak. As you can guess, this is a publicity nightmare for the Morton label. Bad timing too, as we were about to go national."

"The winery was going national?" I asked. I couldn't think of any of the wineries in the village that had made that big leap.

He nodded. "That was the plan." He shook his head. "At least before all this happened. We were taking our ice wine to the national market first. My father was going to announce it tonight at the end of the signing." He paused. "You saw how the signing ended."

My grandmother removed her gloves. "Why aren't you helping your parents in this 'council of war,' as you call it?"

"They don't need me," he said bitterly. "They have Nathan. You know my brother, being the good politician that he is, can spin bad news into good news."

"I don't know how even Nathan can spin a woman's death into good news," I said.

"If there is a way to save the national launch, he will do it." Grant frowned. "Just ask my parents."

Grandma Daisy looked Grant up and down. "You should be trying to help instead of complaining about your brother. I swear, neither one of you boys has matured past middle school."

Grant's face flushed red, and I had to bite down hard on the inside of my cheek to stop myself from laughing.

He cleared his throat. "I'll go see if Nathan needs help."

"That's a good man," Grandma Daisy said to his back. After he had gone, she shook her head. "I like to think the best of people, but that boy tries me to my last nerve."

"I'm sure you're not the only one," I said.

"Surely not," my grandmother agreed. "Let's go back into the main room and pack up what books we have left. There aren't many. Belinda had many fans here tonight."

I nodded. "That's what makes this so sad. This was supposed to be her triumphant return to the village, and now she's dead." I bit down on my lip. "I keep thinking about the awful scene with Lacey. It's going to haunt me until I know she's okay."

"I'm sure it will haunt Lacey as well. I'm sure this is *not* how she wanted it to go." She removed her hat and coat and hung them over her arm.

"Can you start packing up on your own. I want to find Lacey if she's still here. She may not know . . ." I trailed off.

"That's a good idea, my dear. Lacey needs

a friend right now. Remember the times that she was there for you. You need to be there for her now." She patted my cheek. "All will be set right. Do not worry." She lowered her hand and made her way down the hall.

After she was gone, I stepped into the kitchen.

The sous chefs and waitstaff who had buzzed around the room when I first arrived were gone. Lacey and Adrien were alone in the kitchen. Adrien was polishing his knives before setting them back into his knife case. Lacey had her head down as she dried wine glasses and put them back into the white overhead cabinet. Her eyes were focused on the task. Her silver barrettes were still falling out of her hair, and when I saw her face, her eyes were red from crying.

I swallowed hard, thinking about the knife sticking out of Belinda's back again. I wished I could forget it. I wished Belinda were still alive.

Adrien smiled at me, showing off his bright white teeth. "Violet, we were wondering if we would see you again before heading home. I have some chocolate-covered strawberries left over. Let me wrap up a little box of them for you and Daisy to take with you."

I smiled. "That's very kind of you, Adrien.

You know I'll eat whatever you make, but chocolate-covered strawberries are my very favorite. Well, second only to your crepes. I love your crepes the most."

He laughed. "You are a good cheerleader for a chef's fragile self-esteem. Like any chef, I am only as good as the last meal I prepared."

"Every meal you make is great, Adrien, so you have nothing to worry about."

"You are too kind." He smiled.

I searched for some way to bring up the topic of Belinda. It was clear that Lacey was upset, but I knew it must be over the argument with her sister, not over her death. Adrien wouldn't be cracking jokes if they knew Belinda was dead. But how did I tell them? And should I let the police chief tell them? I knew what Rainwater would say.

I had finally made up my mind to tell them when Emerson popped his head out of Nathan's coat.

"Sacré bleu!" Adrien cried. "You have your cat with you."

That comment made Lacey turn around and look at me. Her eyes were even more bloodshot than I had first thought and her cheeks were sunken in.

"Why do you have the cat here?" Adrien asked. "I don't think that Camille Morton will be happy to know you brought a cat in the kitchen," he said with a slight chuckle. But his merriment didn't reach his eyes, which kept flitting in the direction of Lacey. Lacey, who usually found joy and amusement in everything, wasn't smiling. That was the most heartbreaking part of all.

"Emerson's trip out to the winery wasn't planned. He was a stowaway. He snuck into my car, and I didn't have time to take him back home." I tucked Emerson further down into the coat.

Adrien shook his head. "You have a very peculiar cat."

Lacey turned back to the cupboard and the wine glasses. I raised my eyebrows at Adrien and nodded at Lacey. He simply shook his head.

"Lacey," I started.

She spun around. There must have been something in the tone of my voice that told her whatever I was about to say was important. "Violet, what's wrong?"

"There's been an accident in the vineyard." The words came out in a rush.

Adrien nodded. "We heard. Camille stopped by the kitchen and asked us to let the waitstaff go home and to pack up. She said that someone fell in the vineyard. I hope there weren't any broken bones. I have always thought that frozen grape cutting was dangerous. It does make the best ice wine, but there are many chances for injury. The knives they use are quite sharp."

I shivered at the mention of knives. "It was more than an accident. I'm sorry, but —"

"Violet," Rainwater's voice interrupted me. "I need to speak with Lacey and Adrien alone."

Lacey looked from Rainwater to me and back again. "What's going on? What happened in the vineyard? What are you doing here, David? You wouldn't be here unless something terrible has happened." She grabbed on to the large kitchen island for support, and immediately Adrien was at her side, holding her up. She seemed to melt into his body as she wrapped her arms around his waist. "Please, someone tell me."

Rainwater looked to me. "Violet, can you go find your grandmother?"

I wanted to stay and be there for Lacey when she heard the news, but Adrien would be enough. He was the person she would want most at a time like this. I nodded and headed out of the room. I paused outside the door. I couldn't seem to make myself walk any further.

There was a wail that stabbed me in the

heart. I wished I could run into the kitchen to comfort my friend, but I knew Chief Rainwater wouldn't allow it. I reminded myself that Lacey and Rainwater were friends and he would be kind to her. But how long would the kindness last after he found the letter? He or one of his officers must have found it by now. I wished I knew what it said.

I turned to walk down the hallway and stepped through the archway that led into the tasting room. I had unfortunate timing, as I ran directly into Camille Morton, who fast-walked in my direction.

She glared at me. "Violet Waverly, do you make it a personal mission of yours to ruin everything good my family has? The frozen grape harvest is the most important and time-honored event at Morton Vineyards, and you ruined it."

Mr. Morton was a few feet behind his wife. He glared at me too. He was a tall, handsome man who looked like an older version of Nathan, with graying at the temples and a few fine lines around his mouth. In all the time I had known him, I had heard him speak only a handful of times, and everything he did say held criticism.

"If it hadn't been for you, we wouldn't be

in this mess. I doubt Lacey Dupont would have come and made that terrible scene if you hadn't been here to support her. I wouldn't be the least bit surprised if it is found out that you put her up to it," Mrs. Morton said.

I blinked at her. "I had no idea that Lacey would be here tonight. I didn't even know Le Crepe Jolie was catering. You're the one who hired Adrien to cater. Lacey works with him. Why wouldn't he bring his wife? How can any of this be my fault?" I asked.

"Please, let us keep our voices down. There are still a few guests left in the tasting room. We can't have any more scenes. I won't allow it," Mr. Morton said in his measured tones.

I glanced over his shoulder and saw that the crowd of guests had greatly dwindled, but there were still a handful sipping ice wine around the ice sculptures. Grandma Daisy had our table packed up and was loading the last remaining box of books onto the dolly. As soon as the police chief gave us permission, we would be able to go home.

Emerson chose that moment to pop his head out of Nathan's coat, and Mrs. Morton screamed. Her right hand covered her chest.

"Is that a cat?" Mr. Morton asked.

"Yes," I said. "He wasn't supposed to be here. I'll take him home just as soon as we can go."

"You need to get that animal out of here right now. I don't allow animals in the winery."

"I understand that," I said. "I'll keep him with me until I leave."

Mrs. Morton grabbed my arm. "I won't let you bring more disgrace on my family or on Nathan. Do you understand me?"

I yanked my arm away from her. "I have nothing to do with what happened here today. I didn't even know Belinda."

"Belinda?" Mr. Morton asked. "What does this have to do with Belinda?"

I stared at them. They didn't know. "Didn't Nathan tell you?"

"He said that someone fell in the vineyard, you found the person first, and you called for help. He's taking care of it. Of course, we worry about a lawsuit, but surely whatever happened isn't our fault, and that's why we ask guests to sign a waiver before they can help with harvesting. If one of them is hurt, it is at their own risk."

I blinked. Nathan had told his parents the same story he had told Lacey and Adrien. Why hadn't he at least told his parents the truth? Maybe I could understand why he wouldn't tell the Duponts, but I didn't know why he'd told Grant and not his parents.

"Do you really think that the police would be here if someone simply fell?"

"The police are here?" Mrs. Morton asked. "I thought the sirens were an ambulance."

Mr. Morton grabbed the sleeve of Nathan's coat again. I slipped out of it and away from him. "You can give that back to your son." I moved Emerson on my shoulder. "And you might want to talk to Nathan again. Chief Rainwater will want to speak with you soon."

"Why is Rainwater here?" Mr. Morton asked.

"Is this another scheme of yours, Violet?" Mrs. Morton narrowed her eyes. "I have heard rumors about you and the police chief."

I stared at the Mortons. Even with everything I knew about them, I couldn't believe how horrible they were being. I might have forgiven them for what had happened twelve years ago, but they most certainly had not forgiven me.

"Camille and Ron?" Rainwater's deep voice asked behind me. "Can I have a moment?"

I turned and was so relieved to see him. I would have taken any excuse in that moment to get away from Nathan's awful parents. Behind the police chief, Adrien shepherded Lacey out the servants' entrance. Lacey was bent at the waist, the hood of her coat covering her face, but even from a distance I heard her heartbreaking sobs.

CHAPTER NINE

I broke free from Rainwater and the Mortons. I had no interest in being there when the police chief told the couple that a woman had been killed on their property.

In the tasting room, I found my grandmother near the signing table.

"We are packed and ready to go." She glanced behind me. "I see the police chief is caught up with the Mortons. I wonder how long that will take. I certainly would like to get home soon. It's past my bedtime."

"Mine too," I agreed. "Maybe he can get our statements tomorrow."

As I said this, Officer Wheaton walked toward us. His back was straight and his gait was purposeful. Like he had received orders and was bound to carry them out. The stocky officer was a few years younger than I was and wore a buzz-cut military hairstyle. No one had ever said so, but I wouldn't have been the least bit surprised if he had been in the service before becoming a cop. Even in the middle of January, he wore a short-sleeved uniform. I assumed that he wore a coat when he went outside, but you never knew with Wheaton. "Since the chief is occupied, I'll be taking your statements," Officer Wheaton said.

Of all the members of the department who could have interviewed us, Wheaton would have been my last choice. The young officer and I hadn't gotten off on the right foot when I moved back to the village, mostly because he had thought my grandmother and I were murderesses, which was a tough way to begin any relationship. I knew the officer waited for the day he caught me breaking the law so he could finally arrest me. He would take much pleasure in that, even if the only infraction was jaywalking.

He held a small notebook in his hand and a pencil in the air, as if he was standing at attention to hear what we had to say. As much as I wanted to wait for Rainwater and give the chief my statement directly, I could see Grandma Daisy was exhausted. If Wheaton misrepresented what I said to Rainwater, I could clear it up with the chief later.

Wheaton looked up from his notes. "Did

anything out of the ordinary happen this evening before the incident?"

The image of the copy of *Little Women* sitting at the bottom of my bag came to mind. Rarely did the books put themselves in my way in the shop unless there was some sort of problem to solve.

"I would say this entire evening was out of the ordinary," Grandma Daisy said. "It's not often that we have a book signing at a winery, and certainly not so late at night." Grandma Daisy went on to describe the evening up until she'd found me with Nathan and Belinda's body. I was only half listening. All I could think about was the novel lying at the bottom of my bag.

"Violet?" Grandma Daisy asked in a way that told me it wasn't the first time she'd said my name to try to get my attention.

I gave my head a little shake.

"Where did you go just now, dear?" my grandmother asked.

"I'm sorry." I forced a laugh. "It has been a long night."

Wheaton appraised me. He wasn't buying it. He turned back to my grandmother. "You didn't mention the argument between Lacey Dupont and the deceased just an hour before Belinda was killed. I find that interesting."

"Why's that?" I asked. "I don't think it was that important. Siblings fight."

"It's important and you know it," he countered. "This murder was a lifetime in the making, and your friend is smack dab in the middle of it all. What do you know about the argument?"

I glanced at Grandma Daisy, and by her expression, I could tell that we agreed on how to handle Wheaton. "We can't add anything to what you already must know."

He scowled. "I would like to hear your accounts without being altered by what others have said."

"Lacey didn't do this." Grandma Daisy glared at him over her cat-eye glasses. "And we aren't going to say anything that makes it look like she did."

Wheaton gave the smallest smile. "I don't remember saying that Lacey Dupont was a suspect."

"Don't play games, Officer Wheaton." My grandmother shook her finger at him. "Your questions are certainly implying it. If David wants to talk to us about this, he can come see us at Charming Books. It's been a long night, and I, for one, am tired, cold, and ready for home." She marched over to the table and picked up her bag. "Violet, are you coming?"

I glanced from Wheaton to my grandmother and back again. "Yes." I hurried over to her.

"Then give me that cat, and you get the dolly, dear."

"I still need to find my coat."

"Here it is," Nathan said, seemingly popping out of thin air. "I was just bringing it to you."

I thanked him but couldn't help but wonder how much of our conversation with Officer Wheaton he had overhead.

Nathan opened his mouth as if he wanted to say something more, but I turned away from him to hand off Emerson to my grandmother. When I turned back again, he was gone.

I shivered from the chill I had caught outside. I couldn't wait to return to my little apartment over Charming Books and burrow under my bed covers and sleep, but I knew that was a long way off. I had to find out why the shop's essence had been pushing me in the direction of *Little Women*. I knew it must be related to Belinda's murder. I just didn't know how. Reading was the only way to know.

Grandma Daisy, Emerson, and I left the winery through the back door. Out in the vineyards, large spotlights had been positioned around the area where I'd found Belinda's body. Again, the image of the knife came to me. It seemed to be such a cruel weapon. Certainly a convenient one with the grape cutting that night, but not an easy weapon to stab a person in the back with. Grape-cutting knives had a curved blade for cutting the grapes vines more easily. It would have required a great deal of force and anger, rage even. Who could have hated Belinda Perkins that much? The man from Bone and Hearth Vineyards? Had anyone told Rainwater about him? Grandma Daisy and I hadn't thought to mention him during our statements. I made a mental note to tell him about it at first opportunity.

Officers and crime scene techs moved back and forth from the scene. Chief Rainwater was somewhere in there among them. I wanted desperately to know what he had said to Lacey and Adrien in the kitchen.

"Violet, dear, let's hurry. It's too cold to drag our feet," Grandma Daisy said.

I followed her to the parking lot, and the drive back to the village was short. Grandma Daisy was uncharacteristically quiet, which I took to mean that she was extremely tired. It was after two in the morning at that point, and I was exhausted too.

I dropped my grandmother off at her

house a couple of streets over from Charming Books. As soon as Emerson and I walked through the front door of the bookshop, Faulkner cawed and puffed his wings. He perched on his favorite spot, the second branch from the top of the birch tree, and wasn't happy we'd woken him up.

"We shouldn't disturb his beauty rest," I whispered to Emerson before letting the cat jump out of my arms.

The crow cawed again, so I knew he had heard me. Emerson ran over to the foot of the tree and stared up at the large black bird. I could almost read his thought. "Someday, I'll catch you. Someday."

Personally, I hoped that that someday never came. I was fond of Faulkner even if he was a little bossy.

I removed my coat and hung it on the coat tree at the front of the shop. I didn't put the shop lights on to guide my way. There was enough ambient light coming in from the skylight above the tree and from the gas lampposts on the street glowing through the front window.

I slipped out of my snow boots and wished for summer. It was such a production to come and go in the winter. There was so much to put on and off every time you stepped through a door. I would much rather have just curled up in a cozy spot in the shop all winter with a book. That was the only reasonable way to survive the cold, dark months.

Emerson seemed to have forgotten his goal to reach the crow, because he patiently waited for me at the foot of the spiral staircase like he always did when it was time to go to bed.

Slowly, I followed the stairs around the tree trunk. Emerson galloped up ahead of me, looking back every few leaps to make sure I was still there. Finally, I reached the children's loft and shuffled to my apartment door. I couldn't remember the last time I had been so tired.

I opened the apartment door, and Emerson slid around my ankles and made a beeline for the bedroom. He really must be tired, I thought. Usually the mischievous cat wasn't so enthused about bedtime, but it was late. I needed to grab a few hours' sleep before it was time to get up and open the shop for another day of business. Thankfully, I taught only twice a week at the community college where I was an adjunct English professor, and tomorrow was an off day for me.

I flicked on the light in the bedroom and found Emerson sitting in the middle of my bed. His yellow eyes sparkled with mischief. There was a good chance he was going to keep me up half the night by walking on my head and making a general nuisance of himself.

It wasn't until I sat down next to him on the plush comforter that I realized why he wore such a smug expression. He'd led me to something, a book, *Little Women* to be precise. The novel sat in the middle of my bed as if I had been reading it and left it there that very morning.

But that's not what happened. I hadn't been reading the book, and I hadn't put it there. It wasn't the same edition that was on the bottom of my tote, which was most assuredly covered with cat fur after Emerson's trip around the winery in the same tote bag.

When I saw the copy of the book, it left no doubt in my mind that the shop's essence somehow, some way, had known that Belinda was going to be killed that night. The shop had warned me the best it could by giving me a book. Only I didn't understand the signs and didn't even know how I could have understood them.

Even though it was a novel I had read before, I had to read it again, of course. That's what the shop wanted me to do. I lay back on my bed and opened to the first page. " 'Christmas won't be Christmas without any presents.' " The March girls were in their little home preparing for Christmas with very little money. Their mother worked all day to support them. The two eldest girls, Meg and Jo, worked too. Their father was away as a chaplain for the Union Army in the Civil War. Despite all that, they were simple, normal girls complaining about a Christmas with no gifts like any child would. That had been Louisa May Alcott's gift to children's literature: relatability to real children and real people. It's why she stood the test of time.

But as my tired eyes read, the back of my mind was thinking of another set of sisters. Lacey had had three sisters. Belinda was the oldest, then Lacey, and then the two younger girls. It couldn't have been a coincidence.

Four March girls. Four Perkins girls. One March girl dead. One Perkins girl dead. The shop's essence was being a little more direct than usual.

CHAPTER TEN

I read for another hour, but it got to the point that the words on the page blurred and I knew that I had to sleep. I wouldn't be able to make head or tails of what the shop was trying to tell me if I was too tired to think.

Even as desperate as I was for sleep, it eluded me at every turn. My thoughts were jumbled with Belinda, Lacey, *Little Women,* and the murder. Families were complicated and mine was no exception, even though as far as anyone else knew, my family consisted of my grandmother and me; that was it. I was the only who knew that wasn't true. There was another potential member of my family. I just didn't know if I would accept him as such.

Just three months ago, Fenimore James, a traveling troubadour, had stopped me outside my shop, claiming to be my father. I would have dismissed his claim if he hadn't had a letter written in my mother's hand addressed to him. He gave me the letter as his proof. I read it only once, but that was enough. It was sitting at the bottom of my sock drawer, and that's where it was going to stay until I could afford the energy to deal with him.

Until three months ago, I had never had a father. My mother had never revealed who he was, and my grandmother didn't know. My mother had been very private about her romance with Fenimore because she knew she would one day be the Caretaker of Charming Books and the tree, and she knew that she would one day be alone. That was the fate of all the Waverly women who cared for the tree. At least that had been the pattern. I didn't let my mind dwell too long on the fact that it would most likely be my fate as well.

I must have fallen asleep at some point, because the next morning, I woke up to my cell phone ringing. I groaned. It was still dark outside, so I knew it wasn't my grandmother calling me to open the shop. I almost ignored the call, and then everything that had happened the night before came back at me at a rush. I rolled over and snatched the phone from my nightstand, expecting it to be Lacey or perhaps Chief

Rainwater. It was neither. It was Sadie. As much as I loved my friend, I almost didn't answer it. I knew that she must have been calling in hopes of getting a report as to everything that had happened at the book signing last night. I was still processing what happened. I didn't want to talk about it.

However, just before the call clicked over to voicemail, I answered. " 'Lo."

"Violet, what took you so long to answer? You honestly had me worried that something might have happened to you. I was about to call David and tell him to break into Charming Books to see if you had been kidnapped or something."

I grimaced at how Chief Rainwater would react if he was called to my shop on a false alarm. Not good.

"Good morning, Sadie," I croaked. My throat was dry from the bookshop's old furnace running all night.

"Are you okay?" she asked. "You sound funny."

I grabbed my bottle of water off the nightstand and took a swig. "I'm fine. Why are you calling so early?"

"Why do you think?" she demanded. "I heard about what happened at the book signing last night. I stopped by Le Crepe Jolie this morning, and everyone was buzzing about it. Danielle said it was all anyone could talk about, and because Belinda was Lacey's sister, she had been deflecting questions about Lacey all morning."

Danielle worked as a waitress for the café. She also happened to be Chief Rainwater's younger sister. She and her adorable five-year-old daughter Aster had moved in with the police chief after she went through a very contentious divorce. I knew Rainwater would allow her to live there as long as it took her to get back on her feet. He also adored his niece, and I knew he liked having her around.

I set the water bottle back on the nightstand. There was a slight thud on the end of the bed near my feet. I peered in that direction and saw that Emerson had decided to join me. He walked up the length of my body and lay on my chest. I raised my eyebrows at the little tuxie. This wasn't typical Emerson behavior. He was a sweet and loving cat, but he most certainly wasn't a lap cat. He had a need to roam. "What about Lacey? What was Lacey saying?"

"I don't even know if she was there. I didn't see her, and Danielle was playing interference so much, I doubt she would tell me." There was a pause. "But of course, she wouldn't be there; it was her sister that died. Who could go to work after something like that?"

"Did you see Adrien?" I rubbed my eyes with my free hand. My eyes felt grainy and tired. Coffee was the only way I would have any chance of survival that morning.

"No," Sadie said. "But he could be in the back. A lot of times when I run through the café for my morning coffee, he is in the kitchen. Usually Lacey is the one that gives me my coffee to go. She always knows that I'm coming in. I hope she's all right. I wanted to ask Danielle more about her, but I didn't want to be like all those other gossips from the village, running to Le Crepe Jolie with some hopes of more news."

"You couldn't be farther from a gossip if you tried," I said, meaning it. Sadie Cunningham was sweet, actually the sweetest person I had ever met. In all the time I had known her, I had never seen her so much as speak a cross word about anyone, including her good-for-nothing ex-fiancé Grant Morton. Sadie was one of the few people in the village, other than Grant's own mother, who had a nice word to say about Grant, and he'd broken her heart. That said a lot about Sadie's sweetness. I, on the other hand, was not nearly as nice and could think of a whole slew of unkind things to say about the younger of the Morton brothers.

"I need to talk to you about this," Sadie said. "We have to help Lacey. I'm just not sure how we can do it. I'm not sure what an appropriate reaction is when someone's family member is murdered. It's just so unexpected. It's hard to know how to react."

"She just needs her friends now." Emerson head-butted my arm. I patted his head. "I should be in the shop most of the day. You can stop by anytime. It's cold out, so I expect business to be slow."

"I can't wait until you open your shop for the day. I need to talk to you now. I'm already at Midcentury Vintage. I'll be over in two minutes."

"Sadie," I groaned. "I was up until three in the morning. Can I talk to you in two hours?"

"I have coffee from Le Crepe Jolie. One with a lot of cream and sugar, just how you like it."

I groaned again. She might as well have wafted the coffee right under my nose. Le Crepe Jolie made the very best coffee on their French press, and they always loaded mine up with plenty of sugar and cream. Adrien constantly teased me because my cup of coffee was the smallest portion of the beverage.

"And beignets," she said. "Fresh from Le Crepe Jolie."

Argh. She knew my weakness for all things sugar, and to add fried dough to that was just cruel.

"Okay, fine," I said when she slapped doughnuts on the table. "Give me five minutes."

Sadie laughed and ended the called.

I sat up in bed and found myself surrounded by books and notes. This time *Little Women* wasn't among them. After not being able to sleep for so long, I had started to study to defend my dissertation. I wouldn't travel back to the University of Chicago to defend in person until May, but I wasn't one to leave schoolwork to the last minute. I never had been, and especially wasn't now when I was so close to the finish.

The interesting thing about reading my dissertation again was that the topic, the transcendental writers, reminded me that Louisa May Alcott's philosopher father had been a staunch transcendentalist and close friend of Ralph Waldo Emerson. Emerson even gave the Alcotts money from time to time because the family was so poor and once hired Louisa to teach his own children. It seemed that even when I was trying to pay attention to my own studies, the shop's essence still got its point across. I only wished it would be just a little clearer as to what that point was.

I knew that Sadie would make good on her threat of two minutes. Midcentury Vintage was just across the street from Charming Books. I rolled out of bed and threw a hoodie over my pajamas.

I spotted Emerson, who now lay lion style in the middle of the unmade bed.

"Sadie is coming."

He stood up and followed me. Sometimes he behaved much more like a dog than a cat.

I hadn't even made it to the top of the stairs when the front doorbell rang. Faulkner cried from his tree, "Who dare disturb my rest?" Emerson batted at the tree limb that he could reach, and the crow shook his beak at him. "Be gone!"

This only made Emerson whack at the branch harder.

The doorbell rang again, and I pressed a hand to the side of my head. I was decidedly not a morning person, so it was far too early for me to referee a crow-versus-cat argument. I continued down the spiral staircase, taking care in my haste not to trip and fall to the bottom. The original hardwood floor of Charming Books was not a forgiving place to land.

The doorbell rang a third time before I reached the door and threw it open.

"Violet!" Sadie cried. "What took you so long? I thought something had happened to you. I almost called Chief Rainwater again."

The right side of my head where the ache had begun started to throb. "Sadie, I was all the way upstairs in my apartment. It took me a couple of minutes to get moving."

"I'm so sorry about that. Did I wake you up when I called?" Her voice was anxious.

"Yes." When she looked like she might cry, I added quickly, "It's fine. I'm glad you woke me. I have a lot to do today. I might have slept for another two hours at least." Just saying that I might have slept for another two hours sounded like a dream come true. I could hear my bed calling my name from the second floor.

"Coffee?" She held out one of the cups to me.

"Yes, please," I said, barely above a whimper. I took the cup and held it under my nose. I knew Adrien had made it just how I liked it.

Sadie bustled into the room with the second coffee in her hand and a white bakery box with a Le Crepe Jolie signature sticker on it taping it closed. My mouth watered just seeing the box. I knew all kinds of goodness lay in wait for me there.

Of all the friends I had in my life, none of them took fashion as seriously as Sadie. Even on her worst days — and she'd had some bad ones since we'd met — she dressed to the nines. Today's outfit was a mint-green coat with a Peter Pan collar and fake pearl buttons. At least I guessed the pearls were fake. She wore the coat over a gingham dress complete with petticoat underneath. She'd paired the dress with black patent-leather heels. Sadie had just walked across the ice-covered River Road, one of the last original brick streets in Cascade Springs, in those shoes. I wouldn't have been able to walk across the room in them.

As River Road reached the Niagara River and turned left to follow it, it became blacktop. That section of River Road had the highest traffic in the village, so it was impractical to have brick there, but the brick added charm to our portion of the busy street. Most of the year, the brick was fine. During the winter, it was a pain, because the road could never be completely cleared of snow and ice, which was the reason I was aghast that Sadie had walked across the street in those shoes.

I sipped my coffee and felt a little more human again. At least I felt human enough to have a rational conversation. "How did you cross the street in those shoes?"

She laughed. "These shoes are nothing. They have a thick heel. I couldn't fall over in these if I tried."

"I could," I said. "Without trying at all."

"Tell me what happened at the winery." She perched on the arm of one of the two couches that flanked either side of the stone fireplace that faced the tree. After another sip, I set my coffee down on the table and knelt by the hearth. I could at least start a fire while we talked. Customers loved the fire in the winter months. It made them want to stay longer in the shop, and the longer they stayed in the shop, the more likely they were to buy something.

I shoved pieces of newspaper between the logs and put a fresh log on top of the pile. Using a long-handled lighter, I lit the fire, and the flame caught the log. I smiled in satisfaction as I put the grate back in front of the hearth.

Sadie opened the bakery box and set it on the coffee table in front of the couch. She'd even thought to bring a little stack of napkins. Most of the time I wished I could be half as organized as her.

I stood up and sat between the fire and the beignets, holding my coffee. Life really didn't get much better than this.

I selected a pastry from the box, and as soon as I bit into it, I knew why Lacey had married Adrien. He had many wonderful qualities, but his doughnut-making skills were off the charts. Between bites, I told Sadie what had happened at the winery. When I got to the part about finding Belinda's body, the image came back to me so vividly that a piece of beignet lodged in my throat.

"That's awful," Sadie said. "No wonder everyone is talking about it. How terrible for the Mortons to imply that she did this." She pressed her lips together. "I expected as much from Mrs. and Mr. Morton, I suppose. They care a lot about their family, and I'm sure are just trying to protect their home and business. But I know Grant would never say anything like that about Lacey."

I shoved another beignet in my mouth to hide my expression. I wished that Sadie could see Grant for who he truly was, but this was a case where her good nature got in the way. They had broken up three months ago, but she was just as much in love with him as she ever had been.

Sadie selected the smallest beignet from the box. "Do you think Rainwater will miss the Red Inkers meeting tonight? Renee Reid and Simon Chase, our new candidates, will be presenting for the first time. He really should come if he can. He can't let Richard and me make the decision on our own."

The Red Inkers was a local writing critique group that met in Charming Books twice a week after the shop closed. They had been using the meeting space for years, long before I'd returned to the village. Last fall, two of the members had left the group rather suddenly, and it had been a very long process to find new members who meshed well with the current group. The current members were Sadie, Chief David Rainwater, and Richard Bunting, my English department chair at the local college, Springside Community College. I supposed that, since I attended the meetings because they were in the bookshop, I was an honorary member of sorts. I wasn't a creative writer, but I did enjoy listening to the others share their work.

Of the two new potential members, Renee Reid, I was certain, would be a good fit for the group. She was a librarian at Springside who had befriended me when I started teaching there as adjunct professor in Richard's department. It wasn't until Richard had emailed all the Red Inkers to tell us who had submitted works for review that I had learned that Renee wrote. She'd never mentioned it to me before, and Renee wasn't a person to keep her own secrets.

But knowing Renee and how smart she was, I wasn't the least bit surprised her piece was one of the best in the bunch. The only one I would have said was a tad better was the piece by Simon Chase, whom I didn't know at all. In fact, Simon was completely unknown to everyone in the group. This was most surprising to Richard, because as chair of the English department at Springside, he saw himself as an expert on what was happening in the world of literature in the entire Niagara region.

But he did admit that Renee being a writer had taken him too by surprise, especially since he was half in love with the boisterous college librarian and made up every excuse he could think of to visit the college library as often as possible. No one had more overdue books than Richard Bunting.

Sadie wrinkled her nose. "It feels strange to let new people into our group. We have been together so long and know each other's writing so well. What if I have nothing constructive to say about Renee or Simon's writing, or what if they hate my style? I would be devastated if they trashed my work."

"First of all, you're a great writer, Sadie, and you know your stuff. You'll think of something helpful to say to these other writers. Second of all, I know Renee. She is loud and outspoken, but more than that, she is kind. She will tell you what she thinks, but she won't trash yours or anyone else's works. Third of all, we don't know Simon, but I seriously doubt that he would say anything to upset you or Richard or Rainwater early on. He's the one who wants to join your group, remember? He's not going to do anything to hurt his chances."

She grabbed my hand. "But you will be there at the Red Inkers at least and will give us your honest opinion? Even though you don't really get to vote, your opinion matters to all of us."

"I'll be there," I said.

Sadie thought about this a moment. "Still, I really hope Rainwater will be there. I don't want it to be up to Richard and me to make the decision to see if Simon is a good fit. Rainwater is so wise. He will know what to do."

"I'm sure you will know even if Rainwater isn't at the meeting. He will have his hands full now with the murder."

Sadie shook her head. "Another murder. I can't believe it. It seems the grim reaper has been a frequent visitor to our little village over the last several months, and I feel just terrible for Lacey."

"Me too. Do you know anything about Lacey's relationship with her sisters?"

"What do you mean?" Sadie's already big blue eyes went wide.

"Did they get along? Do you know her other sisters?" I asked.

Sadie thought for a moment. "Both of her younger sisters have shopped in my store. But Michelle, the older of the younger two, more frequently. She had a couple of kids with her the last time she was in, so I assumed that she was married. I could be wrong about that. I knew that she was Lacey's sister, but every time I mention Lacey, she changes the subject."

"And the youngest sister?" I asked. "Adele? I think I remember that was her name."

"Right. Adele is nineteen. She's an artist. When she came in Midcentury Vintage, I didn't have anything that was her style. She's a little edgier than the stuff that I sell, but she gave me her card and told me that she had her own studio in the bird neighborhood and I could stop by anytime to see her work. She thought a piece or two would look nice in my shop. She wondered if I would sell her artwork on consignment. That was weeks ago, and I haven't been over there and haven't had a chance to seriously think about it yet."

The "bird neighborhood," as everyone in the village called it, was the eclectic arts district in the village, full of art studios and galleries catering to the many tourists who made their way through the village every year. I was surprised that someone so young would have an art studio over there. The rent was steep.

"She's nineteen and has a studio in the bird neighborhood? Does she do anything else to pay the rent?"

Sadie shrugged. "She didn't say, and I didn't ask." She stood up. "I should head back to my shop and get ready for the day, and um, you probably want to get ready too."

I touched the messy bun on the top of my head. "It's that bad, is it?"

"You always look nice, Violet."

I chuckled and stood up too. "Sadie, if I didn't know you better, I would swear you were lying."

She looked aghast. "I would never lie!"

I laughed. "I never said that you did."

CHAPTER ELEVEN

Grandma Daisy and I had a rush of customers in the morning, but most were there for gossip about Belinda Perkins's death. The copies of her book that we had left from the signing sold out by eleven. I handed an elderly woman the copy of the wine book she had just purchased.

She smiled at me. "I've never taken a drop of spirits in my life. My father always said liquor was of the devil."

I pressed my lips together. "Can I ask why you bought the book, then?"

She pulled on her leather gloves. "It will be a collector's piece now that the author is dead."

After the customer left, I went in search of my grandmother, who was dusting the bookcases in the back of the shop near the kitchen.

"All of the copies of Belinda's book sold," I said.

She held her feather duster in the air like it was a wand and she was about to cast a spell on me. The only spell she could have conjured would have been allergies if she shook that duster in my face. I took a step back to get out of range, just in case.

"All of them."

I nodded.

"Should we order more? Would that be crass?" she asked.

"I doubt the publisher would think so."

She pressed her lips together in thought. "Well, if anyone really wants the book, you know the shop will materialize a copy for him or her."

I knew that all too well. I straightened a book on the shelf closest to me. "The shop has quieted down now that all the gossips have left and gone somewhere else to find their news. I think I will head over to Le Crepe Jolie to see how Lacey is."

"Why would she be at the café today of all days?"

I shrugged. "I don't know what time she got there, but when I texted her a little while ago, she said that she was at work."

"Poor child. She's been through so much. I hate to see this latest tragedy disrupt her life."

"Are you thinking of her mother?" I asked.

Grandma Daisy nodded. "Lacey lost her mother young, just like you did. Not as young as you were, but young enough."

"How did her mother die?" I asked. I knew that Lacey's mother had died while I was away in Chicago, but not the particulars.

"I thought that you knew, dear. Lacey and you are good friends. I thought that she would have told you."

"Any time that her mother came up, she changed the subject. I got the feeling that she didn't want to talk about it, and I didn't want to pry," I said.

Grandma Daisy lowered her feather duster and shook her head. "Car accident coming home from work in Niagara Falls on a cold winter's night, just like the one we had last night. Her car slid on black ice on River Road, and she hit a tree."

"Did she die instantly?"

Grandma Daisy frowned. "Not from what I heard, but the family was very private about it. I think she died a week after the accident. I went to the funeral, of course; most of the village attended. Nela Perkins was well loved. She was a tough, hardworking woman, raising those four girls on her own. Her husband left her when the youngest, Adele, was still in diapers. The girls were just devastated. They adored their mother."

I remembered Lacey's mother. In my memory, she was a lot like Lacey was now. A soft woman with a ready smile and a kind face. She was the kind of person you'd find yourself telling your life story to. I felt like I might be sick. "I wish I had known at the time."

"It happened while you were away, maybe three or four years after you left."

"Why didn't you tell me? I would have come back for the funeral."

She frowned. "Would you? When you left the village, you were so angry over what happened after Colleen's death that you swore up and down you would never set foot in the village again."

I opened my mouth as if to protest, but she was faster. "Maybe I did the wrong thing by not telling you, but it wasn't that long after you left, and you still hated this village so much. I wanted you to forget how you hated it so you would come back to it someday not just for me, but for the tree and your job as the next Caretaker." She nodded at the tree behind me. "I thought if you came back to the village too soon when you were still hurt by it, you would never permanently return."

My heart constricted, and I felt terrible that I hadn't known about Lacey's mother's death. If I had been a true friend to her, I would have known that. When I'd lost my mother at age thirteen, Lacey had come over the next day with a plate of sugar cookies she had made herself. They had tasted awful. It was a good thing that Adrien was the chef at Le Crepe Jolie and not Lacey, but the cookies had been a gift to help me in my grief. I had done nothing for her when her mother died.

I couldn't blame Grandma Daisy. She'd thought she was doing the right thing by not telling me. I had been so hurt by how I'd felt the village had betrayed me, I had told my grandmother I didn't want to hear anything about this place or anyone in it. I realized now how much I had missed by turning my back on the village and my old friends here and how selfish I had been. I could make up for it by helping Lacey now.

Faulkner flew over our heads as he did a loop around the shop and cawed.

Grandma Daisy shook her finger at the bird. "I know that you are also a member of Charming Books staff as well, my dear Faulkner, if that's what you're afraid of, but you don't have be in on every meeting."

"Doubt thou the stars are fire; Doubt that

the sun doth move; Doubt truth to be a liar; But never doubt I love," the crow said, and came in for a landing on top of one of the bookshelves.

Emerson watched Faulkner from the staircase. His black tail swished back and forth along the wooden step.

Impressive. I squinted at my grandmother. "Are you teaching him Shakespeare?"

She grinned. "I thought if he planned to go around here talking all the time, he should say something of worth. Besides, how poetic is it to have a shop crow who can quote Shakespeare? It will attract more customers when the word gets out. I assure you of that."

"Some people seemed to get all sunshine, and some all shadow," Faulkner quoted as he walked along the top of the bookcase. His talons made a click, click, click on the wooden surface.

"That's not Shakespeare," my grandmother said.

"No." I swallowed because my mouth suddenly felt very dry. "It's not Shakespeare at all. It's Louisa May Alcott. It's from *Little Women.*"

Grandma Daisy set her duster on a bookshelf and too a closer look at me. "Violet, what is it? You're white as a sheet."

I swallowed. "Last night right before I left for the signing, *Little Women* appeared."

"Appeared, you say? Delivered by the shop's essence?"

I nodded.

"You know what that means, then, don't you, my dear? The clue for what happened to poor Belinda Perkins is found in that book. You must study it."

"I have been. At least I started to last night after I got home, but it was so late, I didn't get very far. I know the story about the March sisters and their mother Marmee of course."

She nodded. "Four March girls, four Perkins girls. This must be the reason that the shop picked it to deliver the clues to you."

"I can see that too, but I can't make sense of what the clues are. All it has done is put the book in front of me, little else. The book itself is over five hundred pages. I'm a fast reader, but there is no way I would be able to read it word for word and know what the shop's essence is trying to tell me. I don't know where in the story that it wants me to look."

My grandmother set a slim hand under her chin. "Then, I think, you have to ask it."

"Did you ever ask it when you were Caretaker?"

She shook her head. "No, but when I was the Caretaker, it wasn't having me solve murders like it does you."

"That's a good point." I scanned the large room, and my gaze ended as it always did on the majestic tree in the middle of the shop.

"Wait to ask the shop when you get back," my grandmother said. "It has a different sense of timing than we do. It would be best that you were here for a while after you ask. Right now, you should go check on Lacey. She could use a friend."

I nodded and told my grandmother goodbye as I walked to the front of the shop. As I walked past the birch tree, I looked at it. I wished, not for the first time, that the shop's magical essence worked a different way. That it was a little more direct and just told me exactly what to do to solve the murder. The cryptic clues were getting old. As a literature scholar, I thought getting messages through books was all well and good, but it left a lot up to personal interpretation.

As I left the shop, I half expected to find a stack of *Little Women* novels blocking the front door, but there was nothing there. I glanced at the tree. What was the essence not telling me? I didn't know. Emerson, still on the stairs, blinked at me.

I grabbed my coat, hat, and scarf and then left the shop. Normally when I traveled around the village, I used my mother's old aqua cruiser bike that my grandmother had refurbished for me just before I moved back. Now that I thought about it, she'd had my apartment redone at the same time. She must have been pretty confident I was going to move back to Cascade Springs when she'd spent all that time and money.

This deep into winter, however, the bike was an impractical choice. There was too great a risk of wiping out on the ice. Instead, I made my way to Le Crepe Jolie by foot.

In my calf-high snow boots, I walked out of the front yard, which was surrounded by a white picket fence. Across the street, all the lights were on in Midcentury Vintage, and I could see Sadie moving around the shop as she spoke to two customers. I continued toward the Niagara River and the Riverwalk. Just before the river itself, River Road took an abrupt left-hand turn to follow the path of the river.

I walked along the sidewalk on the side opposite the river. Across the street from me, beyond the park on Riverwalk, was the large half-frozen river. Although there were a few boulders that the water splashed over, Cascade Springs sat on a relatively quiet stretch of the Niagara. But in the deep, dark part of winter, the water was much more turbulent. The river was frozen on either side, three feet from either bank. In the center of the river, the water flowed freely.

In the park, huge chucks of ice had been chiseled into unicorns, skiers, and lions from the ice-sculpting contest the previous weekend.

"You're blocking the sidewalk," an irritated male voice said to me.

I looked up from my hands to see who was speaking. Much to my surprise, it was Belinda's fiancé Sebastian. He recognized me as well. "You're that lady from the bookstore who found Belinda."

I nodded. "I'm so sorry for your loss. I know that it must be particularly painful to be in the village where she grew up."

"The sooner I get out of this sad excuse for a town, the better." He wasn't wearing a hat, but he turned up the collar of what looked like a very expensive overcoat, maybe even more expensive than Nathan's, and the mayor liked nice things. He added, "I have never been treated so poorly in all my life!"

I raised my eyebrows. Cascade Springs

was known for being a friendly place to visitors. Tourism was the village's bread and butter. It couldn't survive without it. "Did something happen?"

He glared at me. "Of course something happened. My fiancée is dead, and no one in this village wants to do a thing about it."

"I'm sure Chief Rainwater is giving the case his full attention. I know he is investigating. He will get to the bottom of this."

"Rainwater! He's the worst of them all. I told him who did this and who he should arrest for Belinda's murder. He refused to move on the tip." He held leather gloves in his hands but didn't put them on. His hands were slightly blue. I felt cold just looking at them.

"Who did it, then?" I paused. "I know the police chief rather well and might be able to talk to him."

He looked at me like he didn't believe what I was saying. "Her sister. The one who crashed her book signing last night. Lacey. She's the killer. I'm as sure of that as I have been sure of anything in my life."

"She didn't crash the signing. Lacey's husband was catering the event. She was there to help him."

"I don't care. She should have never tried to talk to my love. Do you even know how torn up it made Belinda to see Lacey? She had to leave the signing for a break after that. I wanted to go with her to comfort her, but she wouldn't let me. If she stayed in the tasting room or if she would have let me go with her, she would still be alive." Tears filled his voice. "Can't you see that? But she left the signing, and her sister was waiting for her and killed her."

"I don't think —"

"After everything Lacey has done to her . . . It's terrible how she came to the winery last night. She came there begging Belinda's forgiveness, but after what she had done, she had no right to ask for that."

I opened my mouth to say something, but he stopped me. "My fiancée was terrified of her."

"Terrified of Lacey? Lacey Dupont? Are you sure we are talking about the same woman?" I was certain that no one had ever been afraid of Lacey, well, ever. With her round cheeks and bright, shining smile, she wasn't the type of person that you were afraid of. She just wasn't.

"She was. She told me many times. After what Lacey did to their mother, it made sense. The police wouldn't do anything about that suspicious death then either."

I froze. "What do you mean?"

"I thought everyone in this village knew the reason Nela Perkins is dead is because Lacey killed her."

"No," I said. "No, they don't."

Before I could say anything more, he walked away, leaving me standing in the middle of the sidewalk in shock.

Chapter Twelve

I stared in the direction Sebastian had gone. As he disappeared around the corner, I realized I'd missed an opportunity to ask him about the murder and what his part of it might have been.

No matter what Sebastian said, I knew that Lacey hadn't killed her mother or her sister. There had to be another side to the story of Nela Perkins's death, and the only person who could tell me that story was Lacey. I continued down the walk to her café.

Le Crepe Jolie had one of the nicest spots in the village. It stood directly across from the riverside park and beside the town hall, a surprisingly large building in a village as small as Cascade Springs.

In the summer, the Duponts arranged for wire tables and chairs outside their café so that customers could admire the view of the park and river while they enjoyed Adrien's delicious food, but in the middle of winter, those tables and chairs were tucked away until spring.

Before I entered the café, I peeked through the front window. Le Crepe Jolie was busy. Danielle Cloud hopped from table to table, filling coffee cups and nodding to diners' comments. Her long black ponytail floated behind her while she moved. Danielle was as beautiful as her brother David Rainwater was handsome, and her daughter Aster was a mini version of her mother.

My stomach rumbled as I watched. Danielle set a strawberry-covered crepe in front of a customer. Even though I had eaten two — okay, three — of Adrien's doughnuts for breakfast, my mouth watered. I was never too full for Adrien's food, especially his crepes.

I removed my stocking cap, tapped down my unruly waves, and walked to the door. As soon as I walked into the café, the room grew dead silent. I glanced around and looked down at my coat, wondering if I had put it on backward or something. Danielle stared with the rest of them, but I realized she wasn't looking at me at all.

Lacey stood just outside the kitchen, and all eyes fixed on her. Lacey appeared to be trapped in fright. She was pale, and her hair was falling from its usually neat barrette. It wasn't hard to guess what the main topic of conversation had been just a moment ago.

I, of all people, knew what it was like to be the center of village gossip. The talk surrounding Colleen's death had kept me away from Cascade Springs for twelve years. I supposed that as a teenager, I had expected my village to be more trusting of me, and when they'd turned on me, I'd been so disappointed that I had fled, leaving behind Charming Books, my grandmother, and Lacey, who had dealt with her mother's death without me. I wished my grandmother had told me about Nela's death at the time. I wanted to think I would have done the right thing and returned to Cascade Springs to be at Lacey's side, but I didn't know if I would have. My grandmother had saved me from making a choice.

Lacey's hands shook. I might not have been there all those year ago, but I could help her now.

"Lacey!" I said, beaming from ear to ear. "Are you ready for our walk? It's a perfect day to start our New Year's resolution."

"Our walk?" she asked. "Resolution? But it's already the third week of January."

I laughed. "Better late than never, right?"

"To start a resolution?" She still sounded

confused. I would have been confused too, since I had just made up our resolution on the spot.

"Sure!" I picked her coat off the rack by the door. "We talked about this. We both want to get more exercise this winter. It's tempting to stay in when it's cold, but we should be outside enjoying the beautiful winter months just as much as summer."

Her eyebrows disappeared into her hairline. "I guess so. But don't you hate winter?"

"I'm turning over a new leaf this year." I chuckled. "If I tell myself I like winter, I might actually like it. Let's head out." I handed her the coat.

She put it on. "I can't be gone long. Adrien needs my help. We're very busy."

"Danielle will tell him where we've gone." I smiled at Rainwater's sister, who smiled back at me as I ushered Lacey out the door.

Even in the cold, Cascade Springs was still a tourist town, and there were several determined horse-drawn carriages parked by the Riverwalk waiting for passengers. In the winter, the carriages were equipped with warm bricks for the tourists' feet and blankets to drape over their laps.

The white horse at the front of the carriage shook his bridle as we crossed the street and stepped onto the ice- and snow-covered path along the river.

The Niagara River flowed beside the path. I marveled at how powerful the river remained even when half of it was frozen. The rushing water forced its way through the large chunks of ice, spraying upward when it hit a large piece of ice as if it had run into a rock.

Lacey pulled a stocking hat out of her coat pocket. "Thank you back there. You saved me." She pulled the hat down over her ears. "I know they were talking about me. The entire village is." She turned back into the wind and started to walk north along the river toward the livery where the horses and carriages were kept.

I skipped to catch up with her. "I'm so sorry for your loss, Lacey. I know that seems like a hollow thing to say at a time like this. Platitudes like that frustrated me when my mom died, but I've since learned that people say them because they don't know what else to say."

She looked at me with tears in her blue eyes. "I know. But the truth is, I lost Belinda a long time ago. What I lost last night was the chance of ever making things right between us, which makes me saddest of all. I so much wanted us to be a family again, and now that will never happen."

I shoved my hands deep in the pockets of my coat. "What happened between the two of you? As soon as Belinda saw you, she lost it."

Lacey sighed. "It's very painful to talk about."

"You don't have to tell me, but it might help if you did. Lacey, I have to be honest with you. It doesn't look good that you got into an argument with Belinda and a little while later she was dead."

She removed a crumpled tissue from the pocket of her down coat and rubbed it under her nose. "I know that. Chief Rainwater told me the same thing. He wanted to know what our argument was about last night too."

"And did you tell him?"

"Sort of," she said.

"Sort of?" I asked.

"I told him it was over our mother's death, which was nine years ago now."

I touched her arm. "Grandma Daisy told me about your mom. I'm so sorry that I didn't know. I wish I had been here for you."

She shook her head. "It's all right, Violet. You have been a good friend to me, and you had your own tragedies to deal with back then. I wouldn't have wanted to add to them."

Her sweet and typically Lacey response only made me feel worse. "Grandma Daisy told me about the accident." I paused. "But she said that your mother didn't die until a week later."

"That's right." She looked at her feet while we walked down the path. "In the accident, our mother was paralyzed from the neck down. She was on life support from the moment she arrived at the hospital." Her voice caught. "We never got a chance to talk to her. She was in a coma too. The second day, the doctor told me she wasn't waking up and had significant brain damage. I can't tell you what it was like to see my vibrant mother in a state like that. She was just a shell." She stopped in the middle of the sidewalk and removed a crumpled tissue from the pocket of her coat. She pressed it to the corner of her eye. "The doctors told me that I had to make a decision whether or not take her off life support."

My heart broke for my friend. My mother had died too, but I had never had to make a tough choice like that. My mother had known that she was dying and so had made all the arrangements. The doctors and nurses knew what she wanted without Grandma Daisy or me having to tell them.

"But you were just a kid having to make that decision. Didn't you have anyone else to help you?"

"I was nineteen. I was legally an adult and the only adult in the family who was there. I asked the doctors to wait because I was trying to find Belinda."

"Find her? Where did she go?"

"Traveling Europe and studying wines. She'd already wanted to be a sommelier all the way back then. Belinda had big dreams. There was so much she wanted to see and do. Look how well she did for herself. She wrote a book. I didn't know anyone who wrote a book before. My mother would have been so proud of her. The trip was her chance to make something great of herself. I had to be the one to make the decision. Michelle and Adele were too young."

"But she didn't leave any way for you to contact her?"

"The last phone number I had didn't work. I sent her an email, but she never responded. I had to make a decision." She started walking again. "So, at the end of the week, I told the doctors to cut off life support, and my mother died that day. The next day, I finally tracked down Belinda and told her about the funeral. She flew home and was furious with me. She claimed that I killed our mother and that I robbed her of her one chance to say goodbye to her. I understood that. She was grieving and wanted someone to blame. I was the obvious choice." She wiped at her eyes. "But I know in my heart that I did the right thing, but maybe I could have tried harder to find my sister, called her friends or reached out to her sommelier school. I didn't think of any of those things at the time."

I squeezed her arm. "Lacey, you did the very best you could have. I know that. You were dealing with so much at such a young age. You did so well."

"Belinda wouldn't agree with you."

"But you should," I said as I squeezed her arm a second time and then let go.

"After Mom died, I still had to take care of my younger sisters. My mother said in her will that if I was of age when she died that I would get guardianship of them."

"You, and not Belinda."

She nodded. "Mom knew Belinda was destined for bigger things. She wasn't going to stay in little Cascade Springs to raise two girls. Adele was only ten at the time, and Michelle was twelve. They still needed years of care. Belinda wouldn't be willing to wait for them to grow up." She sighed. "Even so, Mom's directives hurt her, and she accused me of coercing our mother into giving me guardianship of the younger girls."

"Is this why she was so angry at you?"

She sighed again. "That's most of it. To take care of Michelle and Adele, I had to make money, so I got a job at a fancy French restaurant in Niagara Falls as a waitress. I was awful at it. One of the young chefs took me under his wing to help me learn the restaurant business. He was so kind and handsome. I had no idea why he had taken an interest in me. I have always been round and plain."

"Lacey," I said. "That's not true. You're beautiful inside and out."

She shook her head. "I don't have any illusions about my appearance, Violet."

I wanted to say more, but she went on. "That chef saw something in me that I didn't. You can guess it was Adrien, and before I knew it, we fell in love. He talked about opening a café in Cascade Springs, and if he did, he wanted me to work there with him. I felt like for the first time I had a little hope at a happy ending. The girls were doing fine — as fine as they could be, considering what they had been through. I was hopeful.

"Adrien did buy the café and move to Cascade Springs. I didn't know until much later he did it all because he loved me. Starting out, he acted like it was the next logical step for his career and Cascade Springs was a tourist destination. It was a perfect place for his café. I had thought the fact that I lived here was just a coincidence."

"But it wasn't." I smiled.

She smiled at the memory too. "No, it wasn't." She took a breath. "The café was set to open in October. About a month before the grand opening, Adrien asked me to marry him. I said yes. Because of what happened the last time something big happened in our family, I tracked Belinda down. She was only in California then and much easier to find. I told her that I had met a wonderful man and that I was getting married. She was furious again and claimed this was my plan all along when our mother died. She'd spoken to all the doctors that had cared for my mother and asked them if there was any hope that she might have lived. One said something like only by some miracle. That was all my sister had to hear to conclude I murdered our mother. After that she made it her mission to turn my younger sisters against me." Tears ran down her face. "And she succeeded in that. Now that the girls are grown, they won't even speak to me."

"Oh Lacey. I'm so sorry," I said, wishing I had something more meaningful to say. "How could Michelle and Adele believe that after everything you did for them?"

"Belinda was the cool older sister who traveled all over the world and sent them expensive gifts. Of course they would take her side. I understand that. It was a difficult few years because I had custody of Michelle and Adele until they each were eighteen. They hated me for most of it." A tear rolled down her cheek. "I haven't spoken to any of my sisters in years." She pressed the tissue to the corner of her eye. "I shouldn't cry. It's so cold that my tears might freeze to my face, and we should go back. You must be so cold. No matter what you said in the café, I know you hate the cold."

I smiled. "I'm fine." It was just like Lacey to think of someone else's comfort when she was crying.

"I thought if I could talk to Belinda last night that I could make amends and we could all be a family again, but you saw what happened when I tried to talk to her."

"What happened after she yelled at you in the tasting room? Where did you go?"

She shoved the tissue back into her pocket. "I went back into the kitchen. I told Adrien what happened. He wanted us to leave, but

I said that we couldn't. We had a contract with the Mortons to supply the food. I stayed in the kitchen the rest of the night. I didn't hear about the murder" — she stumbled over the word — "until David Rainwater told me about."

"Did anyone else come into the kitchen after your argument?" I asked.

She looked out to the river. "Mrs. Morton did. She was very upset with the scene Belinda and I caused, and she threatened not to pay us over it. Adrien told her that Belinda was the one who made the outburst, but it didn't matter. Mrs. Morton blamed me for it. She said that she wouldn't pay us for catering that night because we ruined her party."

I bit the inside of my lip. Lacey might not realize this, but Mrs. Morton's threat gave her even more motive to kill her sister. Because of Belinda's behavior, she and Adrien were out a lot of money — I would have guessed several thousand dollars between all the expensive food they had provided and the extra waitstaff they had hired for the event.

I could see the scenario in my head that Rainwater must have already visualized. Lacey sees Belinda head out to the vineyard after their argument. Lacey follows her and confronts her again. Belinda says she wants nothing to do with her and she will do nothing to convince the younger Perkins girls to make amends with their sister. Belinda turns her back, and Lacey stabs her with one of the grape-cutting knives that can be found almost anywhere in the vineyard on the night of the frozen grape cutting. When she does so, the letter that she tried to give her sister falls from her pocket.

It worked. Rainwater would have seen that it worked, but that didn't make it true.

"We should head back to the café. Adrien will be worried." Lacey turned back in the direction from where we'd come.

"Lacey, can you tell me what happened to the letter?" I asked, falling into step next to her.

"The letter?" She shoved the crumpled tissue back into her pocket and pulled on a pair of cotton gloves.

"The one that you tried to give your sister at the book signing."

Her face clouded over again. "I — I don't know. I haven't seen it since last night. In fact, I completely forgot about it, to be honest. I have no idea what might have happened to it. Maybe it's still in my purse or in the pocket of the coat I wore to the winery."

I sighed. "I would be surprised if you found it in either place."

She stopped in the middle of the sidewalk. "Why do you say that?"

"Because I saw it last night."

"At the signing?"

"After the signing." I swallowed. "I was the one who found your sister, and the letter was with her. I recognized your handwriting."

She shook her head. "But that can't be possible. I never gave her the letter. You saw her throw it back in my face."

"I know, but somehow she got it. Or —" I stopped myself from going on.

"Or what, Violet? You have to tell me now."

"Or the killer found it or maybe even stole it from you with the intent to kill her."

Lacey covered her mouth with her hand. "Who would do such a terrible thing?"

"The same person who would kill someone," I said. "Let's keep walking. You're right. Adrien will be getting worried by now."

She nodded, and this time she fell into step with me.

"Lacey, answer me as honestly as you can. Do you know of anyone who would have reason to kill Belinda?"

She shook her head. "No, I haven't spoken

150

to my sister in years. I don't know what her life is like anymore beyond the articles she writes." She looked down at her feet. "I save them all, you know. I have a binder of them back at the house. I was very proud that she reached her dreams."

I bit the inside of my lip, wondering if I should tell her to get rid of the binder. Would Rainwater suspect her more if he knew she had been following all of Belinda's movements since they'd had their falling out?

"Violet?" Lacey asked as we stopped to wait to cross the street. "Are you all right? You are very pale."

A horse and carriage clopped by with a young couple snuggled under a blanket in the back of it.

"Would your sisters have any reason to . . ." I trailed off.

"No," she said, clearly understanding what I was trying to say. "They have no reason at all to wish any ill will on Belinda. Like I said, she was the favorite sister."

"Were Michelle and Adele at the signing? They were so young when I left the village, I don't know that I would recognize them as adults. If they were close to Belinda, wouldn't they have gone?"

She bit the inside of her lip. In that time,

two cars passed us on the street. When the traffic cleared, neither of us made a move to walk the rest of the way to Le Crepe Jolie.

"Lacey, were you sisters at the event?"

"I saw them," she said, barely above a whisper. And against her will, added two more suspects to my list.

"I'm going to help you through this, Lacey."

She grabbed my hand. "I appreciate that, Violet, I really do, but I know the police chief wouldn't want you involved, and I don't want to cause any trouble between the two of you."

"Let me worry about Rainwater, okay?"

She nodded. "Okay."

Chapter Thirteen

I left Le Crepe Jolie carrying a large takeout bag filled with baguettes, lemon madeleines — my grandmother's favorite — and all sorts of other delicious goodies. Adrien never let me leave the café without enough food to feed the Canadian Mounties. He was especially generous this time because there seemed to be a shift in Lacey after our walk. She stayed in the front of the house, spoke with diners, and was in general her old cheerful self. Only a person who knew her well could see the lingering sadness in her eyes.

I turned right out of the café toward the bookshop and in the direction of the town hall. I stepped in front of the hall just as Chief David Rainwater, who was in his winter police uniform, complete with black bomber jacket, ran down the steps. His chiseled face fell into hard lines. He appeared so upset that I almost continued on my way.

I knew he wouldn't be happy if he thought that I was meddling in his murder investigation, and he was clearly already in a foul mood.

Before I could make up my mind, Rainwater called my name. "Violet." His face cleared as he reached the sidewalk. He nodded to the café bag in my hand. "I see you've been to Le Crepe Jolie."

"I wanted to check on Lacey."

He nodded. "You're a good friend."

I thanked him.

"And a curious friend, I take it." He studied me. "Lacey say anything to you that I should know?"

I took a step closer to him. "She didn't do this. I know that Belinda's fiancé thinks that she did, but you know Lacey. She doesn't have it in her to hurt anyone."

He sighed. "You spoke to Sebastian Knight too?"

"I didn't go out looking for him," I said, maybe a tad too defensively. "I ran into him on the street walking to the café."

Rainwater pressed his lips into a line. I had a feeling that he didn't completely believe my story. I knew this must be the result of the times I had spoken in half-truths because I didn't want him to know that I was embroiling myself in one of his murder investigations. I knew that wasn't the way to build a friendship or whatever it was that he and I were trying to create together. I knew that I liked the police chief. He was a strong, noble man and I wanted to learn more about him. If I wanted get to know him better, I would have to be honest with him. I didn't think there was any other way to know David Rainwater. "I'm going to help Lacey."

He folded his arms. "What do you mean?"

"Well," I cleared my throat. "Sebastian Knight thinks that she is behind her sister's death because of old hurts from the past."

"The death of her mother," Rainwater said.

"Right," I said. "But I know" — I pointed at myself — "and you know" — I pointed at him — "that she's not capable of murder. I'm not going to let Sebastian or the Mortons railroad her."

He frowned. "Why bring the Mortons into this? Have you been talking to Nathan?"

"No," I said, surprised. "How was your talk with Nathan?"

"How do you know I saw the mayor?"

"You just came out of the town hall. Belinda's death is the most obvious reason for you to be there right now."

"Touché," Rainwater said. "But I still

155

don't like the idea of you getting involved here. You saw Belinda's body. I wish that you hadn't, but you did. It was a terrible scene. Whoever murdered her was furious or strong or both. It takes a lot of force to stab someone with a curved blade like that."

I shivered. "I had thought the same thing."

"So you can see why I don't want you to make yourself a target."

"I won't make myself a target. I'm just looking out for my friend."

He ran his hand back and forth through his jet-black hair. "I can see that I'm getting nowhere with you."

I knew better than to comment on that. "What did Nathan have to say? You were interviewing him?"

Rainwater frowned. "No, this meeting was his idea."

"What did he want?"

The police chief glanced at the hall. I wouldn't have been the least bit surprised if Nathan was watching us from one of its many windows.

"He wanted to threaten me," Rainwater said.

"Threaten you?" I asked.

"It wasn't in so many words, but his message was delivered loud and clear. He reminded me how important his family was to the village, both socially and economically, and that he was the mayor and therefore my boss."

My face fell. I couldn't help but feel disappointed in Nathan for doing that to the police chief. Rainwater was a good man, and I knew and Nathan knew he would treat everyone in the investigation fairly.

"He even mentioned you."

I blinked. "Me? What about me?"

He shook his head as if he regretted revealing that much.

"You have to tell me. You can't leave me hanging like that."

"I shouldn't have told you any of that. I'm certain if the mayor knew, he would be crafting my dismissal."

"I'd like to see him try!"

Rainwater smiled, and his white teeth gleamed against his tan skin. "You are the most determined woman I have ever met. I guess that's why I find you so fascinating."

I blushed and looked across the street as if there were something along the river's edge that had caught my eye.

Rainwater cleared his throat. "If you learn anything, you have to call and tell me. It doesn't matter that I might already know it or what a small detail it might be."

The river, narrowed by ice, bounced along

its frozen banks. I turned back to Rainwater. "Okay," I promised.

"Thank you. I'd walk you back to the shop, but I have a meeting back at the station that I'm already late for."

I shifted from foot to foot. My toes were growing cold, "It's all right. I saw Sadie this morning, and she wondered if you would be at the Red Inkers meeting tonight."

"I know. She texted me and asked too. I don't know." He paused. "It depends on how the day goes. This is a complicated case."

I nodded.

"Tell them I will try to make it if I possibly can."

I nodded, and he walked to his SUV parked on the curb.

He turned back around. "Violet?"

I stared into his amber eyes. I swallowed. "Yes?"

"I'm happy that you're all right. Last night when Grandma Daisy called me to tell me about Belinda, I was so worried about you. I was afraid you were in trouble again. I couldn't even think subjectively like a cop, at least not until I saw with my own two eyes that you were in one piece. I — I don't want anything to happen to you. Please promise me that you will be careful."

"I promise." What could I say when he was staring at me like that?

He nodded and opened his car door, and I continued on my way half concerned that the police chief had been worrying about me and half thrilled.

As I made the turn on River Road toward the shop. I saw a figure with a guitar case in his hand standing in front of the Charming Books gate. I couldn't see the man's face or hair because he had the hood of his parka all the way up, but the sight of him still made my heart skip a beat. Was it Fenimore? As far as I knew, the troubadour hadn't been back to the village since giving me my mother's letter. I wasn't ready for him to come back. I hadn't told Grandma Daisy about him yet.

Part of me wanted to turn around and hide out in Le Crepe Jolie the rest of the day, eating Adrien's quiche and pretending that I didn't live in a world where murder happened or where long-lost fathers showed up on your doorstep.

The man turned. "Are you Violet Waverly?"

My knees went weak when I saw that it wasn't Fenimore, but I felt oddly disappointed.

CHAPTER FOURTEEN

I walked up to him. "I am. Can I help you?"

He pushed his hood back, revealing a middle-aged man with a thin mustache and beard that was so blond it was visible only with the sunlight. He wore thick plastic-rimmed glasses. "I'd like to talk to you about Belinda Perkins."

"And who are you?"

He handed me a business card. I took it from his hand. It read, JOEL REDDING, P.I. NIAGARA FALLS, NY.

"You're a private investigator."

He smiled. "That's typically what the P.I. means."

I frowned and started to hand the card back to him. He shook his head. "No, you keep it."

"Who are you working for?" I shoved the card into the pocket of my coat. It might come in handy.

"Her fiancé, Sebastian Knight."

A light snow began to fall, but even so I didn't suggest that we go into Charming Books to discuss this further. "Sebastian must be nervous if he is willing to pay a private investigator to look into the murder."

Redding adjusted his glasses on his nose. "He wants to ensure that he's not railroaded by the small-town police, but I don't have to tell you what's that's like. You know all about that very well."

It seemed that Joel Redding, P.I., had done his homework on me, but I refused to rise to the bait. "What's with the guitar? Is guitar playing part of the P.I. gig nowadays?"

He looked down at his case. "It's just the case, no guitar. I use it for a briefcase. I have found that people seem to be more open to an investigator who looks like he plays the guitar than one taking notes."

I arched my brow. It seemed to me that, as quirky as he was, Joel Redding would meld into Cascade Springs society well, maybe too well.

"Now, tell me the details of when you found Belinda. Start to finish in your own words."

"If you have already spoken to the police, I don't know what else I can tell you. I told them everything that I know."

"That I don't believe. I have done my

research on you, Miss Waverly, and you have a very colorful past with the police and have a history of withholding information when you think you're in the right."

I tightened my grip on the handle of Adrien's goody bag, and it cut into my palm. "If you are trying to ingratiate yourself with me, this is not the tactic to use."

He stroked his almost invisible beard. "I just want you to be aware of how seriously I take my investigations. I know all about you, Miss Waverly. Of how you were accused and arrested for murdering your best friend when you were seventeen. How you were cleared, charges were never filed, and it has been expunged from your record. How you returned to this village last summer after a long time away and solved a couple of murders. It's quite impressive for an amateur. If it were not for the fact you are a witness to the crime, I would hire you as my girl Friday for this case. You have a startling success rate."

"How do you know all this? My records were expunged."

He laughed. "You can't really hide anything anymore in the age of information. Your official record was cleared, but the village newspaper had a digital archive anyone can access, and Colleen Preston's death was the biggest story to hit this village in decades. All of your more recent escapades are well documented too."

My heart thundered in my chest. "I suggest you talk to Police Chief David Rainwater. He has the information you want." I slid past him and opened the gate in the white picket fence. I stepped through the gate and closed it behind me, hoping that Redding would get the message that he was not invited to follow me.

"Oh, the police chief with whom you are romantically linked? Trust me, I know all about him too," he said to my back.

I froze in the middle of the snow-covered pavers that led to the steps of the old Victorian.

"Or are you in love with the village mayor? You do set your romantic aspirations high."

I straightened my back, refusing to turn around. I walked straight into the shop and closed the door behind me. I leaned my back against the front door, still holding the bag of food from Le Crepe Jolie. After a moment, I went to the front window, pushed the curtain aside just an inch, and peeked out.

Redding was just where I had left him on the sidewalk in front of the shop, holding his guitar briefcase. He wiggled his fingers at me.

I jumped away from the window. This was bad, so very bad. I knew Sebastian was convinced that Lacey was the killer. Had he hired Joel Redding to prove it? It just made me more determined than ever to clear Lacey's name, but with Redding looking like he had no plans of leaving, that was going to be a challenge.

I glanced around the shop. Faulkner was in the tree, Emerson was MIA, and Grandma Daisy was at the sales counter helping an elderly customer. All was normal, but knowing that Redding was lying in wait for me just outside Charming Books' gate did not make all feel normal.

In addition to the man at the counter, a second customer wandered through the book stacks with a perplexed expression on his face. I was surprised that Charming Books, which was the bookshop "where the perfect book picks you," hadn't revealed to him the book he was seeking yet. It wasn't often that I found a confused customer browsing the shelves.

The man, who looked to be in his thirties, was clean-shaven and wore a long wool coat and shiny black shoes. It was clear that he wasn't from the village. I think it was the shiny shoes that triggered the memory, but I knew I had seen this man the night before at the book signing.

"Can I help you?" I asked.

He was peering at a cookbook on a low shelf and looked up at me. "Oh, hello there. Do you work here?"

I nodded. "I'm Violet Waverly."

"Oh, very good." His eyes flitted around the room. The man looked up into the tree. "Is that a real tree in the middle of your shop?"

I glanced over my shoulder. "It is, and that's a real crow too."

He shuddered. "I don't care for birds."

As if he understood, Faulkner hopped down to the next branch on the tree. The man shuddered. Faulkner, sensing the man's discomfort, reveled in it by walking up and down the branch.

"You don't have to worry about Faulkner. He's very well behaved." I gave the large black bird a beady glare.

Faulkner bobbed his head and unfurled his wings before settling them back against his sides.

The man with the shiny shoes paled.

"I know that we didn't have a chance to meet, but I think I saw you at the book signing last night at Morton Vineyards. Am I correct?" I asked. "Charming Books was there as the official bookseller for the event."

He peeled his eyes away from the bird.

"Jake Zule. I was at the event last night. Belinda invited me. She knew I was on my way up to Ontario. I'm working on a book about Canadian wine country. I'm sure my book won't be as widely praised as Belinda's book was, but I plan to do my very best at it."

"Belinda was a friend of yours?"

"In her way, yes," he said.

I stood there trying to decide what he meant by "in her way." Was there a particular way to be a friend that I didn't know about? Out of the corner of my eye, I saw Emerson eel out from around the tree. The cat moved low to the ground like he was stalking something. I prayed that he didn't pounce on the nervous-looking man.

"I actually stopped by because of another writing assignment that came up rather suddenly, so I find myself scrambling to gather the research I need in time. I want to do a thorough job. The article is for a very prestigious food-and-wine magazine, a great opportunity."

"I'm happy to help you find the materials you need. What's the article about?"

"It's about Cascade Springs and ice wine.

I was asked to review the wineries in the village, and I need a little bit more background on each of them before I can do that. I have searched online, of course, but I was hoping that you had some books on it as well."

"We do," I said carefully. "Ice wine is a popular vintage in the Cascade Springs area, and other than the springs themselves, our wineries are the greatest tourist draw." I paused for a moment. "I thought Belinda was writing an article on the same topic. Someone mentioned it to me at the signing last night before . . ." I trailed off.

His cheeks flushed a light shade of pink. "Yes, well, Belinda was supposed to write this article, but the assignment was given to me after, well, you know."

After she was murdered, I thought. I did know.

"As you can imagine, I'm not completely comfortable with the assignment, considering what happened, but the local wineries, including Morton Vineyards, are looking forward to the publicity the article will generate."

I was certain the Mortons wanted good publicity, especially after the disastrous party the night before. It couldn't have possibly gone worse for them.

"The local history and travel section is by the front window," I said. "We keep it near the front of the shop so it's easy for tourists to find." I led him back to the front near Faulkner's perch. Luckily, the crow remained in the tree. I didn't think the uptight wine critic would respond well if the large black bird zoomed in for a landing just then.

Emerson bounded onto the top of the low bookshelf. Jake gasped. "You have a cat!"

"Emerson is his name." I gave the tuxedo cat a beady look.

Jake lifted a book from the shelf and stared at it. "I thought you said this is where you keep local-interest books."

"It is . . ." I trailed off as I noticed the book in his hand. It was another copy of *Little Women.* It was a different edition than the ones the shop's essence had revealed to me before. I forced a laugh. "Now, how did that get there?" I took the book from his hand. "Why don't I take a look at what we have?" I angled myself in front of the shelf, blocking his view of titles on the books' spines. "I'm sure that the book was just mis-shelved," I said in a singsong voice. "It happens now and again. When customers like to browse, they don't always put the books back where they found them. We have found books in the oddest places in this shop."

I faced toward the shelf, and every last spine facing me was *Little Women*. Emerson walked back and forth the length of the bookcase like a lion in a cage. My palms began to sweat.

CHAPTER FIFTEEN

I set the copy of *Little Women* in my hand on top of the bookcase. Emerson pawed at the book. I reached for another book and came up with Alcott's classic story again. I laughed to cover my dismay. "You know, I'll have to ask my grandmother where she put those books. She must have moved them without telling me. Be right back."

Jake stared at me, and I fled to the sales counter. Thankfully, my grandmother's customer had left. "Grandma Daisy," I hissed.

My grandmother looked up from the book that she was reading. "What is it, Violet? Why are you sweating?"

"I have a problem."

She closed her book and gave me her full attention.

"Don't look over there now, but there is a man by Faulkner's perch by the front window. He says his name is Jake Zule."

Grandma Daisy ignored my directions and stared openly at Jake. "The man with the shiny shoes?"

I groaned. "He is the only man in the shop right now, so yes, that's him. Will you please stop staring at him? He's going to think we're talking about him."

My grandmother folded her hands over the cover of her book and said, "But we are talking about him, my dear."

"Right." I stepped in front of her to block her view of Jake. "He's a writer and has just been given Belinda's writing assignment to review the wineries in Cascade Springs."

"Oh!" Grandma Daisy cranked her neck so that she could see around me. "He will know what she was working on. Maybe he can lead us to the killer!"

"Grandma . . ." I whined.

"Dear, haven't you told me in the past when solving a murder, the more suspects the better? He might know more suspects. He might even be one! I'm just following your direction in crime investigation."

I was really going to have to rethink my life, since my own grandmother took it for granted that "crime investigation" was a part of it. It wasn't like I went out looking for murders to solve. They fell in my lap, or more accurately, I tripped over them.

I winced, praying that Jake hadn't heard my grandmother's comments. She had done nothing to try to modulate her voice. "Well yes, and we have to find out what he knows before he leaves, but I can't do that because the shop is fighting me. If the shop keeps this up much more, he's going to write me off as a complete nut. Then he won't tell me anything."

"Violet, no one could think you are a nut. You're passionate sometimes, maybe a little foolhardy by running into situations where you don't belong, but you're a Waverly, and that's just the way we're wired. You should have seen me as a young woman."

Why didn't I find this comforting?

"How is the shop fighting you? Did you upset it?" she asked.

"Every book that I try to give him, the shop turns into *Little Women*." I glanced over my shoulder and saw Emerson sizing Jake up as if he was deciding whether or not to jump on the wine critic's head.

"The essence isn't being very subtle in telling you to read the book. Have you discovered what it wants you to know from the novel yet?"

"No," I said. "I will try again just as soon as I can learn all I can from the writer, but you have to help him choose a book. I'm

172

afraid if he's given one more copy written by Alcott, he'll bolt."

"What does he want?"

"Local history of the village and books on wine making in the area."

"I'm on it." She floated around the counter. "Hello, Jake, is it?" she asked in a bright, cheerful voice. "I heard that you were looking for local-interest books. I happened to move them, and it completely slipped my mind to tell Violet. How silly of me!" Grandma Daisy walked over to him, took hold of his arm, and turned him toward the street. "As you can see, even in the depths of winter, Cascade Springs is a lovely place. Look at the gas lampposts. Those are the real thing, too, and wait for it! That's a horse and carriage trotting down our original brick street. Utterly charming. I'm sure you can get the idea of how we decided to name our shop Charming Books."

While Grandma Daisy had Jake's back turned to the inside of the shop, dozens of books flew across the room to other shelves. One narrowly missed the back of Jake's head. Faulkner swooped down from his perch in the tree and hovered over the flying books. Emerson batted at them as the books flew into the shelf, and I stood gapemouthed in the middle of the room.

Jake started to turn. "Did you hear something?"

Grandma Daisy turned Jake back toward the window. "It must be the old radiator trying to keep this big Victorian warm. It's a very old house, as you can see. Now, have you been down to the Riverwalk yet? If not, you really should go before you leave the village. It's a lovely piece of green space right in the heart of the village and runs along the Niagara River. Even in the winter it is a beautiful sight, I can assure you of that."

From where I stood, I could see that the books were about to fly in front of Jake. I grabbed his arm and spun him around. "Mr. Zule, I wondered if you noticed the number of books we have on wine in general in our shop. We have a whole section by the sales counter. As you can imagine, it's a popular topic in the area."

The books settled on their shelves just as Jake shook my hand from his arm. "Thank you, but I have more than enough books on wine in general. I'm here to learn about this community. If that's not too much trouble."

"Well, that's no trouble at all," Grandma Daisy said. "Why didn't you just say that in the first place? I thought you wanted to hear about our little village first. Violet misled me. This way to the books." She waved him on. As my grandmother walked by me, she winked.

I stopped just short of rolling my eyes.

Grandma Daisy led Jake over to the other side of the shop and showed him the new place where local-interest books could be found. "We also have several copies left of Belinda Perkins's previous books on wine, if you have any interest. Her new book sold out this morning. This is the place where we keep books by our local authors, Belinda being one of our stars. We are heartbroken to lose her. What a terrible thing to happen in our little village."

"I got one at the signing last night," he said. He selected a few books from the shelf, and I gave a great sigh of relief when not one of them was *Little Women.*

"Oh!" Grandma Daisy feigned surprise. "You were there too? Was it for the article that you are working on now?"

"No." His voice was clipped. He now had five books in his arms. "You have a very good selection of research books that I can use for my article. There are so many. I don't really know which ones to choose. They all look like they would be helpful to me. I don't have much time to throw this article together, so I'll take all the help I can get."

Grandma Daisy laughed. "We'll sell them all to you if you like."

"I might just do that. These are surprisingly perfect for what I want to write."

"Well, as we say, Charming Books is where the perfect book picks you." She smiled as if she didn't mean that quite literally, which of course, I knew, she did.

"I can see that. It just seems so odd that they are all exactly right. Some of the titles here are obscure." He shook his head.

"Don't look a gift horse in the mouth." Grandma Daisy adjusted her cat-eye glasses on her nose. "Or in this case, a gift book in its pages."

I cleared my throat, afraid that my grandmother would take her clueless act a little too far and tip our hand. "Have you been a wine critic long?"

He glanced up from the shelves to me. "I'm a sommelier first. I write, but I am just starting out on the part of the business of being a critic. It will take me some time to catch up to Belinda's level of success, but now . . ." He trailed off as if he had thought better of what he was about to say.

"Then you must know her fiancé, Sebastian Knight," I said. "I believe he's a sommelier as well."

Jake straightened to his full height, which was even with mine at five nine. "Sebastian Knight is nowhere near in the same league as Belinda or me. He plays at wine. He doesn't know how to describe it or pair it. I have seen him at tastings. It's painful to watch. I suppose a less educated person wouldn't know the difference, but Belinda certainly would. I don't have the faintest idea what she was doing with him. My only guess is she kept him around because she knew that he would never surpass her. She was the one with the money and the power in that relationship. Don't let anyone, especially not Sebastian Knight, tell you differently."

"You seem to feel quite strongly about Mr. Knight," Grandma Daisy said.

"I cared about Belinda. She was my competition, but she was also my friend, and I don't like the idea of my friends being taken advantage of, especially not by someone lesser than them. Sebastian was only with Belinda because she was his ticket to the exclusive world of wine. I overheard him say as much when we were all at a New Year's Eve party in Manhattan. I don't believe that's how someone should create a career. I believe that everyone should fight for their place on even footing."

I didn't like to hear this about Sebastian. It was sad to me that Belinda had died without knowing real love.

"Do you?" Grandma Daisy pushed her glasses up her nose. "Do you think that Sebastian might have hurt Belinda?"

Jake's head whipped in her direction. "Like kill her? Why would he do that? Without her, he was a nobody in the wine industry. It was only his relationship with Belinda that made him relevant. No one will give him the time of day now."

I considered this. It made me wonder why Sebastian had thought it necessary to hire a private investigator to look into the murder, then. He had to know what the wine industry thought of him. Jake acted like it was common knowledge.

"He had no reason to kill her, but even if he wanted to, Sebastian is far too spineless to get his hands dirty. I never met such a lazy person in all my life. That's why being Belinda's fiancé was such a good fit for him. She made so much money, he didn't have to work. He traveled the world on her dime, too."

"I hate to keep bringing up last night," Grandma Daisy said.

I knew she didn't hate it in the least.

My grandmother went on to say, "But did

you see anyone there that you thought might be upset with Belinda in any way?"

"I'd say that woman that she lost it over. She would have a very good reason. Did she say it was her sister? Did I hear that right?" Jake asked. "She would have a great reason. Belinda humiliated her in front of all those people. If I were her, I would have wanted the floor to open up and swallow me."

I winced, knowing what he said was true, or at least the version of the truth that people were most likely to believe.

"And I saw a winemaker there who she had shredded in a recent article. I believe she called one of his vintages unpalatable. It was like the kiss of death, as far as that man's business went. No restaurant or wine store would buy his wine with that kind of review from such a powerful woman."

"What was that man's name?" I asked, trying my best to keep the eagerness out of my voice.

"Miles Rathbone. He owns Bone and Hearth Vineyards."

"I saw that man too," I said. "I remember he came up to Belinda's table and asked her to sign his book to the winery she destroyed with her review, his winery."

Jake nodded. "It's the same man."

"I know it," Grandma Daisy said. "It's a relatively new vineyard in the area. I think it used to be a dairy farm when you were a child, Violet."

"How long has Bone and Hearth been in business?" I asked.

"Three or four years," my grandmother said.

Jake nodded. "This would have been the first year they actually had wine to sell. It takes some time for vines to bear grapes and for the wine to age. As you can guess, Rathbone was thrilled to finally have a wine to take to the market, but Belinda's article ruined him before he could even get out of the gate."

"What will happen to Bone and Hearth now?" I asked.

Jake shrugged.

Clearly, Miles Rathbone was a person to talk to and one to add to my growing list of suspects. "When was the last time you saw Miles Rathbone?" I asked.

He frowned. "When I was leaving the party."

"When was that?"

He wrinkled his nose as if he smelled something bad. "Why are you asking me all these questions? You're acting like you're a cop or something."

Grandma Daisy laughed. "Oh, that's just Violet's way. You should have heard the number of questions she asked me as a child. She never gave me a moment's peace. Such an inquisitive child."

"I see." He pressed his lips into a thin line. "I'm sorry that I can't stay and answer all her questions," he said, not sounding sorry at all. He held up half a dozen books he had selected. "These will work perfectly."

After Grandma Daisy rang up Jake's books, he headed for the front door. I peered out the front window and saw that Private Investigator Redding was still standing outside the gate. He had leaned his guitar case along the fence. The freezing temperatures didn't seem to discourage him in the least. I didn't want Jake to run into Redding until I knew more about the private investigator and why he had chosen to stake out my home and business. He'd said that it was because I could give him leads on the case, but I didn't trust that answer. There had to be more to it. He would do much better chasing down leads of his own than standing outside my door.

"Jake, you don't want to go out that way. Why don't you go out through the back of the shop?" I asked.

Grandma Daisy's eyebrows disappeared

181

into her hairline.

Jake move his bag of books from his right hand to his left. "Why would I want to go out the back door?"

I searched my brain for a reason. "We have a lovely garden in the back that leads into the wooded park where the natural springs are. No one can come to Cascade Springs without seeing the springs for themselves. I'm happy to walk you back there."

He frowned. "As much as I would like to see them. I'm on a tight deadline. I'll look at them when the article is complete if I have the time."

"Violet, the back garden and the path in the woods are covered in snow. Mr. Zule shouldn't walk back there in his shiny shoes," Grandma Daisy said.

Jake's face reddened at the mention of his shoes, but my grandmother had a point: they were exceptionally shiny, and the snow would ruin them. However, I couldn't let Jake go out the front door of the shop to run into Joel Redding. I debated whether or not to tell Jake my real reason. Before I could make up my mind, he walked to the front door. "I will try to visit the springs before I leave the village if you really think it's a must. I have a lot of research to do for this article and have no time to waste. They gave me a couple of days beyond Belinda's original deadline, which isn't much. Belinda had been researching this article for months. I have days. Thank you for the books and thank you for your help, but I really must be going."

I watched helplessly as Jake walked to the front door. I followed him to the door and looked on as he moved along the pavers, through the gate, and out onto the sidewalk where Redding lay in wait. The P.I. stopped Jake and spoke to him for a minute, patted him on the shoulder, and then the two men made their way toward the Riverwalk together. It was most certainly a bad sign.

CHAPTER SIXTEEN

I shut the door and sighed. I walked over to Emerson and shook my finger at the cat. "You tormented that poor man."

Emerson batted at my finger with his paw, and then he took his paw and knocked the copy of *Little Women* sitting next to him on the bookcase to the floor. It landed pages down and splayed on the floor.

I rolled my eyes. "What am I going to do with you, Emerson?"

He started to clean his face with his paw as if he didn't have a care in the world.

"My dear," Grandma Daisy said. "If I was going to peg you as one of the four sisters in *Little Women,* you most definitely would be Jo. You have a very direct way about your questions."

"Not direct enough. He still went out the front door."

"What do you mean? And why didn't you

want that wine writer leaving through the front?"

I sighed and told her about the P.I.

My grandmother put her hands on her narrow hips. "There's a private investigator in the village? Is he here to steal your thunder as a crime stopper?"

I rolled my eyes. "I'm not a crime stopper, and for goodness' sakes, don't ever say that in front of David Rainwater or his head might start to spin *Exorcist* style."

"That would be an interesting trick if he can pull it off."

"No, it wouldn't be." I shook my finger at her. "And don't get any ideas."

"No," she muttered, with as much enthusiasm as a teenager accepting the fact that she had to do her homework.

I frowned. "I wonder if Rainwater knows about Rathbone."

Grandma Daisy walked back to the sales counter. "I'm sure he does, but you should call him and tell him all you've learned. I think he would like to know what his star investigator is up to."

"I'm not his star investigator. I think the mere fact that you called me that would give poor Chief Rainwater heart palpitations."

She opened her mouth as if she was going to protest.

"I'll tell Rainwater just as soon as I see him."

"Good," she said, sounding satisfied. "Now, I think it would do you some good to concentrate on the books in front of you. For some reason the shop's essence very much wants you to read *Little Women.* I'm surprised that you're not further along in understanding what the essence wants you to know."

"It's much denser than people believe. The shop wants me to read it, but it'll take time." I bent over to pick up the book that Emerson had knocked over. I flipped it over and found the book was open to the following passage: " 'Money is a needful and precious thing, — and, when well used, a noble thing, — but I never want you to think it is the first or only prize to strive for.' " Marmee was saying this to her daughters.

I bit my lip. Ultimately, was the murder about money? But whose money? I looked out the window in the direction Jake and Redding had gone. I glanced back at Emerson, who was washing his tail now. Was this clue from the shop or was it from the cat? I shook the thought away. It was from the shop. It had to be.

"My dear girl, you just have to make the

time for this. It seems to me that you shouldn't be asking me these questions but asking the books themselves."

"I know. You're right." I showed her the book. "And the shop agrees with you, too."

My grandmother laughed. "It's quiet now, my girl. Read up."

I walked over to one of the large sofas. A fire crackled in the hearth as I curled up in the corner of the sofa with my feet tucked up under me. I lay the book in my lap and waited. Nothing happened. I waited a little longer, hoping that the book would magically open to the page that would tell me exactly what I should do or give me a clue as to what had happened to Belinda, but again nothing happened.

I glanced up at the birch tree as if blaming it. "If you want me to solve this murder, it might be helpful if you were just a little more direct with your hints."

The tree was silent, just like the book, just like the shop and its essence. Emerson jumped up on the couch, curled in a ball, and pressed against my hip.

"Are you going to help me with this?"

The cat didn't answer me either.

I sighed and opened the novel to the chapter I had left off at the night before, where the girls were all complaining about their work and Marmee was letting them lie about. The March sisters soon realized that they missed the structure of work, and Marmee's valuable lesson was instilled into each one of her daughters' hearts.

The ringing shop phone jarred me from the world of the March sisters and their games of make-believe with their dear neighbor Laurie. The shop phone rang again, and I had no idea how much time had passed since I started reading or how many customers had come and gone during that time. I had been too absorbed in the story to notice.

The phone kept ringing. I didn't know where my grandmother had gone. I hopped off the couch and hurried to the phone.

"Charming Books, where the perfect book picks you. Can I help you?" I asked in a breathless voice.

"Yes," an elderly male voice said over the phone. "This is Charles Hancock. I very much would like to speak to my lady Daisy Waverly."

Oh dear, I thought. Charles Hancock was an eccentric old man well into his early eighties who happened to be in love with my grandmother. Grandma Daisy did not reciprocate his affections, so when Charles called or visited the shop, she always seemed to disappear. I found the old man harmless and even endearing. My grandmother didn't appear to see him the same way.

"Hello, Charles," I said in the brightest voice I could muster. "It's so nice to hear from you, but I'm so sorry, my grandmother just stepped out."

"How unfortunate," he said. "I very much wanted to check on her to see if she was well. I have just heard about the events of last night. I hate to think that my dear lady was anywhere close to a murderer. I should have been there with my sword and my shield to protect her from the dangers of the world such as this."

I winced. No one wanted Charles Hancock walking around the village with sword and shield. I prayed that he was speaking figuratively, but with Charles there was one no way to be sure. He had a little bit of Don Quixote in him, or maybe a lot bit of Don Quixote. I wouldn't have been the least bit surprised if he had ridden up to the bookshop one day on Rocinante with Sancho Panza at his side. As misplaced as his feelings were, I found his gallantry toward my grandmother sweet, but as of yet, I'd had no success in getting Grandma Daisy to view Charles as anything more than an annoyance.

"I can assure you that my grandmother is fine, and I will let her know you called and that you were concerned."

"Please do that. I have half a mind to traverse to Charming Books right now so I can see Daisy for myself."

Traverse. That wasn't a word you heard every day.

"Oh," I said. "I don't think that's a good idea. Grandma Daisy is very tired from being up so late last night from the book signing. We don't want to do anything that will exhaust her more."

"Too true. I want my lady to be in her best form. She is so lovely, and she needs her rest to keep her loveliness fresh. I would hate for her to wilt as some flowers do, but it is her soul that I love most. She will always have that. No matter the scars of the body, it is the soul that is precious to me."

"I'll make sure she gets the message," I said, eager to get back to my reading and cracking this case wide opened.

But Charles didn't seem to get the hint that I wanted to end the call. "I am grieved to hear about the troubles that have fallen on the Perkins girls again. I always told them when they were younger to stay together and love one another, but they have not. Now the most terrible deed has been committed against the oldest, against them all, I daresay. I hope after this tragedy the family will finally make amends."

I stopped myself from hanging up the phone. "What was that you just said?"

"I hope after this tragedy that the family will finally make amends. The girls are the only family that they have left in the world. They should be together. It's what their dear mother would have wanted."

"You know the Perkins family?" I supposed I shouldn't have been so surprised, because Cascade Springs was a small village of only a few thousand people. But he spoke like he knew them more than just as villagers. It sounded to me as if he knew them very well.

"Of course I do. I know the girls quite well. I watched them grow up."

That's when a memory of Charles from my childhood came to me. He had been their neighbor. However, back then, I didn't remember him being around as much. That must have been before he fell in love with my grandmother.

As if he could read my mind, Charles said, "I was their next-door neighbor for nearly twenty years. I still live next to the house that the girls grew up in. They've all moved away after the youngest finished high school;

that was well after their mother died. Terrible tragedy. I spent a lot of time with them when they were girls and their dear mother, God rest her soul."

An idea came to me, and I asked, "Charles, would you be up for a visit?"

"A visit?" he asked as if he had never been asked such a thing before.

I felt sorry for the old gentleman. "Yes, I'm wondering if I could come over to your house and talk to you about the Perkins family."

"Will Daisy come with you?" His voice was so hopeful I almost wanted to ask my grandmother if she would tag along with me on my field trip, but I stopped myself. Someone had to stay back and mind the store while I was gone, and my grandmother had made it very clear on more than one occasion that she wanted nothing to do with Charles Hancock.

"I'm afraid she can't," I said. "She has some very important business to attend to at the store, but I can be there in twenty minutes."

"My dearest Daisy works far too hard. It is time for her to retire and enjoy quiet days, but instead she won't give up her work. It's something I love most about her, but that infuriates me as well."

"Yes, well," I said, not sure how to respond to that. "Are you home now? Can I stop by?"

"It would be my great honor to have the granddaughter of the one I love in my home. Please do come."

I said I would and ended the call.

The kitchen door swung closed at the back of the shop, and my grandmother walked toward the tree holding two mugs of fresh coffee. The heavenly aroma wafted my way. She handed me a mug. I took it gratefully in my chilled hands.

"Did the books tell you something?" she asked. "You have a certain sparkle in your eye like you get when you are up to something. When you were young, the look always made me a bit nervous."

Little Woman lay in the middle of the long sofa where I had left it. "Nothing yet. It's so strange. I know the shop's essence wants me to read the book, but what part? It's not exactly a short read." I sipped the coffee. "But I am on to something else. I'm going to go talk to the Perkins' neighbor who knew them when they were young. I hope that will give me insight into the sisters' dynamics and maybe more understanding as to why they had such a terrible falling out." I took care not to tell my grandmother that the neighbor was Charles Hancock.

My grandmother put her hands on her hips. "You're going to go talk to Charles Hancock, aren't you?"

"How on earth do you know that?"

She rolled her eyes. "Violet, I have lived in this village all my life. Don't you think I know where Charles lives? The man pesters me enough that I have to make a point of staying away from his street."

I sipped my coffee, hoping to buy myself some time.

"You do know by doing that that you're only encouraging Charles in his pursuit of me, don't you?"

"Maybe. Probably," I admitted. "But if he knows something that can help Lacey, don't I have to find out what it is?"

"If you are going, then you must assume that Belinda's death has something to do with the sisters."

I walked over to the couch and picked up Alcott's novel. "This is what makes me think that." I dropped the book back on the couch.

"Fair enough." She pressed her lips together and sighed. "I agree, you should go and hear what Charles has to say. However, don't be surprised if it's a whole lot of gibberish." She straightened a book that was crooked on the bookcase next to her. "I care for Lacey too and feel terrible for the poor girl. She's been through so much in her life. More than a woman of her age should." She squeezed my hand. "You have too, my dear. I think deep down that's why you are so determined to help her. You've been in her shoes before, both in the loss of a mother and being accused of doing something terrible when you were completely innocent."

I swallowed and leaned over to pick up the novel again. Before I touched it, the book flopped open and the pages fluttered.

My grandmother and I watched in amazement. Even though we had witnessed this odd phenomenon many times before, it was still a wonder. Finally, the fluttering stopped, and the book lay open.

I picked up the book. My eyes fell on the following line, which I read aloud in a shaky voice. " 'There are many Beths in the world, shy and quiet, sitting in corners till needed, and living for others so cheerfully, that no one sees the sacrifices till the little cricket on the hearth stops chirping, and the sweet, sunshiny presence vanishes, leaving silence and shadow behind.' " I looked up my grandmother. "What does that mean? It's not possible that Belinda Perkins would have been considered a Beth."

My grandmother shook her head. "Quite the opposite, I would say. She was brash, loud, and driven. Nothing like Beth March in the story."

I agreed. "If anyone is like Beth, it would be Lacey." My heart constricted. "Are the books trying to tell me something will happen to her?"

Grandma Daisy shook her head. "I don't know, but if speaking to Charles Hancock will answer that question for you, you should go and go now."

CHAPTER SEVENTEEN

I left for Charles Hancock's home on foot. Since Lacey had been my childhood friend, I knew exactly where to find Charles's house with little thought. It was a path I had trod many times when I was young.

Cascade Springs was a tourist village, and most of the neighborhoods near the historic downtown area where Charming Books stood had a theme. The neighborhood where Lacey had grown up had been the "tree neighborhood." Every street in the small neighborhood was named after a type of tree. Lacey's old home was on Black Walnut Street. The houses on the street were old historic homes, and I hadn't been back to visit since returning to the village.

To reach the neighborhood, I crossed River Road and took a shortcut between Midcentury Vintage and the candle shop next door to Sadie's store. Usually I would have taken the long way around to the tree neighborhood, but I wanted to get to Charles as soon as I could. It had been almost twenty minutes since I'd told him I would see him. Knowing the old gent, he might storm Charming Books with that shield and sword thinking something terrible had happened to my grandmother and caused my delay.

The snow crunched under my boots, and I left behind obvious tracks. I came out on the other side of the block in the tree neighborhood on the street. Before turning the corner, I looked back toward the river and saw a man carrying a guitar going in the opposite direction. Redding again. Was the private investigator following me? If he was trying to stay undercover, the guitar case was a poor choice.

When I turned around again, the man and the guitar case were gone. I wondered if I should continue on to Charles's house. I might just be leading Redding right to the old man. Then again, I decided that I should go. The sooner Lacey was free of any suspicions, the better.

I continued on my way to Black Walnut Street. Even if I didn't know where Lacey's old house was, I would have easily found it, as Charles Hancock stood in the middle of his yard without a coat or hat.

"Miss Violet," he said in his booming voice, and threw up his arms. "I was just about to begin a search party for you. As you can imagine, I have been dreadfully worried about you, since you were supposed to be here a quarter hour ago. I had great fear in my heart that something terrible had befallen your grandmother, my one true love."

I hurried up the sidewalk toward him, taking care not to slip on any of the icy concrete. "I'm so sorry, Charles. It took me a little more time to break away from the shop than I expected. I can assure you that everything is fine, and my grandmother is fine too."

Charles lowered his arms. What was left of his white hair was combed over his pink dome of a head. "I am happy to hear it, because if my lady was in danger, I would be the very first to run to her side."

"I don't have any doubt about that, Charles." I turned and faced Lacey's childhood home. As I stared at it, memories of coming to the house with Colleen flooded back to me in a rush. Colleen and I had traipsed all over the village together, so there weren't many places in Cascade Springs where I didn't think of her. However, standing in front of Lacey's house, it was especially strong. Colleen had always been there with me. I couldn't remember ever walking up to that blue front door alone.

The house that had once been Lacey's was a small white Cape Cod that was almost invisible in all the snow surrounding it. While the other houses in the historic neighborhood stood out, with bright Victorian paint and decorative gingerbread, this house blended in. Charles's home to the right stood in sharp contrast to the Perkinses' old home. It was a large brick home. It was hard for me to believe that the old man had lived there alone all these years.

"I spent a little bit of time at the house growing up," I mused.

"I remember seeing you here often with Colleen Preston." He tried to smooth down the few wayward hairs on the top of his head. "I don't know if I ever told you this, but I never believed you were behind that girl's death, no matter what others in the village were led to believe by the Mortons. You did a good thing to cast Nathan Morton aside. There are much finer men who would raise up their arms to earn your affections. He was not worthy of you."

"Thank you," I said, liking Charles more by the second. He wasn't as bad as my grandmother thought.

He smiled at me. "I was grateful when I called the bookshop today and you said that your grandmother was hard at work. That must mean that she is finally on the mend. I will go see her in a day's time to give her more time to recover. I do know, too, like any true lady, she will want to look her best for her knight, and I must allow her that."

"Recover?" I asked.

"Why yes," he said, aghast. "I have called Charming Books a number of times in recent days, and every time I call, your sweet grandmother has been overtaken by a coughing fit and said she was too unwell to talk or take callers."

I'll bet she did, I thought, trying my best to suppress a smile. No wonder Grandma Daisy hadn't wanted me to meet with Charles when I first mentioned it. I was completely blowing her cover. "She's much better now. A complete recovery."

He placed a hand to his chest. "That's such good news! It does me good to hear it."

He seemed so relieved that I realized that Charles Hancock really did love my grandmother. It wasn't one of his dramatic acts. He had been worried about her all this time. I felt sorry for him and promised myself that

I would put in a good word for the older man with her. Maybe that would help.

"Will you give her my good wishes for her health and prosperity?"

"Oh, I will. You can count on that," I said, realizing that I was picking up some of Charles's flowery language in the process of speaking with him. If I wasn't careful, I would be talking about knights and ladies before the end of the day.

He shook his head. "What she needs is a life of leisure. She shouldn't toil so in the bookshop. I could give that to her. My Social Security checks are quite good."

It was time to change the subject. "When the Perkinses lived here, what was the family like? When did they move away?"

"It is quite cold out here. Let us go into my home, where we can discuss this at length by the warm hearth."

I frowned. I hadn't planned for this little errand to take so long, and I most certainly hadn't planned to go inside Charles's house. However, the old man was visibly shivering. If we stood out here much longer, he was at real risk of catching pneumonia. "Lead the way," I said.

He bowed and walked forward. I followed Charles up the walk to his home. He moved surprisingly quickly.

He opened the rounded front door of the home and stepped inside. I followed him and ran directly into the business end of a mace.

"Ahh!" I hopped away from it and whacked my shoulder against the edge of the open door. I stared at the mace, which was in the hand of a full suit of armor. The knight holding the mace wasn't the only one. There were three other full-sized knights in the corners of the room.

I rubbed my hip. Luckily, I hadn't run into the weapon hard enough to break the skin. "Are those real?"

Charles raised his eyebrow at me. "Of course they are. I had them shipped here all the way from Europe. The one with the mace, I had to outbid a museum in Zurich to add to my collection."

I raised my eyebrows. Charles had never struck me as a particularly wealthy man, but he had to be doing quite well to outbid a museum for artifacts. I wondered what his career had been as a young man and what was in those Social Security checks he had bragged about.

"These are just a few of my treasures," Charles explained.

His treasures. I wasn't sure I liked the sound of that.

Charles led me around the suits of armor, and I kept my eye on them all the while. I wouldn't have been the least bit surprised if they had started moving. That wasn't something I would have thought a year ago, but since I had become the Caretaker of a bookshop with message-giving and flying books, I had been able to bend what was possible a little bit more. However, I was happy the suits of armor didn't appear to have any magical properties and didn't move an inch.

I followed Charles into a room that I guessed was a library of sorts, but it would have been better described as a museum. The walls were lined with glass-enclosed cases that held every sort of ancient artifact I could imagine. There were Grecian busts, pieces of Egyptian hieroglyphs, and Mayan sundials. I couldn't believe what I was looking at. It wasn't possible that all these artifacts were real.

Charles seemed to accurately interpret my inability to speak, because he said, "I had been an archeologist for many years. I made my fortune that way. Now I'm an old man and just a collector."

I blinked at him. "Like Indiana Jones."

He chuckled. "Maybe not just like that."

I walked over to one of the display cases. "I thought archeologists find things for museums, not for private collections."

He smiled at this, and for the first time I caught a glimpse of the adventurous young man he'd once been. "It depends what kind of archeologist you are."

My eyebrows went way up. Had I come face-to-face with a geriatric tomb raider?

"I plan after I die to will my collection to a museum, but until then, I do like enjoying the spoils of my more adventurous youth. When I was a true knight in the field and worthy of a fair lady such as my beloved Daisy."

"Does Grandma Daisy know about all this?" I knew my grandmother would be fascinated with Charles's collection.

"It is not a knight's way to brag of his successes."

"Did the Perkins girls know about your collection?" I asked, thinking that this was a thing Lacey might have told Colleen and me when we were teens. Colleen and I had been a tight pair, and Lacey was always trying to break into our duo. Rarely did we let her in, and I regretted that now. If we had let Lacey be a part of it, I thought, we would have made a dynamic trio as friends. She certainly would have won us over with information about Charles Hancock's collection.

"Only Lacey knew. She was the quietest and sweetest of the girls. I knew I could trust her. I asked her not to tell anyone about my collection, and as far as I know, she never has."

I had been right in thinking that Lacey knew about the collection. The quote that the shop wanted me to read came back to me. Even though she was the second of the four girls, Lacey was very much the "Beth" in the family if they were all assigned roles from *Little Women.* She was not Jo, who was so sure of herself, or selfish Amy. It made me just that much more determined to prove her innocence of Belinda's death.

"Lacey came into the house?"

He nodded. "I know the Perkins girls very well, very well indeed. I always knew from the start how they would end up. Belinda would be a powerhouse and a great success. She had a great determination about her and didn't care who she stepped on in the process of reaching her goals. Lacey would have a quiet and happy life when she gave herself permission to have it. It took some time, and I am grateful to Adrien, who was the one to bring that to pass. Michelle would be happy as a wife and mother because she was always playing house and liked things in a certain order. Finally, little

Adele would be the free spirit to go her own way and create."

"Where are Michelle and Adele now?"

"Michelle is married to an accountant with just the kind of life that she wanted, and Adele has a little painting studio in the bird neighborhood."

My brows knit together. Again, I wondered how Lacey's youngest sister could afford studio space in such an expensive neighborhood. There was no question that I would have to ask Lacey more about her youngest sister.

"And their mother?" I asked.

"God rest her soul. She was a good woman and did all she could for the girls. By the time they moved into that house, their father was out of the picture. I believe Adele was just a baby at the time, no more than three months old. Their mother worked like a dog for years raising those girls on her own. I never once heard her raise her voice or complain in all the time that I knew her. The girls all adored her."

"And it must've been hard on all of them when she died."

"Hardest on sweet Lacey, I daresay. Belinda, by that time, was off seeing the world, just like she always planned that she would. She left behind her younger sisters to fend for themselves." He wrinkled his nose. "Of the girls, Belinda was my least favorite. She was a selfish girl, and it boggled my mind that she could have been raised by such a selfless mother and turn out the way she did. If anyone is most like their mother, it is Lacey, but she takes it to the other extreme. I never heard her defend herself to her sisters, when many times from where I was sitting it seemed to me that she was in the right." He shook his head. "Poor girl."

"She always went along with what the others wanted?" I asked.

"That's not completely true. There was one time when she dug her heels in. It was with Belinda, of course, after their mother died. I remember it like it was yesterday. Belinda roared in here in her fancy car and yelled and screamed at Lacey for killing their mother and keeping their younger sisters from her. The whole neighbor heard, and half of them came outside to witness the trouble. I think Belinda expected that Lacey would hand over the two younger girls, but she didn't. Lacey said the girls would stay with her because it was their mother's wishes. Belinda was so taken aback by it that she promised she would never speak to Lacey again. I hoped that she didn't keep that promise, because not speaking to someone is the worst kind of punishment you can inflict on another person, especially someone you were meant to love as a sister."

I frowned. It seemed to me that Belinda had kept that promise all the way to the grave.

Charles settled into a leather armchair that could have held three of him. The chair dwarfed him, making him look very small and even older than he actually was. "I was happy when I saw that Lacey married Adrien, who is a good man. She was just a sweet, cheerful girl. Never screamed or yelled, even when the others did. She always said hello and waved to me when the others ignored me. She was a sweet cricket."

A sweet cricket. I felt goosebumps on my arms. There was something my brain was trying to click into place. It almost felt like if I could grasp hold of it, I would be able to discover who had killed Belinda.

Then it hit me. The passage that the shop essence had wanted me to read came back to my mind. *There are many Beths in the world, shy and quiet, sitting in corners till needed, and living for others so cheerfully that no one sees the sacrifices till the little cricket on the hearth stops chirping, and the sweet, sunshiny presence vanishes, leaving silence and shadow behind.*

I had to do everything in my power to make sure Lacey didn't meet the same fate that Beth had.

CHAPTER EIGHTEEN

If Belinda's death was related to her sisters, then I needed to talk to each of the other sisters, and I planned to start with youngest. I called my grandmother and told her what I was up to. "Do you know where Adele's studio is?" I asked.

"It's on Sparrow Street," Grandma Daisy said.

I told my grandmother that I would be back to the shop as soon as I could and ended the called.

Adele's studio was an old Cape Cod home that probably dated all the way back to the same period as Charming Books. I knocked on the door, but as I did, the door fell open.

"Hello?" I called into the place.

The house retained its original architecture on the outside, but on the inside the former home had clearly been altered. Many of the walls had been blown out to make one large great room that was brightly lit with large windows and sunlight. Every color of paint in the rainbow was spattered on the floor and walls. I hoped that Adele wasn't renting the work space, because there was no way she was getting her deposit back.

"Ahhh!" A scream came from the back corner of the room, which was hidden from the rest of the place by a paint-spattered Chinese screen.

"Hello? Are you hurt?"

"Ahhhh!" the scream came again.

Maybe talking to Adele wasn't necessary, or maybe I could come back later when she wasn't screaming her head off.

"Hey, who's there?" a voice asked, perfectly calm and composed. A small woman popped out from behind the Chinese screen. She wore a pair of earbuds, and even from where I was standing by the front door, I could hear the pounding heavy metal she was listening to.

The last time I had seen Adele, she had been ten and blonde. She wasn't either of those anymore. Her hair was jet-black and fell all the way down her back. She wore a black beret on her head, and it was tilted at a jaunty angle. Both her hair and her hat were splatted with red, yellow, green, and purple paint. So were her clothes, which were also black, or at least they had been.

She was the girl all in black that I had seen at the book signing, which meant that she had been there the night her oldest sister died.

"Who are you?" Adele asked.

I shouldn't have been surprised that Adele didn't recognize me. "I'm Violet Waverly. I'm friends with Lacey."

She nodded. "Why are you here?"

It was a very good question and one I should have expected her to ask. I didn't have a good answer, so I settled on the truth. "I wanted to talk to you about Belinda."

"No," she said, and disappeared behind the Chinese screen again.

I stood there for a second, unsure what to do.

"Ahh!" she cried from behind the screen again. Her cry made me move, and I peeked around the side of the screen.

She stood in front of a six-by-six canvas that had a lovely view of the Riverwalk in the village. I recognized the scene immediately even though it was blotted and streaked with red paint. "What are you doing?" I couldn't keep the horror out of my voice. The Riverwalk scene was so lovely and tranquil, and the red paint ruined it.

"Starting over. All I can do is start over."

"But the painting was lovely."

"I hate this painting," she said.

I stared at it, and my heart broke a little at the sight of all that red over the lovely woodland scene. "Why? It's the best of the Riverwalk I've ever seen. You captured the heart of the village so perfectly."

"That doesn't matter. There is no point in it anymore. There is no reason to perfect my art when I'm going to be living on the street."

"Why do you say that?" I kept my voice as calm as possible.

Adele dipped her broad brush into the red paint and flicked it at the canvas. It immediately reminded me of blood and brought back the memory of her oldest sister's death. "Is it Belinda? I can see why you're upset."

She set her brush on the paint spatter table next to her. "My sister is dead, but before she died, she killed me."

"How?" I asked.

"It doesn't matter."

"You were at her signing. I was there selling books with my Grandma Daisy. I saw you there."

She frowned. "I suppose I stood out with all of Belinda's fancy friends, didn't I?"

"Did you get a chance to talk to your

sister before . . . ?"

"No. I almost did, but as soon as Lacey walked in, I knew it was a lost cause, so I left."

"You left before Belinda was found."

She gave me a level look and wiped her hands on a dirty paper towel. It didn't look to me like it helped much. If anything, it ground the paint deeper into her skin. I wondered if she walked around all day with permanently blood red–stained hands. "I didn't hear about the murder until the next day when Lacey called me."

I frowned. She hadn't exactly answered the question.

"You and Lacey are on speaking terms?"

"Not exactly, but she does call now and again. I never pick up when she calls."

This made me very sad for Lacey. I could see her continually calling her youngest sister with the hope that one day Adele's anger would soften toward her and Adele would pick up.

She wiped her paintbrush on her jeans, leaving a swath of yellow paint across the fabric. "There's no point in any of this."

"What do you mean?"

"All the work I had done will come to nothing."

"I'm happy to help any way that I can,

and I know Lacey would too. She's your sister and loves you very much."

She laughed. "Can you pay my rent for this space? Because that's what I need. That's what Belinda promised she would do because she said I had talent. I should have known that she was lying. I should have known, if I couldn't make any money, that she would change her mind. I can't believe I trusted her." She flicked more paint onto the canvas, and spatter flew everywhere, including on me.

"Sorry," she said. "You might want to put on a poncho if you're going to stand there." She waved the brush, and globs of red paint fell onto the top of my shoe.

I looked forlornly down at the shoe that I'd had since college. It was clearly a goner. "It's fine," I said, unable to keep the sadness from my voice.

"I really am sorry," Adele said, looking as if she might cry.

I smiled at her. "It really is okay. Both Grandma Daisy and my friend Sadie have been trying to get rid of these shoes for weeks. They will be very happy when they hear the news, and I'm certain that Sadie will love finding a new pair for me."

"They are really ugly shoes," she agreed. Then her face fell. "Belinda always had the nicest shoes," she said. "What do you think will happen to all her nice shoes?"

"I — I don't know."

She burst into tears. Between gasps, she said, "They were really nice shoes."

"Are you crying over the shoes?" I found myself asking.

"No." She shook her head. "I just can't believe she's dead. It doesn't seem possible, you know? Belinda would be so mad that she was dead, and even madder if she knew that someone had killed her. Do you think she knows she was killed?"

"I don't know," I said, feeling at a loss to comfort the girl. Her tears washed away some of her harsh makeup, and she looked so very young under that hard exterior.

"And do you know the worst part?"

I nodded, waiting for her to tell me.

She wiped away a tear from her cheek with the back of her hand, smearing paint and black mascara. "The day before she died, when she told me that she wouldn't be paying my rent anymore, I told her that I could . . ." She didn't finish her sentence.

"You told her what?" I prompted.

"I told her that I could kill her." She took a breath and said, barely above a whisper, "And I really meant it."

CHAPTER NINETEEN

Adele was inconsolable after that and asked me to leave the studio. I asked her if there was anyone I could call to be with her, maybe Lacey or a friend? But the young artist said she wanted to be alone with her paints. As I walked out her door, I couldn't help but realize that she had as good a motive to murder her sister as anyone else did.

After leaving Adele's studio, I went straight to Charming Books. The after-school crowd of children and parents were there, so business was brisk. It seemed that every middle-schooler who came into the shop needed a copy of *The Adventures of Huckleberry Finn* right away. Luckily, Charming Books was the kind of shop that, even if we didn't know what books our customers would want, always came up with extra copies of the books our customers would need.

The sun had set right at five when the

shop closed, and with the loss of the sun, the temperatures outside dropped into the single digits. Grandma Daisy struggled into her winter coat and pulled a hat so far down over her silver bob that it touched the top of her glasses. Then she wrapped a six-foot-long scarf around her face half a dozen times. By the time she was done, the only parts of her that were visible were her glasses and eyes.

"Are you sure you don't want me to drive you to your house? It's very cold out there."

She pulled the scarf down. "Violet, you act like I'm an elderly woman on my last leg. I am more than capable of walking the three blocks to my home from the shop. It's not even snowing. The sky is clear with a bright blue moon. I have been making this trek back and forth for decades, and I won't let you take it from me."

I held up my hands in surrender. "All right, all right. On the bright side, if you run into Charles Hancock, he will never recognize you in that outfit."

She grinned. "Maybe I will start wearing it all year round." She narrowed her blue eyes. "We were so busy when you got back to the shop, you didn't tell me how your visit with Charles went."

"It was interesting," I said, thinking of his

219

artifact room. "He knew the Perkins family quite well." I stopped myself from saying anything more about Charles's home. He had not outright asked me to keep his secret about his in-home museum, but it felt like a betrayal of sorts to say anything about it. "He's an old gentleman, really. You might like him better if he toned down the knight stuff."

She shook her mittened hand at me. "Don't you be getting any ideas about Charles and me."

"What ideas?" I asked innocently.

She glowered at me. "I suggest that you spend what time you have tonight reading *Little Women*. That book will be the key to whatever is going on in this village."

As if on cue, Faulkner flew across the shop and dropped a copy of Alcott's novel on the sales counter. It landed with a resounding thud that echoed through the shop.

"See, Faulkner agrees with me," Grandma Daisy said.

After my grandmother left, I took her advice and sat down on one of the two couches by the hearth with the novel and a legal pad. I set the book in the middle of my lap. Emerson jumped onto the coffee table as if in anticipation. Faulkner too seemed interested in the proceedings, as he swooped down from the birch tree and settled on the corner of the hearth. He held his wings out from his body as the fire warmed his feathers.

I glanced at my two companions. "Are we all settled now?"

The cat and crow stared at me expectantly. I shook my head. If my friends back in Chicago could have seen me now, looking for guidance from magical books and talking to animals, they'd have had me committed.

I lay the book open in my lap to the passage that the shop's essence had last shown me. Nothing happened. "Come on," I said to the tree. "Why are you making this so hard this time?"

Still nothing. The front door of the shop opened, and a gust of cold wind ruffled the pages of my book, causing me to lose my place. I jumped up. Had I forgotten to lock the front door after Grandma Daisy left? "The shop is closed!"

"Then you might want to turn around the open sign and lock the door," Grant Morton said. He held a narrow bottle of ice wine in his hand.

I scooped *Little Women* off the floor and held it to my chest. "What are you doing here, Grant?"

He smiled and held up the bottle. "I brought this by as an apology gift. My parents gave you a hard time the other night."

They had. I couldn't deny that. "They were understandably upset."

He set the wine bottle on the sales counter. "They are always upset." There was a hint of bitterness in his voice. "And I am sorry about how they acted. I don't want the winery to have a bad reputation. It has so much potential."

"National potential?" I asked.

He smiled.

"You said you were going to take the ice wine to the national market."

He nodded. "I'm starting with specialty stores, but if it goes well, the sky is the limit. It's the first time Morton Vineyards has tried to do this. My parents don't have the same vision."

"But you and Nathan do?" I asked.

The fire had died down, and I shifted the logs with an iron poker.

"I do. Nathan has nothing to do with this deal." He started to pace. "He's like my parents, really. They are all too afraid to branch out. They think what we're doing is enough. It never is. You can always push further."

I set the poker back in its stand and studied him. "And Belinda's death. What impact will that have on your plan?"

He snorted. "Nothing. I'm sorry she died, but it has nothing to do with my family business."

"Does the name Joel Redding mean anything to you?"

He snorted again. "You mean the private investigator Sebastian hired?" He rolled his eyes. "The man is a nut, carrying around a guitar case all the time. He came to the winery this afternoon. He wanted to see where she died. I kicked him off the property. He's not a cop, and I don't have to give him access to anything."

"Don't you care what happened to Belinda?" I asked.

"Not enough to dwell on it. I'm sorry that it happened, even sorrier that it was on my family's land, but I didn't know her, not really. No one can expect me to be sad. The only shame for my family is the loss of publicity from her article. She was writing a piece on the wineries in the village. I had hoped to announce our move to a national market through that article."

"The magazine found another sommelier to write the article," I said.

"They did? Who?"

"Jake Zule."

"Really? I've never hear of him." He looked like he wanted to say more when the front door opened again. I would really need to lock it.

"Violet, I know you have been crazy busy today, so I baked some cookies for the Red Inkers meeting tonight. I just wanted to drop them off early so I didn't forget them. You know how absent-minded I can be." Sadie floated into the room holding a tray of cookies. She froze in place when she saw Grant standing there.

I closed my eyes for a moment. This was the worst possible time for Sadie to drop by early.

"Sadie," Grant said. "It's nice to see you."

She blinked and seemed unable to talk.

Grant smiled in the way a person would at a misbehaving child. "You must have one of your writing meetings tonight. Are you still working on your little novel, Sadie? It's such a sweet hobby."

Grant's comment seemed to shake her from her stupor. "It's not a hobby."

He laughed.

I clenched my fists at my sides. "Grant, I think it's time for you to go."

He smiled. "I didn't mean any harm."

"Yes, you did," Sadie said. "You always

224

do. I wish I had seen that sooner."

A strange look crossed his handsome face. "I do too." He walked out of the shop without another word, slamming the door behind him.

"Are you okay?" I asked Sadie.

"I will be. Someday," she said. "I should have known Grant wasn't the right guy for me. He never thought I was going to be a writer."

"You are a writer."

She gave me a watery smile. "Okay, a published writer. He always called it my hobby. I thought it didn't bother me. I told myself that it didn't bother me, but hearing him say that again, I realized that it bothered me a lot."

"I'm sorry, Sadie," I said. "If a person loves you, he should believe in you and your dreams."

She wiped a tear from her cheek. "Right." She gave her head a little shake. "I'm going to go back to my shop until the meeting. I just need some time."

I wanted to argue with her, but she set the cookies on an end table and was out the door. I went back to my book, more confused than ever, and more disappointed than ever that the shop's essence wasn't telling me more.

CHAPTER TWENTY

I read for another hour until there was a brisk knock on the front door of Charming Books. The Red Inkers had arrived. I jumped out of my seat and hurried over to the sales counter before going to the door. I hid the bottle of ice wine that Grant had brought me under the counter. There was no sense in reminding Sadie that Grant had been there.

Emerson sat in the middle of the coffee table with his paws tucked up under his body, and he blinked at me slowly, while Faulkner cawed and flew from the edge of the hearth to the top of the tree.

There was another bang on the front door. My cell phone rang, and I removed it from my back pocket. "Violet." Sadie's high-pitched voice came over the line. "Are you going to let us in for the Red Inkers meeting? It's freezing out here. I can't feel my toes anymore."

"I'll be right there," I said, and ended the call. I did my best to clean up my papers and notes on the couch. I patted down my unruly hair, and when that didn't work — I could feel my long strawberry waves zooming off in every direction — I twisted my hair in a messy knot on the top of my head. As I walked to the door, I rubbed grit from my eyes and pinched my cheeks to add some color to my pallor. Chief Rainwater might be on his way here or even outside with the other Red Inkers, assuming he hadn't been caught up with the murder investigation. That would never do, since I looked like I had been hit by a truck.

I opened the door and smiled. I found Richard, Renee, and Sadie on my doorstep. I was both relieved and disappointed not to see Chief David Rainwater among them. His absence would give me more time to be presentable, but it wasn't until that moment that I realized how much I had been looking forward to seeing him again that evening.

The three of them trooped inside and removed their layers of coats, scarfs, hats, and gloves.

"The worst thing about winter," Renee said, "is you practically have to disrobe as soon as you enter any building."

Richard, who was just a few feet away from her, neatly folding his scarf in his hand before tucking it into the sleeve of his coat, blushed.

"I think winter has a certain kind of beauty," Sadie said wistfully.

"Sadie Cunningham," Renee said. "You could say something nice about a snake."

"What's wrong with snakes?" Sadie asked, confused.

"My point exactly." Renee gave me a hug. "It's nice to see you off campus, my friend. Wouldn't the students be surprised if they knew we had lives outside of that place?"

"I'll be there tomorrow. I have two morning classes back to back. Both are freshman comp, and therefore, no one in either room wants to be there, including me."

"Yes," Richard said. "It can be a challenge to teach language arts to those who have no interest in it, but I truly believe that anyone can be a writer. I myself have worked on my craft for years, and I still see so much room for improvement."

Renee eyed him. "Richard, your writing is very good. In my opinion, you are at the point you are ready to submit. I know I'm new to the group, but I have known you all for a very long time and feel like I can be frank. I think you are afraid to let your writing go."

Richard's eyes were wide behind his round glasses. "I value your opinion, of course, but I still have much work to do."

Renee shook her head. "In any case, I'm excited to be joining this group. I've wanted to for a long time. Richard talks about it so much when he visits the library."

Richard looked like he wanted to burrow through the wooden floor of Charming Books and hide. I suppressed a smile. It was clear to me that Renee was oblivious to the impact she had on the austere English professor. Sadie winked at me. She hadn't missed it. I was relieved to see that she was back to her cheerful self after her encounter with Grant just a little while ago.

"I have read samples of all of your work as you asked me to in preparation to join the group, and I think part of my job for this group will be just to encourage you all to go for it. You are all so talented in your own genres. Now it's time to get out there." Renee stopped just short of pumping her fist in solidarity.

I inwardly smiled, thinking that Renee would be a welcome addition to the Red Inkers. I agreed with her assessment of everyone's writing. There comes a time for any writer when you have to decide if you really want to share your work or keep it to yourself. None of them were going to get published if they didn't put their work out there.

"*Little Women*," Richard said as he picked up the book I had left on the coffee table. "I assume you are preparing to defend your dissertation, are you not? You have that glazed look of someone who has been studying for many hours. I know it well."

"I thought you would be researching the murder," Renee said. "I know you are poking your nose in where it doesn't belong because both Lacey and Nathan are both involved."

"Nathan's not involved in the murder," I said. "Not really. It just happened to happen at his family's vineyard. I think that's the end of his involvement with it."

Renee shook her head. "I wouldn't dismiss him or any of the Mortons so quickly. There has to be a reason that murder was committed at the vineyard. It seems to me it might be a message to the Mortons."

I raised my eyebrows. Renee had a point, but the best way for me to figure out why the murder had happened at the vineyard would be to go back up there. That wasn't something I was eager to do.

"Where is the other writer?" I asked, looking for a way to change the subject. I most certainly didn't want to talk about Nathan with any of the Red Inkers.

"Simon should be here soon." Richard adjusted his bow tie. "I'm quite eager to meet him. I have read his samples, and they are very good. However, just because someone can write does not mean he is a good fit for the group. We are a cohesive band, and every personality must fit in our little family of sorts."

"I think it will be fun to have another new member of the group," Sadie said, bouncing in her seat. "Simon will bring a new perspective and challenge us as writers. Sometimes I think we are too comfortable with where we are. We should always be evolving if we want to improve."

"Well said," Renee agreed. "I say that we give this young man a real shot to be part of the group. I know technically I am supposed to be trying out too, but I like to think that I have already been accepted."

"Oh, you have, Renee," Richard said quickly, as if he was terrified that she might think anything else. "I can vouch for you as someone who gives a wonderful critique. You push me to make my writing better with every page of mine that you review, and I was so pleased to learn that you were writing original work of you own."

To my surprise, Renee blushed at his compliment. In all the time that I'd known her, I'd never once seen the brash and outspoken librarian blush. I hid a smile. Richard might have a real chance with the college librarian after all.

Just then, there was a timid knock on the front door.

I stood up from my seat. "It must be Simon."

"It certainly is not Chief Rainwater," Richard said. "He would know to come right in."

I opened the front door and found Simon Chase on the other side. He was a tall, African-American man with a slightly hunched back as if he had been taught to be ashamed of his height. His black hair curled at the collar of his Oxford shirt and his dark-brown eyes were downcast. Simon Chase looked like he needed a hug.

"Simon?" I held out my hand for him to shake. "Violet Waverly."

He shook my hand. "I know who you are. You own a lovely store. Every time I come in here, I feel like I never want to leave all these beautiful books."

I smiled. "Let me introduce you to the

rest of the group." When we came to Sadie, he fidgeted in place.

Sadie, being the sweetest person who had ever walked the face of the earth, also noticed the man's discomfort. "We're so glad that you're here, Simon. We've all read the piece that you submitted and love it. You have a real gift."

Sadie's compliments only made Simon fidget more. "I'm sorry that I was late," he said, giving the same apology he had given me earlier. "I had to work overtime."

"What is it that you do, Simon?" Richard appraised him as he spoke. Usually Richard was far more welcoming, but the Red Inkers had been his brainchild years ago, and he was very protective of it. I could sort of imagine what he was like when he gave an oral exam now, and why my students at the community college much preferred to take tests from me.

Simon's face turned bright red. "I'm an insurance adjuster. I live here in the village, but I work in Niagara Falls. I grew up outside of Rochester, and my family used to vacation here when I was a child. I just fell in love with the charm of this village, and when my firm wanted to move me to Niagara Falls, I knew that I wanted to live here. It's a short drive, but it seems to be worlds away from the city."

That was most certainly true. Cascade Springs was only a fifteen-minute drive from busy Niagara Falls, but it was like living on another planet or at least in another time when things were simpler — except for the murders, of course.

"How long have you lived here?" Sadie asked.

"About a month. I'm still getting my bearings. This is a very close-knit community. I was beginning to think that I wasn't going to fit in." He blushed. "I work long hours and I don't have much chance to make new friends, and then I saw your advertisement for the critique group in the local paper. I knew that was just the way that I could find a place for myself here."

"That's so wonderful to hear." Sadie beamed at him. "I'm so glad that our ad grabbed your attention and that you answered it."

"I just hope that I don't embarrass myself by trying to be a writer," he said.

"You're a writer," Sadie corrected. "One of my writing teachers told me that the first step to actually getting published is owning the title of writer. You don't have to be published to call yourself by that name."

Richard nodded as if he was happy with

that answer as well. "Let's all take a seat and begin."

We sat in the circle of folding chairs I'd set up in the middle of the room for the meeting.

Renee smiled at Simon. "If it makes you feel any better, this is my first Red Inkers meeting too. I've known everyone for a long time, since I've lived in the village for a good while, but this is the first time I have shared my writing with any of them."

"I'm still surprised that not one of us knew you wrote, Renee," Sadie said.

She laughed. "I thought it was common knowledge that one out of five librarians has a dusty manuscript hidden in his or her desk. What do you write, Simon?"

He glanced this way and that as if he was looking for the nearest exit. Faulkner looming above him in the tree couldn't have helped his anxiety. "I write poetry mostly."

Sadie smiled. "Wouldn't it be lovely to have local poetry reading here at Charming Books sometime? It will be a way to showcase all the talent in the village."

Richard nodded. "I have some free verse that I would love to read."

"I — I don't know that I could read my poems to the entire village," Simon stammered. "It took all I had to send you a sample to be considered for this group."

Sadie smiled. "It was so brave of you to come. I know the first time I came to a meeting, I was scared to death, but you will grow to love it. The Red Inkers is like a family."

"Family is what I need," Simon said, giving Sadie his first real smile of the night.

It could have been just me, but I had a sneaking suspicion that insurance adjuster Simon could grow to love Sadie too. Kind, stable, he had a great job, and he was responsible. He checked all the boxes. I glanced at Sadie, and a kernel of an idea began to form. She smiled pleasantly at Simon, completely unaware of the number of times he sneaked a peek in her direction when he thought no one was watching. I wouldn't have been the least bit surprised if Cupid was hovering somewhere in the shop ready and waiting to strike, and I couldn't have been happier about it.

CHAPTER TWENTY-ONE

We were halfway through the Red Inkers meeting when there was another knock on the front door of Charming Books. Renee, who was reading from her novel, stopped midsentence.

"Who could that be at this time of night?" Richard asked.

"I'll get it; you all keep going with your meeting," I said.

I walked to the front door and heard Renee reading again. I opened the door to find Chief David Rainwater standing on the other side. He wore jeans, boots, a heavy winter coat, and a blue stocking cap on the top of his head. His hands were buried deep in his jeans pockets, and he rocked back on his heels. He smiled at me, but the smile didn't reach his amber eyes, which looked as if they threatened to close due to sheer exhaustion. "Is the meeting still going?"

I stepped back and let him in the shop.

"Renee is reading her piece right now. They'll be so glad you're here. No one expected you, considering . . ."

He glanced at me. "Are you glad I'm here too?"

Before I could answer, Richard called out, "David, how wonderful that you made it. We were just listening to Renee's piece. Come and meet Simon."

Rainwater glanced at me before he went over and joined the group. I took a deep breath. I didn't know if I was happy or disappointed that Richard hadn't given me a chance to answer Rainwater's question.

Rainwater held out his hand to the other man and stared at him. "What are you doing here?"

Simon blinked at him. "Excuse me?"

Richard chuckled uncomfortably. "David, what is the matter?"

"I saw this man earlier today in Niagara Falls."

Simon looked like he might be ill. "Yes, I remember. You were the police officer who came to our office with questions about a life insurance plan."

I stepped forward. "Who was the life insurance for?" I asked.

Simon shook his head. "I'm not at liberty to say."

I looked to Rainwater, and he wouldn't meet my eyes. This had to be about Belinda.

"Well," Richard said. "Let's continue on with the meeting."

We took our seats, and Renee continued to read her piece, which was very well written, but I couldn't concentrate. All I could think about was Belinda's murder, and I was dying to know what Rainwater had spoken to Simon about at his office. I wasn't sure that either man would tell me though.

"Well," Richard said, snapping me out of my daze. "Renee and Simon, I must say you both seem to be a fine addition to our group, and we're very happy to have you join. We meet twice a week right here at Charming Books. We're so lucky that Violet can provide such a nice place for us to gather. Next time, I believe it will be Sadie's turn to share."

Sadie stood up and hugged her notebook to her chest. Tonight she wore a tea dress with butterflies fluttering all over the fabric. Her black hair was pulled back into a high ponytail. "I can't wait to share my latest revision of my book right now." She paused. "I think I'm ready to send it out on submission to agents."

"My goodness, Sadie," Richard said. "That's quite a big step."

Sadie glanced at me. "Like Renee said, we aren't going to be published without putting our stuff out there. I really feel like the book is as good as I can make it."

"I'm sure it's wonderful," Simon said. "I'm looking forward to reading it." He blushed.

I bit the inside of my lip to hold back the smile.

Everyone started to pack up their things. I packed the last of the cookies from the meeting and set them on a paper plate on the sales counter. I noted that Richard had cornered Rainwater in a conversation. This was my chance to speak with Simon if I didn't want the police chief interfering.

Simon started to fold up his chair, but I stopped him. "I can take that. I know you all want to get home soon on such a cold night. What did you think of the group?"

He smiled. "The group is fantastic. I feel so encouraged and energized to go home and write. This was really the shot in the arm I needed."

"That's wonderful. I think both you and Renee will bring new life to the group too."

He blushed. "Thank you. I'm just happy about meeting more people in the village. All I do is work, and I realized that I was working my life away. I have to make room in my life for other things and for other people." His face turned a burnt-red color. "That was quite a speech. I'm sorry."

I laughed. "No need to apologize. It's one I needed to hear. Before I moved to the village, I was living like a robot. This place changes you and reminds you of what's really important. You'll see."

"I'm looking forward to it."

Across the room, I saw Rainwater watching me over Richard's head. I looked away as Simon pulled on his coat.

"I just had a question before you leave," I said.

"Oh?" he asked.

"It's about the insurance business. Do the police often visit your offices?"

His brow furrowed. "No. I work for a large national insurance company. We have offices all over. The police chief's visit today was the first time that I had any dealings with law enforcement."

"Were you able to help him?"

He picked up his notebook from a nearby bookshelf. "I can't really talk about anything relating to a client policy."

"So, he was there about a client's policy?" I asked.

Simon shifted from foot to foot.

Sadie bounced over to us holding the plate

of cookies. "Simon, we all agree that you should take the last of the cookies home."

He waved them away. "I could never eat all of those."

"Then take them to your office and make everyone's day." She looked up at him with her big blue eyes.

The man caved, taking the plate from her small hands. "All right. They will be very pleased."

Only an ogre could have said no to Sadie and a plate of cookies.

She beamed and turned to me. "I can help you clean up."

I shook my head. "Don't worry about that. I don't want to keep you too late. It looks like more snow is on the way. I'd feel better knowing you all made it safely home before it hits."

Sadie gave me a hug. "Are you excited that the Red Inkers is whole again?" She beamed at Renee and Simon. "I'm so thrilled to have you two in the group too."

Renee grinned back, and Simon fidgeted. I suppressed yet another smile.

Richard offered to give Renee a ride home since they both lived near campus. Renee looked like she was about to turn down his offer, saying she was very fond of walking, but Sadie stepped in and encouraged her to go because it was so cold outside, well below zero.

Sadie winked at me as she was ushering the pair of front door. It seemed to me that my friend was playing matchmaker. I watched Simon as he shuffled out the door, seeming to be reluctant to leave until the others did. Or maybe, I thought, he was reluctant to leave until Sadie left.

Richard, Renee, Sadie, and Simon all left at the same time, and I smiled as I watched them walk down the porch steps two by two. I closed the door.

"What's that smile on your face for?" I turned around to find Rainwater looking at me with a twinkle in his eye. In the last few months after meetings, Rainwater had opted to stay behind and help me clean up. At first, he had left as soon as the chairs were put away, but over time he had stayed longer and longer, and we would end up talking about his book, his niece, my students, and my dissertation. I had come to cherish these quiet moments with the police chief, whom I now considered a dear friend.

"What smile?" I asked as innocently as I could, but the innocence came off as false and I knew it.

"I have a feeling that you have a plan for Simon, and it has nothing to do with his poems." He folded the last two remaining chairs.

I took one of the chairs from him and walked it back to the storage closet behind the spiral staircase. Rainwater followed with the second chair. "I don't have any plans for Simon. He seems like a nice guy and a very good writer. Both he and Renee will add a lot to the group."

He laughed as he handed me the second chair and I put it away in the closet. "I saw how you were looking at him and Sadie. My advice is to stay out of it. If they are meant to be, it will happen."

I frowned. "You really believe that? That if people are meant to be together, it just happens? I think that discounts how much work a relationship takes. You can't just coast along and assume you end up in the same place with the right person." I took the chair from his hand and tucked it into the storage closet with the others.

When I turned, he was looking at me, and there was no more teasing in his eyes. "I do believe that. It gives me the strength I need to be patient. Don't take that away from me."

My throat felt dry. I couldn't talk about this any longer. I felt like it was a slippery slope where my traction was already in question. As much as I liked Rainwater, how could I be involved with him or any man when I knew that I would have to keep my identity as the shop's Caretaker secret from him? Keeping that secret hadn't worked out for any of the Waverly women that came before me, including my mother and grandmother. It sounded to me like a recipe for heartache. I wasn't prepared for more of that in my life.

"So, you went to Simon's office today?"

Rainwater sighed.

"Did your visit have anything to do with Belinda's death?"

"Violet," was all he said.

"I know that it must. Had she bought an insurance policy recently? Was there a dispute about her insurance claim? Is Simon somehow involved in the murder? I really need to know that before I start planning his wedding to Sadie."

"Violet, take a breath. You don't even give me an opportunity to answer one question before you bulldoze to the next."

I waited.

"Yes, the visit was about Belinda Perkins. No, I have no reason to suspect Simon at all. He wasn't even the one who opened the policy in question. It was in the New York City office of his company. I went to his office because I had some questions about the legality of the policy that I thought would be easier to have answered in person."

"What were those questions?" I closed the closet door and moved around the tree.

He followed me and then pressed his lips together into a thin line.

"Oh-kay, then, let me guess. My guess is that you went to the insurance office because Belinda had a life insurance policy on herself, and you wanted to see who was on the policy and therefore had the most to gain from her death." I folded my arms, feeling quite pleased with myself.

"No," Rainwater said.

I dropped my arms. "What do you mean, no?"

He sighed. "If you must know, a policy was recently opened on Belinda's life, but not by Belinda."

"What? Then by who?"

Rainwater looked as if he regretted even saying that much. Above his head, Faulkner walked back and forth on his branch in the birch tree, and Emerson sat on the top step of the spiral staircase dividing his attention between Rainwater and me and the bird.

"It was Sebastian, wasn't it?"

He didn't say anything.

"I know I'm right," I said. "It has to be him."

Again, nothing from the stone-faced police chief.

"But they weren't married," I said, talking myself out of my theory. "You can't take an insurance policy out on someone that you're not married to."

"That's not true," Rainwater said. "You can take an insurance policy out on anyone if you can prove that their death would cause you financial hardship."

"Aha! Then I am right!"

Rainwater sighed.

"This explains the private detective."

He folded his arms. "The what?"

I went on to tell him about meeting Joel Redding outside the shop earlier that day. "Honestly, I was surprised that you didn't run into him outside. I thought he would come back at some point to take up his post. He seems to think I know more about Belinda's murder than what I told the police."

Rainwater gave me a level look. "And is he right?"

I gave him the same look back. "No."

The police chief was the first to look away this time.

"Doesn't this make Sebastian look guiltier?" I asked. "Hiring a private investigator is a lot of trouble to go to."

"Or it could be he wants this case closed quickly so that he can file his insurance claim."

"Oh." There was that.

Rainwater didn't say anything, and we stared at each other in silence. Neither of us willing to give in. Behind Rainwater, a book fell onto the floor with a bang. Both he and I jumped. Rainwater turned around and picked up the book. Even before he handed it to me I knew it would be another copy of *Little Women.*

He put the book in my hand. I was right. It was a thick paperback edition of the novel, much like the one I'd had as a little girl when I read it for the first time.

"An American classic," Rainwater said. "There is a lot of wisdom in that novel."

I looked up at him. "You've read *Little Women?*"

He smiled. "I have. I hope you aren't one of those people that think the book is only for women."

I blushed. "Of course I don't."

"Admittedly, I read it not that long ago," Rainwater said. "Within the last few years. I thought if I want to write for children that I should read some of the masters. Alcott was at the top of my list. You have to respect a novel that lasts the test of time so well."

I smoothed my hand over the book's paper cover. "You do." I removed my hand from the cover and the book flew open. Its pages flew.

"What the . . ." Rainwater began.

I stared up at him in horror. What was the shop doing by opening the book in front of the police chief? I spun around, trying to shield the fluttering pages from Rainwater's view.

"Violet, what's going on?"

The book stopped moving as abruptly as it had begun. My eyes fell onto the passage in front of me. " 'I want to do something splendid before I go into my castle, something heroic or wonderful that won't be forgotten after I'm dead. I don't know what, but I'm on the watch for it, and mean to astonish you all someday.' "

I stared at the passage for a moment. The words were spoken by Jo March, the second-oldest and most famous of the March sisters from the story. She was the tomboy. The girl who wished she was born a boy, so she could be rough-and-tumble and go to college. Were they directing me to Lacey because she was the second sister in her family? But these words didn't suit Lacey at all, especially now that I'd heard Charles's account of her as a child. She'd never had such aspirations.

Belinda. Belinda was the sister with big dreams who had wanted to make her mark before she died. And she had, both in life and in death.

"Violet." Rainwater stepped around. "What's going on?"

I swallowed and look up at him.

"You look like you've just seen a ghost."

"No ghost."

He frowned. "Was it a ghost that opened that book?"

I laughed. "That's ridiculous. I was just flipping through it."

"I don't think so." He studied me.

I laughed again. "You can't be implying that anyone else opened the book but me. I was the only one touching it. Honestly, I think you have been writing fantasy novels for far too long."

His face clouded over, and I wished that I could take back my harsh words. At the same time, I had to shoot this conversation down. Rainwater couldn't know about the shop's magical essence. This was my burden as the Caretaker. In the succession of Caretakers, I didn't want to be the one who gave away the Waverly family's greatest secret.

He took a step back from me, and for the second time in a short period, I thought that I had made the wrong move with him. But it had to be done. No one could know about the shop's essence, not even Rainwater, no matter how much I was dying to tell him about it. In a way I felt like he was the one person in the village other than my grandmother who would understand, but still I couldn't tell him.

He sighed and stepped back. "You want me to tell you everything that I know about my investigation into Belinda's Perkins' murder, but you don't trust me."

I snapped the book closed. "What are you talking about? I trust you."

He shook his head. "No, you don't. I know that something odd is happening in this shop and with you. I know that you don't want to tell me what it is because you don't trust me."

"There's nothing odd going on." My denial sounded hollow.

"And Violet, look at the tree. Someone shot it last October and it's completely healed. The mark where the bullet hit it isn't even there. That's not normal. The tree even being alive is not normal. A book that opens under its own volition is not normal."

I chewed on my lip. After the tree had been accidently shot, it had started to die, so I had done the only thing I could think of and poured the mystical spring water into the hole in the trunk that the bullet had made. I had been so relieved when it healed the tree, I hadn't thought of concealing this miracle from the public. Rainwater had taken note of it right away.

"If anything between you and me is going to work, you have to trust me with whatever you are hiding."

"What are you talking about?" I felt like I was losing my breath.

"You know what I mean. You have to choose."

"You're speaking in riddles."

"You know the riddle, but you're the only one who can solve it. You have to choose to trust me. Whatever you're hiding, I can handle it. I promise you that, but if you don't make up your mind, you could very well end up alone."

I stared at him. *Alone.* But wasn't that my destiny anyway as the Caretaker of Charming Books? Not a single Waverly woman had any luck at romance. They always ended up single in the end. Why should I fight it?

I stared into Rainwater's understanding

amber gaze. *Because of him,* I thought. I couldn't say it though. I wasn't that brave. I wasn't sure if I would ever be brave enough to say what I wanted so desperately.

Faulkner flew over our heads from the tree to his perch by the window and cawed, "Some people seemed to get all sunshine, and some all shadow . . ."

I shivered.

Rainwater watched the bird. "You can't tell me a crow quoting Alcott is normal either."

I didn't know what to say. I was afraid if I opened my mouth, I would tell him everything. When I did, there was no going back.

The police chief leaned toward me and kissed me softly on the lips. "Good night, Violet Waverly. Make the right choice for both our sakes."

And then he left.

CHAPTER TWENTY-TWO

"Please read chapter six in your textbooks for next week. We'll have a quiz on the content," I said to my freshmen composition class as the students shuffled out of the room with a groan.

I gathered up the papers that they had turned in at beginning of class. Several students in the class were natural writers. I wished that they would embrace that instead of hating the course so much. But as I left the room, I was more distracted by Belinda's murder than by my students' papers. Usually after my second class for the day, I went back to Charming Books to work until my afternoon class at two, but this time I decided to stay on campus and do a little research at the college library. I texted my grandmother to tell her not to expect me at the shop until after the afternoon class was finished.

My English classes were in the humanities

building, which was on the other side of campus from the three-story library. The day was warmer than the past week had been, but the snow blew hard outside. Through the glass door leading into the humanities building, I could see shapeless figures bending forward against the drafty squalls as they forced their way through the blustery campus. My car was parked semi-legally in front of my building and I was half tempted to give up the library idea all together and go home.

However, I knew the shop, and my grandmother would give me no peace until I found out what the shop's magical essence was trying to tell me through the words of *Little Women.* I took a deep breath and headed toward the library.

A few minutes later, I blew through the front doors of the library with a puff of snow in my wake. Renee sat at the information desk typing on a laptop. She grinned when she watched me shake the snow off my coat and out of my hair.

"You take the winter weather with you when you leave," she said.

"I would if I could. It seems to me that the winter is just getting started."

"That's life in Niagara for you. Snow comes down by the feet, not by the inches,

255

and the college never closes. At least it never has for snow in the six years I've worked here."

I wasn't looking forward to that. It was my first winter back in Cascade Springs, and I remembered how nasty the past winters had been. "I came by to ask for your expertise, but you look busy. I don't want to bother you if you're working on something."

Renee closed the lid to her laptop. "I'm a librarian; it is my job to be bothered. Besides, you're pulling me away from a boring circulation report. Whatever you have to ask me I know will be much more enjoyable."

"I don't think it will be too hard to find either, but since you're the searching expert, you will be much faster at it than I would."

Renee cracked her knuckles in preparation. "Flattery will get you everywhere. What do you have?"

"Belinda wasn't just a sommelier. She was also a writer and wine critic. I'm wondering if you could pick up some of her reviews, especially of wineries within a reasonable driving distance."

"That would be a lot of wineries," she said. "It's a big industry around here. Are you thinking on both sides of the Canadian border? Because that really would be a lot."

"Good point. Let's just stick to wineries in western New York to start."

"That's easy enough." She opened her laptop and started clicking on the keyboard so fast I wouldn't have been the least bit surprised if she had the ability to type two hundred words a minute. As she searched, she asked, "What's with the interest in her writing?"

"Her reviews were known to be harsh, harsh to the point that it would affect a winery's business if she gave a bad review."

"So you are thinking that someone who was poorly reviewed by Belinda might have wanted to seek the ultimate revenge against her." Her glasses had slipped to the tip of her nose. "It's not a bad motive."

"Thanks."

She grinned from ear to ear. "I knew it. I knew you were poking around in the murder."

"I'm not poking around," I said defensively. "Also, there is one review in particular that I'm looking for that she wrote about the winery Bone and Hearth."

She looked up from her computer. "That's the newer winery in the village, isn't it?"

I nodded. "I got a tip that she didn't care for it."

"A tip, eh? Now we are really detecting, aren't we?" She cracked her knuckles.

"I'm just looking for other possible suspects so the police will look for someone other than Lacey." I almost told Renee about private investigator Joel Redding but thought better of it. It wasn't the time to get Renee off on a research tangent. I needed those articles.

She rolled her eyes. "Lacey is as gentle as a bunny rabbit, and bunnies don't kill people."

"You've read *Bunnicula,* haven't you?"

"That was a very rare case of crazy bunny. Most rabbits are perfectly nice."

"It just takes one crazy bunny to spoil it for all the good bunnies," I said.

She nodded. "I'll give you that. But you're basically investigating leads. I'm pretty sure that's the definition of poking around."

I was about to argue with her more when she held up her hand. "Here's the review on Bone and Hearth."

"What does it say?" I tried to lean over the information counter to get a look at the screen, but she had it turned away from me.

Renee cleared her throat. " 'The vintage attempting to have a tropical flavor comes off as a mediocre fruit punch. This does not bode well for the rest of the line. Customers would do better choosing ice wines from across the Canadian border than to waste their money on this drivel.' " She looked up. "Can you say, 'Ouch'?"

"And Miles Rathbone is the owner of this winery?"

She made a few more clicks on her keyboard. "Yes, that's what it says here."

"He was at the book signing. He came up to her table and told her to sign her book to the winery she ruined."

Renee blinked at me. "Yikes. So, we can easily say that man is a tad bitter."

"Definitely."

She leaned forward, closer to her screen. "Belinda posted her review of the winery a month ago, and from what I can tell, it completely ruined his sales. It says here on another industry website that Rathbone pulled all Bone and Hearth's wines this year over concerns for the vintage." She looked up at me. "Which means they will make next to nothing in income. Why on earth would he want to be anywhere close to Belinda after she trashed him?"

"Because he wanted to confront her, which he did," I said.

"Or kill her, which we don't know if he did," Renee said. "Seems to me that you have a serious suspect on your hands."

"I have more suspects than I know what to do with. Maybe it's time to just tell Chief Rainwater about each of them and let him handle it."

Renee laughed. "I'd like to see you try. Violet, you and I know that you won't rest until we see this through to the end."

I frowned, wishing that she wasn't so right about me. "Does the article include a photo of Rathbone? I want to see if I recognize him from the book signing."

"No," she said. "But that will be easy enough to find." A moment later, she turned the computer screen in my direction. "There he is."

On the screen there was a photo of a middle-aged man standing in a vineyard. He had his hand on a post and smiled into the camera. He had salt-and-pepper hair and a toothy smile. Even though he hadn't been smiling the night of the book signing, I recognized him immediately. "That's him."

She nodded. "I can do better than that."

I arched my brow. "What do you mean?"

She clicked away on the keyboard. "We need to go deeper and find out more about Belinda." She typed for a moment.

"What are you doing?" I asked, and tried to peer at her screen.

"Patience. You can't rush research." She

clicked a few more keys. "Ah, did you know Belinda was married before?"

"What? I had no idea. How did you find that?" I asked.

"It's all public record. You just need to know how to find it, and with all those genealogy databases on the market that store this information, it's easier than ever."

She clicked with her mouse. "Looks like they were married for less than a year."

"Was it annulled, then, because it was so short?"

She shook her head. "Looks like a straight divorce."

"When was this?" I asked.

"Five years ago."

"What's the man's name?"

"You are not going to believe it."

"Who is it?"

"Miles Rathbone."

I froze.

Not noticing my reaction, Renee went on. "They were married in New York City by a justice of the peace." She looked up. "What wrong?"

"What if her bad review of his winery was retaliation over their divorce?"

I frowned and wondered if Lacey knew that her sister had been married once before. It was very possible that she didn't, since the sisters hadn't spoken in years. "Wow, this changes everything."

She nodded. "I bet Rathbone kicked himself over the divorce after Belinda became a success. From what I've found, her writing only hit the *New York Times* best-sellers list in the last four years. Although once she hit it, she hit it every time." She paused. "And now she ruined his reputation with that article and is going to marry someone else. That seems like a good motive for murder, right?"

I shivered.

She removed her glasses and studied me. "It seems to me that you need to have a chat with Rathbone."

I nodded.

"And there's another person you need to talk to."

"Who?"

"Nathan. You need to find out what his involvement is in all of this."

I stepped away from the information counter. "His involvement?"

"The murder did take place at his family's vineyard. You can't ignore that."

"No, I can't, so it's hard for me to believe they could be involved. There is nothing the Mortons hate more than scandal, and they would never bring this level of notoriety down on their own property. It's just not possible."

Renee set her glasses on the top of her head. "If you want to do right by Lacey, you can't give Nathan or anyone else who was at that book signing a pass."

"Not even my grandmother? She was there too."

"Okay, you can give Grandma Daisy a pass, but that's it." She rolled her eyes.

"Gee, thanks," I muttered. "I think it's more important to focus on Miles Rathbone right now. Also, there is her fiancé, Sebastian Knight. He has plenty of motive." I was thinking about the insurance policy on Belinda.

"They are both good suspects. The bad review of Bone and Hearth was just scratching the surface. There are at least five other scathing reviews of wineries and restaurants I found with a simple search. Who knows what I will find as I dig deeper. Rathbone's might not be the only business she ruined with her pen."

"What does that mean?" I asked.

Renee glanced up from the screen. "Belinda Perkins made a lot of enemies."

Some would have said one too many.

Chapter Twenty-Three

It took all of my teaching skills to make it through my late-afternoon class. All I wanted to do was leave campus and find Miles Rathbone to ask him the growing list of questions in my head. By the end of the hour-and-fifteen-minute class, I congratulated myself that I'd made it through.

As the students filed out, one came to my desk. She was a petite girl with a large hoop through her eyebrow and a thick layer of black lipstick around her pouty mouth.

"Professor Waverly," she began.

I held up my hand. "Jodi, if this is about another extension on your paper, I'm going to have to say no."

"Professor, you have to give me an extension. I don't want to hand in anything to you that's not topnotch."

I raised my eyebrows.

"It's true. You are such a good judge of what good writing is. I would hate to insult you if I turned in something not good enough for you to read."

I sighed. "How much more time do you need?"

"Just one week. I'm almost done. I promise." Her pout morphed into a smile.

I had heard that all before. This was the third time that I had given the same student an extension because she showed promise. The writing samples she had actually turned in were well constructed and imaginative. I marveled at how she could say mundane things in new and exciting ways. I didn't want to discourage her from writing. She had such a gift.

"Okay, but this is the final time. I can't keep giving you an extension. If I do, I will have to give you an incomplete for the quarter. It could ultimately affect your final grade."

"Thank you, Professor Waverly! I will make it up to you. I promise!" She turned and almost ran directly into a woman entering the room.

"Sorry. I'm just leaving. The room is all yours," I said, thinking she was the next professor to teach in the classroom. As at many community colleges, most of the faculty at Springside were adjunct professors like me, which meant I didn't know who many of them were. I believed only a handful lived in the village of Cascade Springs; most commuted in from farther away. "I'll get out of your hair."

I slid my class notes and composition book into my giant tote bag that I used for my classes. The tote was impossibly heavy, weighing more than most seven-year-old children. I heaved the bag onto the desktop.

"Are you Violet Waverly?" the woman asked.

I stopped putting items into my bag. "I am." I smiled, still thinking that she was a professor. "Can I help you with something?"

The woman held a pair of leather gloves in her hands that she had twisted into a tight rope. She was of medium height and build and had dishwater-blonde hair that was pulled back into a severe low ponytail. She dressed like she was a woman creeping up on old age, but I guessed from her face that she was younger than I was. She was vaguely familiar to me, but I assumed that was because I had seen her around campus. "I'm Michelle Hardy. My maiden name is Perkins." She paused. "Lacey Dupont is my sister, and I have been looking for you."

I stared at her. Many times, I had gone looking for someone who might be related to a murder. This was the first time someone

266

related to the victim came looking for me.

"Michelle?" I asked in wonder. The last time I had seen the third of the four Perkins girls had been when I was a senior in high school. I guessed that Michelle had been eleven or twelve at the time. However, now that I knew she was Lacey's sister, I saw the family resemblance. The hair color was close, but Lacey's was lighter and much less drab, and she had Lacey's curvy build. Where the sisters differed, the most was in demeanor. There was none of Lacey's natural exuberance and zest for life. Michelle Hardy appeared to be a woman who had lived a hard life and simply accepted the cards she was dealt instead of throwing them back and demanding a new deck.

"How did you find me?" I asked.

"I knew that you taught here. I work at the college too. When they announced that you would be joining the English faculty, I recognized your name. You're a bit of a celebrity in Cascade Springs."

I winced. I knew that she was thinking about my dramatic exit from the village twelve year ago. It seemed that I would never completely be able to leave that all behind me.

"Since I work for the college, I called your department secretary and asked where I could find you."

I grimaced. "There is a class in here soon. Can we go somewhere else to talk?"

"What about the college coffee shop? It should be quiet this time of day, as most of the classes have finished up and students will have gone home." Springside was strictly a commuter campus. There were no dorms on the property.

I agreed. Michelle and I walked across the campus with our heads bent low, unable to chat in the howling wind. That was fine with me. It gave me time to gather my thoughts about what I wanted to learn from Lacey's sister. Lacey had said she'd been at Belinda's signing, but I didn't remember seeing her. Unfortunately, the third Perkins sister was the kind of woman who was easily forgotten.

The college coffee shop was in the middle of the campus and was the gathering place for all the commuter students to wait between classes and hang out with their friends. It was a large room with café tables and quiet booths peppered throughout, so there were plenty of places for students to socialize or study. It was one of my favorite places on campus, and the baristas there made decent coffee. It certainly wasn't up to Adrien's standards, but it was good.

As Michelle had predicted, the shop was nearly empty. There were two baristas at the counter, looking impossibly bored, and one lone student, who had the volume up so loud on his earbuds I could hear every lyric, was hunched over a laptop.

"Can I get you something to drink?" I asked Michelle.

She looked like she might say no but changed her mind. "Just a small black coffee for me. Thanks."

I nodded and put in our order with the green-haired barista at the counter: small black coffee for Michelle, large caramel latte for me. I had a sweet tooth, and I wasn't afraid to show it. Service was quick, and I paid and carried the coffees to the most secluded booth, where Michelle sat. I set the coffee in front of her and took my place.

Michelle wrapped her hands around the paper cup. "Thank you."

I smiled. "What did you want to talk to me about? I assume it's Belinda."

At the mention of her eldest sister's name, Michelle teared up.

I plucked three white napkins from the dispenser on the table. "I'm so sorry for your loss. I know losing your sister must be awful. She was such a vibrant woman."

"She was a terror."

I jerked my head back.

"I'm not crying because I'm sad that she's dead." She wiped at her eyes with the napkins. "I mean, I am sad. It's sad when anyone dies, but I don't mourn her like you should mourn a sister. She was more a stranger to me. She flitted in and out of my life when it was most convenient for her. Since I had nothing of worth to contribute in her mind, I was of no interest. If it weren't for my children, I don't think she would have communicated with me at all. I'm not Adele."

She said all this in a rush, and I stared at her. I had been prepared for tears, but not for such obvious anger. "What do you mean that you're not Adele?"

Mascara smeared onto the white napkin as she rubbed the coarse paper under her eyes. "Adele was the favorite. Belinda doted on her and gave her favors and money. How else can my youngest sister live as a starving artist?"

"Why did she like Adele so much?"

"Because Adele had a talent. She's a painter. Belinda only cared about people who showed promise of some sort. According to her, I didn't have any useful talents. I was of little interest."

That sounded odd to me. If Belinda

believed only in people with talent, then why was she with Sebastian, who by all accounts wasn't much good for anything?

"But she's interested in your children?"

She sighed. "She had been. She sent us money from time to time to put our two daughters in different activities so that we could discover what their talents were. At Belinda's direction, we put them in everything from gymnastics to singing lessons to dance. Nothing 'took,' as far as Belinda was concerned, because the girls didn't show exceptional promise in any of them."

"How old are your children?" I sipped from my latte.

"They are three and five, and Belinda expected them to be protégées in something. It was too much pressure for a little girl. I refused to put them through it any longer. I told Belinda this a year ago. I said she could give the girls money if she liked, but she couldn't dictate how we spent it." Michelle pushed her untouched coffee cup away from her. "Belinda wouldn't agree to those terms, because even hundreds or even thousands of miles away, she wanted to control the family. I don't know why. She abandoned us when we were children ourselves. I always thought that this was her way of making up for her guilt of leaving the family."

"Seems an odd way to do it."

"Well, Belinda has always done things her own special way." She folded her hands on the tabletop.

"So, what happened when you told her this?"

Michelle licked her lips, and I thought she wasn't going to answer. She finally said, "She cut the money off."

I wasn't sure if Michelle was aware of it or not, but depending on the terms of Belinda's will, she had just given me a very good motive for murder. Love and money were the most common reasons to kill someone. Love lost, in this case. The lost love of a sister, and the money that she might have granted the family had Michelle remained in Belinda's favor.

"You were at the book signing the night Belinda died," I said.

"Only for a few minutes. My husband wanted me to go and talk to my sister about the money, to remind her that the girls needed it. I couldn't bring myself to do it. As soon as I saw Belinda, I turned around and left." She pulled her coffee closer to her and finally took a sip. "I was in such a hurry to leave that I ran into Lacey as I was leaving. It was the first time I had seen her in a long time. She looked very upset."

"What did you tell your husband when you got home?"

"That if he wanted to grovel to Belinda, he'd have to do it on his own. I couldn't stomach it anymore." She set the cup back on the table.

"What about your relationship with Lacey?" I asked. "Since you and Belinda had a falling out, have you reached out to Lacey at all?"

"Just because one of my sisters is being selfish, it doesn't mean that I have forgiven the one that killed my mother."

"Lacey didn't kill your mother."

"She let her die. Do you have any idea what it's like to grow up without a mother?"

"Actually, I do," I said in a quiet voice.

She stared at me for a long moment, and then she said, "I didn't come here to tell you my life story."

Since she had told me so much, I strongly doubted that. "Then why did you come here?"

"I'm here to tell you to butt out. I know your reputation in this village. You're one of the crusader types thinking that you can waltz into a situation that you couldn't possibly understand and fix everything."

At the mention of crusader types, the image of Charles Hancock came to mind. Surely she wasn't thinking I was like that.

She stood up, leaving her barely touched coffee on the table. "You can't fix this family, so don't bother trying. It's broken beyond hope."

"I can't believe that anything is beyond hope," I said.

Michelle buttoned up her coat as she stared down at me. "Stay out of this family feud. It can't be mended. Your meddling will only make it worse and dredge up more pain for us all." She spun and walked away.

I sat in the booth for a moment, going over in my head what had just happened. As an only child, I had always wished for a sister, but if my sisters would have ended up anything like Belinda or Michelle, I was grateful that I had been an only child.

I slid out of the booth and was heading out of the café when something caught my eye. I turned and found private eye Joel Redding in the booth behind where Michelle and I had been sitting making notes in a small notebook.

He smiled up at me. "Well, hello there."

"What are you doing here?" My tone was icy.

He gestured at the paper cup of coffee in

front of him on the table. "I stopped in for a cup of coffee. Is that a problem for you?"

"No," I said. "My problem is that you are following me and clearly listening in on private conversations. I want you to leave me alone."

He smiled pleasantly. "Miss Waverly, I'm going to be sticking to you like glue."

"Why?"

"Because you are my one-way ticket to the murderer."

CHAPTER TWENTY-FOUR

I made it back to the shop, and as I climbed out of my Mini, a gray sedan pulled into the space behind me. Through the snow, I saw P.I. Redding behind the wheel.

I stomped over to his car. "Don't even think of coming inside my shop. Got that?"

He smiled. "Got it. You can keep me out of your shop, Violet Waverly, but you can't keep me off a public street."

I marched away through the front gate and up the steps to the shop. I let the heavy antique door slam closed behind me.

"Violet, what on earth are you doing coming in here like Godzilla storming Tokyo?" my grandmother scolded. She paused in her dusting of the sales counter and thwacked the feather duster against her hand.

I frowned at her. "Thanks, Grandma Daisy. That's what every woman wants — to be compared to Godzilla."

"Someone has ruffled your feathers."

At the mention of feathers, Faulkner jumped down from his spot on the tree and glided across the shop, landing on the sales counter with a click of his talons. Emerson bounded in from wherever he'd been hiding in the shop and jumped up on the stool behind the counter. At present, the animals weren't eyeing each other, planning their next move. Grandmother, cat, and crow all had their eyes fixed on me, waiting for me to share my tale.

I sighed. "Grandma, I'm so sorry for being snippy. That private investigator is following me again. He's outside right now."

My grandmother moved to the window. "Is he the man in the gray car?"

"Yes." I removed my coat and hung it on the coat tree by the door.

"He just waved at me. The nerve of that man."

"He is very nervy," I said. "I don't know what to do. He said he was going to follow my every move. How am I supposed to help Lacey with this guy following me all over the village?"

"If the man is bothering you, call David, and he will get rid of him."

I frowned. "I'm not going call the police chief to protect me." I bit the inside of my lip. I didn't add that I was still emotionally reeling from Rainwater's words the night before.

Grandma Daisy knocked the end of her feather duster on the counter. "Well, maybe two can play at this game?"

"What do you mean?" I leaned against the counter

"If he's so convinced that Lacey is the killer, lead him away from her. Give him other leads to follow while he is following you. The more rabbit holes you have him follow down, the more frustrated he will become. Maybe he will give up."

"That's a good idea. I had another thought too. He was hired to prove that Sebastian is innocent of the murder. Maybe if I can prove Sebastian innocent, that would be enough to get rid of Redding."

"Do you think that Sebastian is guilty?"

I shook my head. "There is no way to tell right now. He has the best motive." I went on to tell my grandmother about the life insurance policy.

She whistled. "Do you know what the amount is?"

I shook my head. "I was lucky to learn about the policy at all. The police chief was being tight-lipped about it."

"What other suspects do you have?"

"This time, my list is full of suspects."

My grandmother gestured to tell me to get on with making my list.

"Okay." I ticked the suspects off on my fingers. "There's the fiancé, Sebastian Knight. He's jealous of Belinda's success. He is a sommelier too, but not as successful as she is. We saw them together if only briefly. She treated him more like a lackey than the man she was going to marry, and we can't forget the life insurance policy that he took out on her."

"I like him for the killer," Grandma Daisy said. "It's clean and easy and makes the most sense." The feather duster slashed like a swashbuckler. "Oh! And he's a double ringer. Money *and* love. It's the logical conclusion."

"Conclusions that make the most sense are not always the right answer." I didn't know what disturbed me more: the parrying duster or her obvious joy in discussing a murderer.

I went on to my next suspect. "Then we have Miles Rathbone of Bone and Hearth Vineyards. Belinda wrote a terrible review of his winery and stopped his wine from having any traction in the market, so much so that he had to pull it from the shelves. Renee found the review for me. It was scathing. But that's not all." I paused. "It turns out Rathbone and Belinda were married."

"What?" Grandma Daisy yelped, and Falkner cawed in protest.

I went on to tell her what Renee had discovered. Then I said, "And don't forget wine critic Jake Zule said that he was there the night of the book signing. Jake Zule is a suspect in his own right because he now has Belinda's writing gig. Perhaps he is thinking that he can take her place in wine society."

"They are both good options, especially the ex-husband, but my money is still on the fiancé."

"And we can't forget Lacey's younger sisters. Michelle works at the college and found me today. She and Belinda had a falling out when Belinda stopped giving money to Michelle and her husband to help raise their young daughters. Michelle is clearly envious of the younger Perkins girl, Adele, who has a studio in the bird neighborhood."

"How can she afford to have studio space there? It's the most expensive part of the village."

"Belinda."

"Ah," Grandma Daisy said. "I have never approved of the tactic of buying someone else's affection."

I walked around the counter and picked up Emerson. The tuxie let me cradle him in my arms. He seemed to sense I needed some fluffy comfort at the moment. "It could be any one of them, and the shop is not exactly being direct as to who I should be looking at the closest."

"Aren't you forgetting a few suspects?" My grandmother studied me.

I tucked Emerson under my chin and felt his strong purr against my throat. "Not that I know of."

"What about the Mortons?" she asked in a low voice. "Nathan even?"

I stared at her. "Grandma Daisy, you can't think that Nathan did this? Or anyone in that family. Look at the bad press it has brought their winery."

"The Mortons were at the signing. You can't count them out," she said, repeating Renee's sentiment from earlier.

I hated to admit that my Grandma Daisy just might be right. Perhaps one of the Mortons had followed Belinda into the vineyard; maybe they'd argued over Belinda's outburst. Hmmm.

"Have you talked to any of them?"

"Only Grant." I frowned.

"When was that?"

"Last night. He brought over a bottle of

ice wine to apologize for how the family had treated me."

Grandma Daisy pressed her lips together. "I don't trust that man."

"Neither do I," I said, thinking of how he'd spoken to Sadie about her writing. "But Grant is far too self-involved to murder anyone. All the Mortons are. They wouldn't want to hurt their business like that. The business comes first."

"Maybe that's where you need to start leading Redding astray then. Lead him back to Morton Vineyards if it's so obviously the wrong direction. He will think you're onto something or he will become so frustrated that he will leave you alone."

"When should I do this?" I asked as I set Emerson on the counter.

"Now, girl. There's no time to waste."

I grimaced. I was tired and looking forward to a quiet evening in the shop, but Grandma Daisy was right: I had to get Redding off my back as soon as possible. "I don't think the Mortons are involved, but at least it will throw him off Lacey."

"That's the idea."

"Just don't make it easy for him. Then he will become suspicious." There was a mischievous twinkle in her eye.

I grinned. "I won't. Grandma Daisy,

you've given me a great idea. I know how to take it from here."

She waved her duster like a wand. "That's what fairy grandmothers are for, my dear."

CHAPTER TWENTY-FIVE

I wanted Joel Redding to follow me to Morton Vineyards, but I didn't want him to think that I wanted him to do that. I knew if he did, he would realize I was leading him on a wild-goose chase, so I left the bookshop on foot. I dashed across the street and between Midcentury Vintage and its next-door neighbor.

As I disappeared between the two buildings, I heard a car door slam shut. I knew it was Redding following me. Instead of going straight, I ran around the back side of Sadie's shop, around the side of the building, and back onto River Road.

Then I sprinted to my Mini Cooper and jumped in.

As I drove down the street and turned left on the road to follow the river, I saw Redding come around the side of the building. Clearly, he had followed my tracks in the snow. He threw up his hands as my car went around the curve.

I wasn't sure that Redding would be able to find me after that, but I basked in the moment of outmaneuvering the P.I.

I followed River Road past the town hall, the Riverwalk, and the livery until it led out of the village to the wooded countryside. After two miles, the woods opened up and the wine country unfolded in front of me. There were rows of frozen grapevines on either side of the road.

After a few turns, I came upon the long driveway that led to the Mortons' white-framed winery and home. The late-afternoon sun reflected off the blanket of snow on the acre in front of the house. Snow balanced precariously on thin limbs of trees, and there was a thin coat of snow on the long drive that had fallen just that morning. I didn't park in front of the house; instead I parked in the guest parking lot, just like I had the night of the signing. I chose a parking place that could be seen from the road so that Redding would spot my car if he happened by. Today the lot was empty.

Sure enough, I saw a gray sedan roll slowly by the end of the Mortons' drive. I knew it was Redding. I climbed out of my car, certain that Redding would see my car from the street and come back.

I walked around the back of the winery to the servants' entrance. The ice sculptures that I had seen in the garden near the entrance to the vineyard were gone. I wondered if Mrs. Morton had ordered them destroyed after the disastrous book signing.

Now that I was at the winery, I wasn't sure what I should do. I couldn't very well knock on the door. Mrs. Morton had made it clear that she didn't want me anywhere near her business or family. At the same time, I couldn't let this opportunity to see the crime scene again pass. This might be my only chance. It was unlikely that Rainwater and his officers had missed any evidence from the scene. Rainwater was a thorough cop, and I knew he would have been back to the scene several times to reevaluate the scene. Even so, that didn't mean I couldn't take a second look too.

Before I had made up my mind, the back door of the winery opened and Grant Morton stepped outside. He wore a winter coat and scarf. His mother was a step behind him, but she wasn't wearing a coat over her twinset sweater and slacks. She was, however, wearing a sour expression. Grant's back was to me, and Mrs. Morton looked too angry to see anything other than the subject of her anger, which happened to be her son.

Not taking any chances, I squelched a yelp that threatened to bubble up in the back of my throat. And ducked around the latticework archway that led into the vineyard. A large bush hid me from view, but I risked it to peek around the side.

"You never listen to a word I say," Mrs. Morton said to her son. "We wouldn't be in this mess if it weren't for you."

"It was Nathan's idea to have the book signing at the winery, not mine!"

"Yes, but you were the one who chose that store."

"Charming Books is the only bookshop in the village. Who else were we going to have sell the books?"

"We should have done it ourselves. Charming Books never should have been involved."

"Do you think the Waverlys killed her?" Grant asked.

I stifled a grasp. I had never thought for a moment that Grandma Daisy and I were suspects in the murder.

"No, but you know how seeing Violet confuses your brother. He needs to remain focused on his political career and on the winery. He can't keep setting his eyes on

Violet Waverly, who never was and never will be good enough for him. Can you imagine that girl as a governor's wife?"

Even though I no longer loved Nathan, her words stung. As a teenager, I had thought that I didn't measure up in Mrs. Morton's view as a worthy partner for her son, and now I knew that was true.

"Governor? My, you think Nathan can do anything, don't you?"

"You ruined your hopes of politics when you were caught in that fraud scheme last summer. That will always come back to haunt you."

"So, nothing I've done in all this time at the winery has improved my image in your eyes, has it?"

"I didn't say that," Mrs. Morton snapped.

But Grant and I both knew that, in a way, she had.

"I don't have time for this." Hurt laced Grant's voice. "I'm going to be late for the winemakers' guild meeting."

"I don't know why you're even going. Nathan will be there. He will represent our winery."

"Because he's the perfect son," Grant said bitterly. "I already know this, Mother." He spun on his heel, and I ducked behind the bush, holding my breath.

I heard footsteps moving away toward the front of the large house, and the back door to the winery slammed closed.

I crouched in my spot for a few seconds more and then slowly stood up. I poked my head around the side of the bush again. Mrs. Morton and Grant were gone. I gave a sigh of relief.

I turned back to the vineyard. In the light of day, the vines were pretty in a dead, frozen sort of way. Thin nets had been placed over all the vines to protect the frozen grapes from birds. The frozen grapes glinted and twinkled in the sunlight like polished marbles.

Bending down low, hoping the grapes would hide me, I crept to where I had found Belinda's dead body. The spot wasn't hard to find. There was crime scene tape around the area. There was a dark-red mark on the snow. I swallowed, knowing that the stain must be blood. I stepped closer to the red mark and leaned over the crime scene tape for a better look. I shivered and stood up.

Standing there, I realized that Grandma Daisy was right. The Mortons could very well have committed this murder. It had happened only a few steps from their back door. They'd had the opportunity. I knew firsthand that there were members of the family angry enough to commit the crime. They'd had the means. However, I kept coming back to the fact that killing Belinda made their lives more difficult. The motive was what I was missing. The murder brought bad press down on the winery and tarnished their reputation. For the Mortons, all four of them, reputation was everything. I just could not believe that they would do something so detrimental to their own business. I could see them hurting someone else's business with no problem.

"I wish I could say I'm surprised to find you trespassing back here, but then I would be lying," a male voice said behind me.

I jumped and spun around. "Grant! How did you find me?"

He laughed. "Vi, your car is in the middle of the parking lot, plain as day. Anyone could have found you here."

I should have thought about the Mortons seeing my car as well as Redding.

"Two kinds of people come back to the scene of the crime: the guilty and the nosy. Which one are you, Vi?" Grant studied me.

"I'm not guilty," I said.

"But you are nosy, too nosy for your own good."

"I prefer inquisitive." I stepped back from the crime scene tape.

"What are you doing here?" he asked.

"I just wanted to come back to the scene to see if it would stir any memories that might tell us who killed Belinda."

He laughed. "You solved a murder or two and now see yourself as a professional."

"I'm not a professional, but Lacey is my friend. I want to help her."

"I can understand that. You were always such a loyal friend to Colleen, weren't you?"

I frowned. Why did he insist on bringing up Colleen?

"If you are looking for Nathan, he's not here. He's off doing mayoral things." He said this with just a hint of bitterness in his voice. "Nathan is the heir to this throne." He gestured broadly at the vineyard. "But he doesn't have to put in the day-to-day work to earn it. It must be nice to be the heir."

"This is your home too," I said.

He smiled. "I'm doing my best to prove that to my parents and to my brother."

"Your parents have always wanted you to take over this business."

"Theoretically," he muttered. He eyed me. "Were you going to knock on the door to announce your visit this afternoon, or did you plan just to snoop around the vineyard like a thief? You're a braver person than me to risk Camille Morton's wrath."

Considering the argument that I had just overheard between Grant and his mother, I doubted that. I knew better than to admit I had been eavesdropping, though. Another thought struck me. "I'm trying to find out who was at the book signing the night Belinda was killed. Do you have a guest list?"

"Yes." He frowned.

"Did you give the police the list?" I asked.

He laughed. "Your Rainwater asked for it that very night."

"He's not my Rainwater."

He smirked.

"Can I have the list?"

"Are you a cop?" he asked.

I frowned. "No."

"Then I have no reason to give it to you. You're the one in the wrong here today, Vi. You're the one trespassing on private property."

I didn't want to admit it, but he was right. I gave up asking for the list, but there was one person I very much wanted to know about.

"Did you see Miles Rathbone at the signing?"

"From Bone and Hearth? Yeah, he was here."

"Did you speak to him?"

He nodded. "For a second. He asked if he could have a moment with Belinda alone. He wanted 'to talk things over with her' and see if she would retract her review of his winery. I told him good luck with that."

I shivered. Had Rathbone gotten Belinda alone when she fled the winery after seeing Lacey and, when she refused to do what he asked, stabbed her?

"Wouldn't you say he's another good suspect then?" I asked.

"Not as good as Lacey."

Behind me there was a faint clicking sound. Grant must have heard it too, because he jumped around me. There was a glint of light reflecting off a lens and then it was gone.

"Hey!" Grant shouted before he bolted away from me through the rows of grapes with no explanation at all.

CHAPTER TWENTY-SIX

"Ahh!" A scream cut through the vines and trellises.

I ran in the direction it had come from and found Grant sitting on a man's chest in the middle of a row of grapes. Redding had found me.

"Tell this Neanderthal to get off me!" Redding cried when he saw me. He kicked at Grant with his legs, but Grant, having been a star wrestler in high school, easily avoided Redding's flailing limbs.

"What are you doing here?" Grant demanded.

"Why don't you ask her?" Redding said. "I can't answer because I can't breathe!"

"You are breathing enough to shout," I said.

"Violet, what's going on?" Grant asked.

Redding's face was turning a terrible shade of red. Perhaps he wasn't lying about the inability to breathe. "This is Joel Redding, a private detective who Belinda's fiancé Sebastian hired to clear his name. He's been following me around and making a general nuisance of himself."

"You led me here on purpose!" Redding gasped.

"That's ridiculous." I rolled my eyes as if that were the dumbest idea I had ever heard. "Grant, you might want to climb off him. He is turning purple."

Grant scowled and looked down at the other man. Finally, Grant got up.

Redding let out a huge breath. "I could have you arrested for assault."

Grant laughed. "I would like to see you try. My brother's the mayor."

I wished that there was less truth in that statement, but I knew from Grant's crimes in the past that he did get away with more than the average villager because Nathan was his brother and the Mortons would do just about anything to avoid a scandal. Unfortunately, when Belinda died, scandal had fallen on their doorstep. This time it was much more difficult to pretend it had never happened.

The sun was beginning to set, and pink and purple light played off the frozen vines and grapes. The beauty of the scenery against the absurdity of the situation was not lost on me.

"Get up," Grant ordered.

Redding struggled to his feet and dusted snow off his coat. "You don't know who you're messing with. I have put tougher men than you in prison. You and your family don't scare me."

"And your weak threats don't scare me," Grant shot back. He turned to me. "What are you really doing here, Vi?"

"I want to know who was at the party and who of those people might have held a grudge against Belinda."

He smiled. "Ah, the more suspects, the less likely you think Lacey will be arrested. I remember that you had the same tactic with Sadie when she was accused of murder."

I ground my teeth, doing my best not to show how furious I was at him for bringing up Sadie's name. I didn't know what my friend had ever seen in him.

"I think it's time for both of you to go. Vi, you don't want my mother catching you here, do you?" Grant smirked.

I frowned. "I'm not afraid of your mother."

This made him laugh.

Mrs. Morton's voice suddenly rang out. "Grant! Grant! Where are you? We need to go over these receipts."

"Speak of the devil," he said with a mischievous smile.

Quite literally, I thought as I heard Mrs. Morton's voice. I would have been lying if I hadn't admitted that the sound of Camille Morton's voice made me cringe.

Mrs. Morton came around the side of the trellis. "What on earth is going on here?" She pointed at Redding. "Who are you? This is private property."

"Mother, I have this handled. Violet and her friend were about to leave."

"He's not my friend," I corrected.

Mrs. Morton glared at her son. "Just like you have other things handled, son. Let's not kid ourselves there."

Inwardly, I cringed on Grant's behalf. It seemed like I had fallen back into a time capsule. I had heard the Mortons reprimand their children many times for not achieving as much as they hoped they would. Even when the boys reached their greatest successes, the elder Mortons had wanted more. They wanted them to be greater and reach higher. There was no final goal — just bigger and better every time. I'd never had to live like that. I put more than enough pressure on myself to achieve, but it was self-inflicted. Grandma Daisy and my mother had never put that type of pressure on me. They'd wanted me to be happy in whatever form that took. Mrs. Morton's words reminded me how lucky I really was.

Redding held out his hand to Mrs. Morton. She glared at it until he finally lowered it. Even so, Redding didn't appear to be insulted by her slight. "Joel Redding, P.I. I'm looking into the Perkins murder."

"I have nothing to say to you," she snapped, and then turned on me. "Why did you bring this man here?" She was bundled up in what I feared was a real fur coat. I preferred not to think about it too much.

"I didn't bring him here. I don't even know him."

Redding smiled. "It's true that Violet didn't bring me here; she led me here. I can't help but think that she wanted me to meet you. Perhaps because you had something to do with the murder. I know that you and Violet have a long history."

Mrs. Morton's face flushed red. I wouldn't have been the least bit surprised if smoke started coming out of her ears.

I grimaced. The plan I had hatched with my grandmother back in Charming Books had backfired. Redding was turning the idea back around on me. It seemed that I hadn't outsmarted him at all.

She took a step toward me. "I want you to stay away from my boys. Do you understand me?"

"Mother," Grant said. His ruddy complexion was a tad redder than usual. I was certain that a twenty-nine-year-old man didn't want his mother telling him who he could and could not interact with.

"Violet Waverly, I want you off my family's property this instant — and never come back!" His mother spat at me. "I won't have you ruining something for this family."

"Gladly," I said, and walked out of the vineyard. I didn't wait to see if Redding followed me. If he wanted to be my shadow in this investigation, he would have to learn to keep up.

CHAPTER TWENTY-SEVEN

I had just reached my Mini when a black Roadster flew out from behind the back of the house and down the driveway. I caught the briefest glimpse of Grant behind the wheel.

The private investigator folded his arms. "Where's he going like a bat out of hell?"

"Why don't you follow him so you can find out?"

He smiled. "You'd like that so I will stop following you, wouldn't you?"

I leaned against my car and folded my arms.

He scowled at me. "What are you doing?"

"Waiting for you to leave," I said. "I won't have you following me anymore."

He mimicked my posture and folded his arms, leaning against the gray sedan. "Like you can stop me."

The sun was past the tree line now, and it was growing darker by the second. "It's going to get really cold, then," I said.

He opened his mouth to say something back, but his cell phone rang. He removed the phone from his pocket. "Redding."

There was yelling on the other end of the line, and even though I couldn't make out the words, I certainly caught the emotions of the other person.

"All right. I'll be right there!" Redding shouted into the phone. He ended the call and shoved the phone back into his pocket with a scowl.

I smiled brightly at him. "Everything okay?"

"I would love to continue our staring competition, but I have to go."

"Anything to do with the murder?"

The corner of his mouth turned up. "I'm sure you would like to know." He studied me for a moment. "After this is all over, you might want to rethink your career. Why work in the dusty old bookshop when you can come work for me as an investigator? You seem to have a natural knack for it."

"That is flattering of you to ask, but I'm good where I am, thanks. The shop's not dusty anyway. My grandmother takes dusting very seriously."

"If you ever change your mind, let me know." With that, he climbed into his car and drove away. I watched the gray sedan's headlights until he turned off the road.

Part of me considered following him. Maybe this time Redding would lead me to something related to the murder, but I thought better of it. It seemed to me that I should take advantage of the private detective's absence and do some more snooping on my own.

I climbed into the Mini and headed for my next stop: Bone and Hearth Winery.

The new winery was only a few miles away from the Mortons'. Most of the wineries in the village were out in this area. Even though the wineries were close together, the sun set fast this time of year, and it was dark by the time I reached Rathbone's vineyard.

Lampposts led the way up Bones and Hearth's long driveway that was still not as long or as impressive as the Mortons'. However, there was no question that this place was a winery, as row upon row of grapevines covered the front lawn.

The stone building was half the size of the Mortons' as well. A dozen or so cars sat in the circle drive in front, and all the lights were on. I slowed the Mini as I drew closer to the last car in the circle. I stopped my car behind it and shifted into park. I sat in the car for a moment, wondering if I should approach the building or come back another time when I might catch Miles Rathbone alone.

But as it typically did, curiosity got the better of me. I wanted to know why there were so many people there, especially since Rathbone's wine was ruined by Belinda's review.

A car parked behind me. A woman got out and hurried toward the building. She was middle-aged, and most of her face was covered by a scarf. I followed her and fell in step behind her. She held the door for me and smiled. "Don't you hate when you're late for these meetings?"

"For sure," I said, even though I didn't have the faintest idea what she was talking about.

As soon as we got inside, the woman took off toward the middle of the room. The Bone and Hearth tasting room was light and airy, with blond wood paneling and a high ceiling defined with matching blond beams. Ten rows of eight chairs filled the room and were all pointed forward toward a long table that had three men sitting at it. The man in the middle seat, whom I recognized as Miles Rathbone from his photos, hit his gavel on the table.

"Miss, standing in the back, please sit down."

Screeching sounds resonated off the ceiling while everyone in the room turned and stared at me. I slid into the closest chair. I sat next to an elderly man with his eyes closed. He was either asleep or dead. I was hoping for the former. I had seen enough dead bodies for the week.

"Can we please focus on the issue at hand?" a voice asked from the front of the room. "The village should do more to support the wine industry in Cascade Springs. I believe that we need to be given some leeway here. Without us the village is nothing, but with us it's a tourist destination. The winemakers' guild needs to have a prominent place in the village."

I raised my eyebrows. It seemed to me that I had stumbled into the winemakers' guild meeting that Grant had mentioned to his mother. I could have been wrong, but it looked like Miles Rathbone, the discredited winemaker, was the leader of the guild too.

"It's the springs themselves that bring the tourists in," another voice argued. "They have been doing that since long before the Revolutionary War."

I agreed with the voice about the importance of the springs. I knew what the water could do.

"The springs might bring them here the first time," the first voice said. "But the wine is what keeps bringing them back. Once you see the springs once, there isn't really any reason to see them again. It's just water."

It was a little bit more than just water, I thought. I certainly wasn't going to say that in front of this group.

"James, if you are so moved about this, I suggest you draft a memo for the village council for the next meeting that will include what we want the village to do for us," Rathbone said.

"Nathan Morton is right here; just hand him the demands of our group and let's be done with it," another man at the table said.

I bobbed my head back and forth, looking for Nathan. I finally spotted the back of his blond head in the second row from the front.

"I'm here as a guild member this afternoon, not as the mayor," Nathan said. Even though he was facing the table, I could clearly hear his voice in the back of the room. Nathan sounded more like a politician than I had ever heard him sound.

"Yes, Nathan is attending today as a member of the guild, but I know that he will present our idea to the city council in a favorable light."

Nathan stood up now. "Of course I will. I am the mayor of Cascade Springs, but I am a winemaker too, and the Cascade Springs Winemaker Guild is an important organization in this village. I will do whatever I can to support this group that has been so good to my family over the years. We are all saddened over the passing of Belinda Perkins, and I want to thank each and every one of you who have reached out to my family at this difficult time." He sat back down.

I frowned. It was true that Belinda had died at Morton Vineyards, but it seemed odd to me that Nathan would be thanking this group for condolences. Lacey and her sisters were the ones who should have been comforted.

The man next to me snorted. I glanced at him. He didn't open his eyes but said out the side of his mouth, "The Mortons think they run this village and the guild. The problem is, everyone lets them believe that. I thought that might have changed when Belinda Perkins turned up dead in their vineyard. This town is too blinded by the Mortons to even see the threat they are."

"Threat?" I whispered back.

Never opening his eyes, the man rested his chin back on his chest and seemed to go back to sleep. I was corrected when the man stood and said in a booming voice, "Not that a single person here today can claim to be upset over Belinda Perkins's death. We've all been touched by her pen. Even when she wrote a good review, she phrased it in such a way that it came off as an insult. You know better than anyone about that, don't you, Rathbone?" He sat down.

Rathbone froze. "How dare you say such a thing?"

The old man burrowed back down in his coat and began to snore. However, what he'd said seemed to cause a stir in the group, and I heard Belinda's name whispered all around me.

"The incident at Morton Vineyards has nothing to do with this meeting. I'm sure that we're all sorry to hear the news about Belinda Perkins's passing. She was an icon in our industry, and we would do well to remember all that she contributed."

"Or destroyed," another voice said.

I couldn't tell where the speaker was seated, but I saw several other people in the room nodding their heads. Perhaps what the old man had said was true. No one in this room cared that Belinda was dead. If that was the case, was I in a room full of suspects?

Rathbone knocked his gavel on the table two more times. "The guild subcommittee will come up with a list for the town council to approve. If we have no more *business* to discuss, I suggest that we adjourn. Do I have a motion?"

"I move to adjourn," a deep voice from somewhere in the middle of the chairs said.

"Second!" several voices echoed.

The meeting started to break up. I looked at the sleeping man next to me, and he didn't move. I was about to ask him more about Belinda and the guild when a hand clamped down on my shoulder. "Did you follow me?"

I looked up to find Grant Morton staring down at me.

I jumped out of my seat. "No. I came here to speak to Miles Rathbone. I had no idea a meeting was happening."

He narrowed his eyes. "Why don't I believe you?"

Nathan joined us and stared at me. "What are you doing here?"

"That's not very welcoming," I said, stalling for time.

My seat companion didn't stir.

Grant frowned. "I'm sure the police chief would love to hear about your snooping around."

I ignored Grant's comment and turned to Nathan. "It sounds like the guild is making up a proposal to give you and the town council about wine making in the village. What is it about?"

He pressed his lips together. "I don't know why it's your concern, Vi. Are you interested in the wine business?"

"Only in regards to how it relates to Belinda Perkins's murder."

He paused. "I heard from my mother."

"That's my cue to leave," Grant said, and walked away.

Nathan scowled at his brother's back.

"And what did your mother want?" I asked as innocently as I could manage.

He studied me with his dark eyes. "She said that you went up to the vineyard and snooped around with a private investigator."

"I wasn't snooping around with a private investigator. I don't even know him. He followed me there. He said that he was hired by Sebastian Knight to look into the murder."

Nathan frowned. "Sebastian doesn't have faith in the police?"

I shrugged. "I think it's a safe bet to say that Sebastian doesn't have faith in anyone. I'm not even sure that he loved Belinda. He

309

certainly loved her money," I said, thinking of the life insurance policy.

"Mr. Mayor," Miles Rathbone said as he joined us. "I'm so very glad that you could come to our meeting. You secretary said that you wouldn't be able to make it."

Nathan plastered on his mayoral face, which I had come to recognize as a pleasant mask. "You know I try to always make time for the guild when I can."

"Of course, of course," Rathbone said. Miles Rathbone was a slim, short man with a perfectly manicured goatee. He couldn't be much more than forty. "I don't believe I have met the lovely woman standing next to you."

"This is Violet Waverly," Nathan said. "She owns Charming Books, the bookshop in the village, with her grandmother Daisy."

Rathbone paled some at the mention of my name. "Oh, I have heard many things about you throughout the village."

"All good, I hope."

"All interesting," he said.

"I've heard some things about you too," I said. "Belinda wasn't fond of your wines. How has that impacted your business?"

His face turned white. "I don't know why it's any of your business."

"She's dead, and the police are looking to

find the person who killed her. It seems to me that a lot of people had a motive to kill her, including you."

"That's ridiculous. I wouldn't kill anyone." He laughed nervously. It wasn't the most convincing claim to innocence I had ever heard.

"But you were upset with Belinda, weren't you?" I asked. "She wrote an unfavorable review of your ice wine that was so bad you had to take it off the market."

"I don't know what you're talking about."

"Of course you do," I said. "I was there when you asked Belinda to sign your book to the winery she destroyed, your winery. I'm sure that is especially hard to take since she is your ex-wife."

Nathan's mouth fell open. "What?"

Rathbone's face turned a deep red. "How dare you come into my winery and guild meeting and speak to me like this?"

Nathan stared at him. "You were married to Belinda?"

"Years ago, for a very short time. It has nothing to do with what is happening now."

"The bad review must have been extra painful, though," Nathan said. "More personal."

"If I wanted to kill that woman, I would have when I was married to her. She was

311

conceited and selfish and I was happy to be rid of her. I know she wrote that review of my winery out of spite, but according to the wine community, Belinda Perkins can do no wrong. There was nothing I could do to stop her." With that, Rathbone stomped away.

He said it with so much venom that I couldn't help but believe that he was capable of murder.

The old man who had been sitting next to me stood up. "Some people seemed to get all sunshine, and some all shadow . . ." The old man hobbled away.

"Vi, what's wrong?" Nathan peered at me. "Do you need to sit?"

I forced a laugh. "No, it's just that quote. I know it."

"Where's it from?"

I shrugged. "I probably read it somewhere."

CHAPTER TWENTY-EIGHT

On my way out of Bone and Hearth, I spotted Grant and Nathan talking to writer Jack Zule out of the corner of my eye. I knew that they would want all press about Morton Vineyards going forward to be good press.

I left the winery more determined than ever to get back to the shop and get to the bottom of what the shop's magical essence was telling me as far as *Little Women* went. I didn't know if I was misinterpreting the passages that it wanted me to read because it was being purposely obtuse or because I had lost my knack for understanding what the shop wanted me to know. In either case, it ended tonight, even if it took all night. I was determined to solve the clues.

When I turned onto River Road, I drove slowly up the street looking for any sign of Redding's gray sedan. It was nowhere to be seen. In fact, the only mode of transport that I passed was a carriage and its white horse making its way back to the livery.

In the winter when there wasn't a special event taking place, Cascade Springs became the quiet little river village that I imagined it had been when my ancestress Rosalee Waverly came here for the first time in 1812. She fell in love with the spring water and with the village as a whole. It could easily be done. It wasn't until I had returned to the village after all that time away that I realized how much I had missed this place. There was something special about Cascade Springs. I just hadn't realized how special until I came back and learned about my role as the Caretaker.

I parked the Mini in front of the shop and walked through the front door. The shop door was still unlocked even though it was after closing time.

Emerson met me at the door and cocked his black and white head. I narrowed my eyes at him. "And what have you been up to all day?"

He wove around my ankles and purred.

"Grandma!" I called into the shop.

There was no answer. That wasn't all that unusual. Often Grandma Daisy got caught up in a project and lost track of time. I was guessing that was why the front door was still unlocked.

I locked the door and went in search of my grandmother. I circled the shop but didn't find her. Then I went into the kitchen, which was the most likely place. She wasn't there either. Shaking my head, I went up the narrow servants' stairs behind the kitchen. The steps creaked under my weight. I pushed open the door and entered the fairy room loft. Emerson sat on one of the red-and-white toadstools as if he had been sitting there for hours waiting for me.

I frowned when I noticed that the door to my apartment was ajar. We always kept the door closed and locked when the shop was open just so customers didn't wander into my personal space.

With my toe, I pushed open the door. Grandma Daisy sat in the middle of my sofa holding a letter. I immediately recognized the letter as Fenimore's and my stomach dropped.

I wanted to scold and yell at her for going through my private things. She had no right to do it, but when she looked up at me, all the harsh words died on my lips. She was pale, and her cheeks were sunken in.

"What is this?" she asked in a hollow voice.

"Did you go through my things?" The

question came out harsher than I meant it too.

She wouldn't meet my eyes. "I didn't mean too. I thought that I was helping you. You've been so stressed lately with the shop, your classes at the college, your dissertation, and now Belinda's murder, that I thought I would do you a little favor and fold your laundry. It's been sitting in the basement for a few days." She took a breath. "I didn't mean to find this, but it was sitting on your nightstand."

"My nightstand? How did it get there? That's not where I kept it."

"I don't know," she said. "But that's where I found it."

The shop's essence had moved the letter. I knew it in my heart.

"As soon as I saw it," Grandma Daisy said, "I recognized Fern's handwriting. I know it was wrong to pick it up, but I couldn't help but touch it. She was my only child."

"Did you read it?" I asked.

She handed me the letter. "I wanted to. That's why you caught me here. I wanted to read that letter so badly. I wanted to hear my daughter's voice in my head again, but I couldn't. The letter is not addressed to me. It's not even addressed to you, even though you are the one who has it. Why is it addressed to Fenimore?"

Fenimore was a traveling troubadour that came to the village every year for the festival. He traveled all over the Niagara region and into New England playing his guitar and harmonica. That's how my grandmother knew him. She didn't know that he was the one man my mother had fallen in love with. She didn't know that he was my father.

"Maybe you should read it," I said. "I'm not sure that I can explain. The letter will do a better job than I can."

She took it from my hand again. "Are you sure?"

I nodded and perched on the armchair across from her.

She stared at the letter and then took a deep breath. She unfolded that piece of yellowed paper and read. Tears gathered in Grandma Daisy's eyes. "Why didn't she tell me? I wish she would have told me."

I didn't have an answer for that, so I asked, "Do you want me to make some tea?"

Tea was always my grandmother's go-to in times of distress.

"Yes, dear, I think we'd both do well with a cup."

My apartment didn't have a kitchen. I

used the one downstairs in the main part of the house, but I did have an electric teapot for emergencies. This was an emergency if I'd ever seen one.

I walked over to the credenza along the wall where I kept the teakettle and teacups. The vintage tea set decorated with classic children's book characters had been a Christmas gift from Sadie. After filling the kettle with water from the bathroom sink, I plugged it in and sat across from my grandmother again.

She folded the worn letter back up and tucked it into the envelope. "I wish that she had told me."

"According to Fenimore," I said, "they didn't tell anyone. They met in the summer, and by the end of the season, their relationship was over." I was quiet for a moment. "When my mother was pregnant, did you ever ask her who the father was?"

Grandma Daisy held the letter out to me, and I took it from her hand. I set it on the table between us. For some reason, seeing it there made me feel better. I hadn't known how much it was bothering me being the only one who knew this secret about my mother. Now that I no longer had to carry the burden alone, I felt so much lighter.

"I asked her several times in many different ways, but your mother was stubborn and wouldn't tell me. I had to make a choice. Did I alienate my daughter by continuing to press the issue or let her tell me in her own time? I decided on the latter. I always thought she would tell me one day, but life got busy, she got sick, and you know the rest of the story."

I certainly did.

"When did you find out?" Grandma Daisy asked.

"Around Halloween," I said. "I'm sorry I didn't tell you. I didn't know how to. I felt like I needed to come to terms with the information before I came to you with it. I wished that Mom had told me herself, but I don't know what difference that would have made. It took Fenimore almost sixteen years to give me this letter. I don't know what good it would have done me knowing all that time. Maybe it would have hurt more to be so young, know there was a father out there but he didn't want anything to do with me."

"Oh, my dear. If he knew what you were like, he would want to know you. I'm sure of that," my grandmother mused.

I wasn't as sure. Fenimore knew what I was like now, and I hadn't heard a peep from him since he had given me the letter.

The teakettle whistled, and I got out of my seat. At the credenza, I poured hot water over tea bags in two of the small teacups.

"English breakfast tea," I said. "You're favorite." I handed her the teacup with a scene from *Charlotte's Web* painted on it. I took the *Alice in Wonderland* teacup.

"You are too good to me, my dear. You've always been a good granddaughter."

I smiled at the kindness of my grandmother's comment. I hadn't been that great of a granddaughter. When I fled from the village, I had seen my grandmother only one or two times a year until I returned to the village. I hadn't been a good granddaughter then.

Grandma Daisy sighed. "I wish your mother told me. I could have helped her more."

"You were a great help. Mom always appreciated what you did for both of us." I sipped my tea. I cupped the teacup in my hand. "Maybe she was afraid to. Maybe she thought something would happen to Fenimore," I said. "Aren't the Waverly women destined to be alone? Maybe she thought it would be easier this way."

Grandma Daisy studied me. "Is this something you've worried about?"

"You must admit it's a pattern."

"There is no rule that it has to be that way," she said quietly.

"But it is that way. It has always been that way. You told me that. Why has it always been like that?"

"You can't keep a secret like that from someone you love so dear. Take it from me, it starts to eat at you. I can't tell you how many times I almost cracked and told my beau Benedict." She sighed. "I was planning to tell him everything," she went on. "When he died suddenly, I was glad that I hadn't said a word."

"Why?" I whispered the question.

"I'm not sure how he would have taken it. It is a lot to absorb." She finished her tea and set it on the side table. "Maybe you will be the one to find the right man to share the secret with. Maybe you will be the luckiest one of us all."

I thought of Rainwater. Could I trust him? I knew my family's secret was the heart of my hesitation with him.

I picked up my grandmother's teacup and took both our cups back to the credenza. Just inches away from the electric teapot lay a copy of *Little Woman.* I knew that it hadn't been there when I made the tea. I reached for it, and the book fell open. There were no fluttering pages, just a gentle *thunk* as the front cover hit the credenza.

I bit my lip and then peered at the page. My eyes dropped to the text. "Unfortunately, we don't have windows in our breasts, and cannot see what goes on in the minds of our friends; better for us that we cannot as a general thing, but now and then it would be such a comfort, such a saving of time and temper."

The passage was from when Jo spoke out of turn to her aunt March and so lost her chance to go to Europe. Amy was asked instead. Was the passage telling me to hold my tongue?

"What's wrong, Violet?" Grandma Daisy asked.

I picked up the book and took it back to the chair with me. "This." I showed her the book.

"Have you learned anything at all from the books?" She frowned. "You seem to be confused this time."

I looked up from the book. "That's because I am confused. I don't know what the shop is trying to tell me."

I made a move to turn the page when the book snapped closed. I moved my hands out of the way and stared at it on my lap. A second later the book fell open, but to a new page. It was to a chapter not long after

Meg married Brooke. She was remembering her mother's warning about her new husband. " 'He has a temper, not like ours — one flash and then all over — but the white, still anger that is seldom stirred, but once kindled is hard to quench.' " I read the passage aloud to my grandmother. "Whoever killed Belinda was angry? At least that much is clear, and this would lead me to believe that whoever killed her didn't do it in a fit of rage, but instead thought and planned it for a long time."

"Do you think the book is saying that her killer was a man?"

"I'm not sure I would take it that literarily." I frowned. I closed the book and stood up. "I promise I will study that book tonight, but first I have something more important to do."

"What is that?"

"I have to water the tree."

She nodded. "That is more important."

CHAPTER TWENTY-NINE

The sooner winter was over, the better it would be for me. Running into the woods in the middle of night to avoid being seen to collect water for the tree from the natural springs was much more fun when I didn't fear frostbite on my nose.

I burrowed deeper into my scarf and pulled my hat down over my ears with gloved hands as I walked at a fast clip toward the springs.

Two nights ago, on the night of Belinda's book signing, I had run to and from the springs in a frenzy, knowing how late I would arrive at Morton Vineyards. It wasn't until Belinda died that I'd realized being late was the least of my worries.

Hoot, hoot, an owl called from somewhere high in the trees. Without their leaves, the trees looked alien against the night sky. I felt like I was in an old Bugs Bunny cartoon where the faceless eyes in the woods were watching me. I shook off the creepy feeling that I knew was more self-inflicted than anything else. This was a time when having a vivid imagination was not a good thing.

I quickened my pace, but I didn't run. Finally, the path opened up and the natural springs bubbled in front of me. Much of the water was frozen. Even the small waterfall that trickled down the rocks was frozen in place. I walked to the edge of the spring and picked up a large rock. I hit the rock on the ice over and over again until it made an indentation in the ice. I hit it again, and water began to pool over the sheet of ice. I collected what I could. My finger cramped from the cold and my gloves were soaked.

Finally, I had enough spring water to fill the watering can. I stood up and hurried back down the trail. I was halfway back to the bookshop when I heard a stick snap to my left. It sounded like a gunshot on the still winter's night. I froze and listened. I didn't hear another sound. I told myself that it was a deer in the woods or another animal. Nothing to be afraid of.

I started walking again, and I'd moved a few more feet when I heard the same sound, followed almost immediately by another. Up ahead a shadow cast across the path, and it was in the shape of a man. The moonlight distorted the shadow, making the shape look like a giant.

My knees knocked together. I didn't know if it was from fear or the cold. "Hey!" I shouted at the figure. "Who's there?"

The giant shadow turned and ran down the path. Forgetting my fear, I held the watering can to my chest and took off after the shadow. Just before I reached the person, there was a scream and then a thud.

I ran to where I heard the fall and found Joel Redding lying on the ground holding his ankle. A giant tree root poked out of the ground to his right.

"Owww!" Redding moaned. "My ankle. Call an ambulance! I'm hurt."

I stared down at him. "Were you following me?"

He groaned.

"Answer the question."

"I told you that you were my lead to solving the case. When I followed you, I thought you were going into the woods to meet someone. I didn't know you wanted a drink of water."

I shivered. Redding had seen me gather water from the natural springs. What did this mean? Would he figure out Charming Books' secret? This was much worse than him just following me to learn more about the murder.

"What are you doing out here in the middle of night anyway?" Redding wanted to know.

"I went for a walk. Not that it's any of your business."

"Who goes for a walk carrying a watering can?" he asked.

I stepped around him and started down the path.

"Wait! You can't leave me here. I'm hurt."

I walked a few more feet.

"You're really going to leave me in the middle of the dark woods with what is most likely a broken ankle?"

I sighed and turned around. "Are you sure it's broken?"

"Look at it!" He pointed at his ankle.

I did, with only the dappled moonlight that came through the cracks in the tree cover to see by. His ankle was bent at an odd angle. The laces of his boot were stretched, as it had already begun to swell. "Maybe it's just a sprain."

"Doesn't feel like a sprain," Redding muttered.

"Then we need to get you to the hospital." I set the watering can on the ground and started to help him to his feet.

"No! Ow! Don't move me. Don't you

know that you're not supposed to move someone with an injury?"

"I'm pretty sure that's someone with a back injury, and your back is fine. I can help you down the path and you can hop on your good foot to my car. It's parked in front of Charming Books. It's not too far."

"It's not too far for someone with two working legs. It will take forever for me. You need a better plan."

"I can't just leave you here."

"Call for an EMT or something."

I chewed on my bottom lip. If I called for an EMT, Chief Rainwater would surely hear about it. I didn't want to bring more attention to my walk in the woods than I already had. "Don't be a baby, Redding. You will probably be on crutches for a while after this. You should get used to hopping."

"I'll never get used to hopping."

"My offer is to take you to the hospital in my car, or we can go to Charming Books and I can call an ambulance from there for you."

He rubbed his knee and glared at me. "All right."

"Can I help you up?" I asked.

He nodded.

I bent and grabbed Redding under the right shoulder. As I straightened up, he cried out.

I grimaced. He wrapped his arm over my shoulder and hopped on one foot.

"Try to keep your balance while I pick up my watering can." I bent down with Redding clinging to my shoulder as I picked up the watering can. Only a very small amount of the spring water splashed out. I righted myself and held the can to my chest with my right hand and supported Redding with my left.

We started our way down the path. Our progress was slow. Redding wasn't a great hopper, and he had to rest every few feet.

"Tap water isn't good enough for you?" he asked.

"What?"

"The watering can. Do you collect water from the spring because you don't care for tap water?"

I searched my brain for an explanation. "It's for my cat. He doesn't like tap water," I said. Inwardly, I groaned. Redding would never believe that excuse, and I couldn't blame him for that.

"Your cat?"

"You shouldn't have followed me into the woods. If you hadn't, you wouldn't be hurt right now."

"I followed you because I wanted to tell

you that you're right."

I stopped in the middle of the path. "What?"

Redding hopped wildly in place trying to keep his balance. "Hey, you can't just slam on the brakes like that. You have to warn me."

"Sorry." I started walking again. "What was I right about?"

"Lacey. I don't think she killed Belinda either. When I got that call at the vineyard and left, I was headed for Le Crepe Jolie. Sebastian was there and wanted me to question Lacey. I did, and I concluded that there isn't a single mean bone in her body. She didn't kill Belinda."

I gave a sigh of relief. "Thank goodness. You should have come to that conclusion a lot sooner, though. So, who do you think the killer is?"

"My money is on Lacey's husband."

"Adrien?" I gasped. "You can't be serious."

"The man is built like a professional wrestler, and he's protective of his wife. He saw her be publicly humiliated when Belinda rejected her. He was angry."

"Adrien wouldn't do that. He's a gentle giant," I said, just as we reached the back gate of the shop. I had never been so grateful to see Charming Books in all my life.

"It's a gut feeling he's the killer, and my gut feelings are almost always right."

I opened the gate. "Not this time."

"I know you didn't go to the springs to collect water for your cat. But whatever propelled you to go into the woods in the middle of the night was important." There was a pause. "I'm going to find out what that is."

Grandma Daisy met us at the kitchen door and held it open for us. She had her coat on. "I was just about to go look for you, Violet; you were gone so long." She stared at Redding. "What's going on?"

"Grandma Daisy," I said. "This is Joel Redding, the private detective that I have told you about who has been following me around the village. He followed me into the woods tonight and might have broken his ankle." I stopped myself just in time from saying that he deserved it for snooping.

"Oh dear, you both come inside from the cold."

I helped Redding through the doorway, and he winced. I knew that he must be in a lot of pain. I settled him on the kitchen stool.

Grandma Daisy looked from the watering can in my hand to Redding and back again.

I gave a slight shake of my head. There was no time to explain now. I had to get Redding out of the shop. "You can have a quick rest, but we need to get you to the hospital so you can have the ankle looked at," I said. "I need to get my car keys."

When I was in the main part of the shop, I looked behind me to make sure the door between the kitchen and the rest of the shop was closed. It was, and with another moment's hesitation, I watered the tree and stored the watering can behind the sales counter. Then I grabbed my car keys.

When I came back into the kitchen a few minutes later, Redding was sipping from a cup of tea.

Grandma Daisy smiled at me, but it didn't reach her eyes. "Mr. Redding was just asking me all sorts of questions about the history of the bookshop. He's very curious about this place."

"Oh," I said, and I felt the knot in my stomach tighten. I turned to Redding. "Are you ready to go?"

He nodded. He was much paler than he had been a few minutes ago. I helped him to his feet for a second time and led him to the back door. There was no way I was taking him out the front of the shop where he would see the birch tree. I knew that it was impossible to keep him from learning about the tree. Everyone in the village knew it was there. I only wanted to postpone that as long as possible.

"Violet," Grandma Daisy said, stopping me. "Be careful." She gave me a meaningful look.

"I will," I said.

CHAPTER THIRTY

The entire drive to the emergency clinic, Redding moaned about his ankle. I finally gave up consoling him about it. At least he had fallen on his own accord in the public park. He had no grounds to sue me or Charming Books over the injury. I didn't doubt for a moment that he would have tried, given the fuss that he was making.

We arrived at the clinic, and it must have been a slow night because they took him right in. While I was in the waiting room, I called Rainwater. I knew I was long overdue to tell him about what I'd been up to.

He answered on the first ring. "Violet, are you okay?" He sounded a little bit out of breath.

"I'm fine," I said. "P.I. Redding not so much. We're at the emergency clinic."

"What happened?" he asked.

"Maybe I should start from the begin-ning?" And I did just that. I told Rainwater about everyone I had spoken to about Belinda: my visit with Adele, running into Michelle, talking to Charles Hancock, learning that Rathbone was Belinda's ex-husband, and the guild meeting at Bone and Hearth Vineyards.

Rainwater remained silent through all of it. I couldn't tell if he was happy, angry, or indifferent about everything I had learned. I didn't know if I was telling him anything new or if this was all old information as far as he was concerned, but I didn't hold anything back. When I finished my story and he didn't say anything, I asked, "Do you have anything to say about that?"

"I have a lot to say about it," Rainwater confessed. "I'm just trying not to say anything that I will regret over it."

"I would do it all over again. Lacey is my friend, and I want to protect her."

He sighed. "I know. You're a loyal friend, Violet, and that is an admirable quality. You should be proud of that."

"Thank you," I murmured.

"We can talk more about this later and in person. Why don't you go home? I'll send Wheaton over to wait and take Redding home after he's released from the clinic."

"You want me to just leave him?"

"Yes," he said, leaving no room for argu-

335

ment. "This man has been badgering you. Just tell them at the desk that Wheaton will be there."

It sounded like a good plan to me. "All right," I agreed.

"I'm tied up at the moment, but I'll come over and see you at the bookshop just as soon as I can."

"You don't have to do that," I said in a low voice.

"I know I don't have to, Violet. I want to." There was a pause. "Now, go home. I'll see you in a little while."

I finally agreed, not because I was willing to take orders from Rainwater but because I didn't want to listen to Redding whine about his ankle any longer.

When I got back to Charming Books, there was a note on the sales counter. Faulkner cawed and Emerson meowed.

I read the note. I WENT TO LE CREPE JOLIE TO CHECK ON LACEY AND GET SOME DINNER. COME JOIN US! GRANDMA D.

Dinner with Lacey, Adrien, and Grandma Daisy was just what I needed. I texted Rainwater to tell him where I would be in case he arrived at Charming Books sooner than he thought.

I bundled up in my winter coat, hat, gloves, boots, and scarf again and headed out the door. Emerson followed me. I shook my finger at the little black-and-white tuxie. "I don't think so. It's far too cold out there for you to be romping about, especially now that the sun has set."

He meowed and placed his white front paws on my legs. He looked at me imploringly. I shook my head, trying to be firm. "No, stay here with Faulkner. He could use the company."

The large black bird flew through the shop and landed on the mantle above the fireplace. "Hogwash."

I narrowed my eyes at the bird. "You're not helping."

Finally, I had no choice but to do the one trick that I knew worked with the cat. I picked up a pen from the sales counter, walked to the front door of the shop, waved the pen back and forth in front of the cat's face, and then threw it as far as I could across the shop. "Fetch!" I shouted.

Emerson bounded after the flying pen, Faulkner took to the air, and I jumped out the front door, locking it behind me.

I heard an ear-splitting yowl from the other side of the door. The cat wouldn't let me forget this injustice, that much I knew. I would worry about Emerson's wrath later. I ran down the steps, onto the snow-covered yard, and through the gate. I slowed my pace as I reached the icy sidewalk. It was nice to know that I could move through the village without being followed by Redding. Not that I was happy that he had hurt his ankle. All right, maybe if not happy, I was a little bit relieved.

I followed the turn where River Road curved to follow the river. Lacey's café was to my left, but instead of going there straightaway, I crossed the street to the Riverwalk. The moon was nearly full, and its white light reflected off the rushing river water. The ice shimmered and the river glowed. A breeze coming over the border from Canada made me shiver, but I walked to the river's edge anyway. The sight was so lovely, I couldn't turn away.

Another figure moved on the Riverwalk. The person appeared to be dressed all in black. I might have been mistaken, but it looked like Adele Perkins. Was she on the Riverwalk to finally make amends with Lacey? I hoped that was the case for both of their sakes. I couldn't discount what Adele had told me, that she had wanted to kill Belinda for no longer supporting her art. Even so, it was hard for me to believe that the youngest Perkins girl had committed murder, and Lacey would be heartbroken if I even suggested Adele as a suspect. I had told Rainwater what I learned from Adele, and I decided that I would leave it at that.

For some reason, looking at the river made me think of Nathan and Colleen and all that we had been when we were young. We had spent so much of our time growing up in this very spot that it was impossible for me to separate this moment from those that clouded my memory. I could always hear Colleen's infectious laughter, but the January wind seemed to carry it away just before I could catch it. It was like losing her again. I knew that if Colleen were still alive, I would have told her about being the Caretaker of Charming Books. I would have trusted her with that information. Was it fair not to trust Rainwater? Could I trust him enough to tell him my secret? I knew I could never really be with him if I had this wedge between us.

I shook my head, doing my best to chase my rambling thoughts away. It was time to go see Lacey and my grandmother. I had started to turn back toward River Road when I felt two hands on my back. Before I could even scream, those hands pushed me into the rushing water below.

CHAPTER THIRTY-ONE

This was how Colleen died! She drowned in this river. I don't want to die too. I don't! The thoughts shouted inside my brain. *Stand up, stand up!*

Somehow in the bone-chilling cold, my muscles listened. I felt my foot touch the bottom of the riverbed, but still my head didn't break through the surface. My body jerked in the current, and I was so cold, so very cold. It would be much easier to lie down. I just wanted to lie down for a minute. I wanted to stop fighting the current for one minute; that was all I needed.

Then I felt a jerk that nearly pulled my shoulder out of joint. I heard the shout. "I have her!"

I felt my body being pulled from the river's current, the back of my coat scraping over the jagged ice on the riverbank. Once I was on the riverbank, I was rolled onto my side.

"Is she all right?" a high-pitched voice cried. In my fuzzy state of mind, I thought that it might be Lacey. "Is she dead?"

"Not dead," my grandmother said.

"She should go to a hospital. She might have hypothermia." Lacey sounded worried.

"I got her out pretty fast," Grandma Daisy said.

"You might have hypothermia too," Lacey said.

"No, no," I said, finally able to speak. "No hospital. I just want to go home."

"I don't think that's a good idea." It was Rainwater speaking. When had he arrived? I wondered.

I tried to sit up. "Please, just take me home."

I felt someone wrap a blanket around me, and then I was picked up by strong arms. My vision cleared at that point, and I realized Rainwater was carrying me up the street. I wanted to protest and tell him to put me down. I could walk perfectly fine, but instead I rested my head on his shoulder and closed my eyes.

When I woke again, I was tucked into my bed under at least fourteen quilts. There were so many blankets on top of me that it was impossible to move.

"David, thank you for helping me get

Violet into bed," I heard my grandmother say just outside the door.

"That was a foolhardy but brave thing you did back there, Daisy. You might very well have saved Violet's life," the police chief said.

"She's all I have in the world." My grandmother sounded choked up. "I'm going to sleep on her sofa just outside her bedroom and keep an eye on her."

"I'll stay the night too."

"You don't have to do that," my grandmother said. "I am more than capable of taking care of Violet."

"I know you are," Rainwater said. "But someone tried to kill Violet tonight, and I'll be damned if I let it happen again."

"You didn't let it happen, David," Grandma Daisy said soothingly.

"I should have been there." There was a pause. "I can't lose her."

Then their voices moved away from my bedroom door. Although my body still felt so, so cold, there was a warmth in my heart put there by Rainwater's words. I snuggled down in the blanket and closed my eyes again.

The next morning, every muscle in my body ached. I touched my shoulder and felt a bruise forming there. I shoved off the pile of blankets and quilts that had buried me alive the night before. Emerson was at the foot of my bed watching me. When I got out of bed, I saw I was in my pajamas. The conversation I had overheard last night came back to me. Grandma Daisy had mentioned something about Rainwater helping her put me to bed. I prayed to God that he had not helped get me into my PJs. If he had, I would surely die from embarrassment.

I stepped out of my bedroom and saw my grandmother sleeping peacefully on the couch in my tiny living room. There was a smile on her face. If I knew Grandma Daisy at all, she was reliving her heroic rescue of me over and over in her dreams. She deserved to. Rainwater was right; she had saved my life.

I tiptoed out of my apartment, into the children's loft, and down the spiral stairs, wondering if I had imagined the night before: the trip to the hospital with Redding, being pushed into the river, Grandma Daisy jumping in to save me, and Rainwater being there when we came out of the water. But as I walked down the steps and saw the outline of the police chief lying on one of the large sofas by the crackling fireplace, I knew that it had to all be true, every last bit of it. Faulkner fluffed his feathers when I passed the sleeping bird on his favorite branch. I knew that the crow must be awake but was determined to pretend that he was still asleep. I wondered if there was a more obstinate bird on the planet. It was hard to imagine such a creature.

Emerson softly padded down the steps in front of me, looking back every few steps to make sure I was coming. The little tuxedo cat moved noiselessly, but the old staircase groaned under my weight.

Rainwater stirred and opened his eyes. He smiled when he saw me standing just a few feet away from him.

I walked over to him and wrapped my arms around my waist. I was wearing my polar bear pajamas that my grandmother had given me for Christmas, and my hair was a tangled mess sprouting out of my head. I wished that I had taken the time to dress or at least brush my hair before I came downstairs. "You stayed the whole night," I said.

Rainwater pushed his blanket to the other side of the couch and sat up. He'd slept in his jeans and plain white T-shirt. Both were impossibly wrinkled. A very faint five o'clock shadow darkened the skin around his mouth, and his amber eyes were alert. He could not have looked more handsome if he'd tried. "I told your grandmother I would. Why do you think I would leave?"

"I didn't think you would leave by your own choice," I said hesitantly. "But you're the chief of police in this little village, and if something happens, you have to go." Tentatively, I sat beside him on the couch. I left six inches of space between us.

He took my hand in his and held it on the sofa cushion between us. "That may be true but unless there's a break in the homicide case or another murder, I told my officers that I was leaving all late-night calls to them. Clipton, Wheaton, and my other officers can handle the traffic stops and minor infractions that happen in the village overnight." He sighed. "When I took this job, I didn't think murder investigation would be a main portion of my duties." He shook his head. "How's Daisy?"

"Sleeping like a log." I smiled. "I'm glad she wasn't hurt. It was so foolhardy of her to jump into the water after me. How did she get to me so fast?"

"She invited me to dinner with you and the Duponts and met me in front of the café. She just took off running across the street. She saw someone push you into the water."

"Did she see who did it? Did you?"

He shook his head. "Neither of us did. We were both so focused on saving you."

"Grandma Daisy could have drowned." I shivered.

"Violet, she saved your life."

"But she risked her own," I protested.

He squeezed my hand. "That's what people do when they love someone. It's what they should do. I just wish that I had been there to pull you out of the water."

"You were there," I protested.

He frowned. "After Daisy had already pulled you out of the water. I knew that you were becoming too involved in the investigation. I didn't protect you like I should have."

"Don't beat yourself up over this. No one could have known this was going to happen, and we don't have proof that it was Belinda's killer who pushed me into the river. All we can do is speculate."

He stared down at our entwined hands.

I studied him, but he didn't look up and meet my gaze. "The truth has always been abundantly clear to me. You're a man worthy of trusting. I just don't know if I can. I can try if you will be patient with me."

He opened his mouth again as if to speak, but I shook my head and continued. I had to get this out before I lost my courage. "My hesitancy doesn't come from Nathan or wanting to be with Nathan, if that's what you think. It comes from what he represents, my life before my mother and Colleen died. He knew them. He was with me when they died. You'll never know them, and that's a hard truth." I took a shaky breath. "You would've thought after all these years I would be over losing them, but the truth is, when someone you love that much dies, you don't ever really get over it. I've learned I have to give myself permission to live happily ever after without them, and not feel guilty because I'm here. Neither my mom or Colleen would want me to suffer and be alone if I have an opportunity to be happy with you. They would want me to take the risk. They would scream at me to take it."

Tears were rolling down my cheeks now, but I made no move to wipe them away. I was showing Rainwater who I really was: a polar-bear pajama–wearing, tangled-haired, blubbering mess. "I choose you. I was always going to choose you; I just had to give myself permission to do it. That's my decision to live in the moment." I took another breath. "What do you have to say about that?"

He didn't say a thing. Instead, he leaned forward and gave me a good-morning kiss.

CHAPTER THIRTY-TWO

Two hours later, I was showered and dressed. Rainwater had left not long after our talk. I felt so much lighter having told him how I felt. I hadn't known how much holding my feelings back from him had been weighing on me. I glanced at the tree. When it came to Rainwater, there was still the issue of being the shop's Caretaker to deal with. I didn't know how I could keep that secret from Rainwater without sabotaging whatever we might have in the future. For the moment, I pushed those thoughts aside and concentrated on the present, and part of the present was finding out who had pushed me into the river.

I moved slowly down the steps, still sore from my tumble into the river. I had half a dozen bruises peppered across my body, but thankfully it was the middle of winter, and by the time it was warm enough to wear T-shirts and no coats again, the bruises would be healed.

Moving slowly, I reached the bottom of the staircase as Grandma Daisy was opening the shop for the day. I was more than grateful that I had classes at the college only every other day, so I wouldn't have to teach that morning.

When I reached the main floor, Emerson turned his back on me and walked away. I knew that was part of his payback for tricking him into stay in the shop last night. He had slept on my bed the night before, but I thought that was probably just to make sure I was all right. Now that I was confirmed okay, he could commence reminding me of what a mean cat owner I was.

"Be careful, dear. Are you all right?" Grandma Daisy was at the front of the shop, putting corn kernels into Faulkner's food dish near his perch. Corn was his favorite breakfast.

He swooped down from the tree and began to peck at the corn. He bobbed his head. "Thank you," the crow said.

I frowned. I really was beginning to think that the shop crow knew exactly what was going on. Emerson paced under the large bird, waiting for any piece of corn that Faulkner might drop. He wouldn't eat it but batted it all over the floor. I had found kernels of corn in the oddest places in the shop. I had once even found a kernel in my bed.

"I'm fine. Just moving slow. You went into the river too, and you look right as rain."

My grandmother smiled. "I feel invigorated. Saving you reminded me that my time isn't up just yet."

I blinked at her. "What do you mean?"

She folded her arms over her chest. "Well, my dear, you may have noticed that I have dusted this shop from top to bottom every other day. I'm bored! Ever since you have taken over being the Caretaker, I don't know what to do with myself. I had that role for so long, I'm at loose ends."

"Oh," I said, feeling awful. "I had no idea. I'm sorry that I took it from you. I didn't want it in the first place."

"I know that, Violet. That is why I haven't mentioned my lack of direction to you until now. I knew that you would feel bad about taking the Caretaker duties. However, when the essence wants to pass on the duties to a new Caretaker, there is nothing anyone can do about it."

"I wish I could give them back," I said, thinking of Rainwater. "I really do."

"I know, dear, but there are other things I can do; saving you last night made me realize that. I just have to find my new niche."

"I hope your new niche doesn't include jumping into the Niagara River on a regular basis."

She held her arms aloft. "Who knows! The sky's the limit."

I didn't like the sound of that at all.

There was a loud thud on the sales desk. Grandma Daisy and I both jumped as we turned to face the desk.

A copy of *Little Women* sat on the sales counter.

I glanced at Emerson. He was sitting by the front door, clearly planning his escape. Faulkner was at the top of the tree preening his feathers. Neither of them had dropped the book out of the sky.

The shop's essence had put it there. I went to pick up the book, and it fell open to the chapter detailing the adventures of Amy, the youngest of the March girls, in Europe. I looked up from the book. *Amy.* If I equated her with the Perkins sisters, she would be Adele, the young artist who had wished her sister dead when Belinda refused to pay her studio rent any longer as well as the young sister I'd thought I'd seen walking along the river last night just moments before I was pushed in.

I looked up from my book. "I think I know

where the book wants me to go this time."

"Go, then. I think we will all feel better when this mess with Belinda's murder is settled," Grandma Daisy said. "Just stay away from the river's edge."

I promised I would.

Grandma Daisy held on to a hissing Emerson as I left the shop. The cat was going to be so mad at me for leaving again when I got home later that day. I decided to walk to Adele's studio rather than drive. I thought that walking would work out some of the aches and pains in my body left over from my dip in the river. I was halfway to the bird neighborhood when I realized that walking was a mistake. I was still impossibly sore. It was a great relief when Adele's Cape Cod studio came into view on Sparrow Street.

I climbed the two steps to the studio's front door. I knocked on the door, but just like the first time I had visited Adele, there was no answer. I pushed open the door and peeked inside. "Adele?" I called.

There were no bangs and yells coming from behind the Chinese screen like there had been last time. Instead, I found Adele sitting on the middle of the studio floor cradling Emerson in her arms. I blinked. "How on earth did he get here?"

She looked up and didn't appear the least bit surprised that I was standing in the doorway. "Do you know him?"

"He's my cat."

"Why did he come here?" she asked.

I shook my head. "I don't know."

She scratched Emerson under his white chin, and he began to purr. "He's a nice cat. I was just sitting on the floor, and he walked through the front door just like you did and sat on my lap."

I sat across from her cross-legged on the floor. "And why are you sitting on the floor?"

"Thinking," she said vaguely. "I need to do a lot thinking to know what I will do next now that I don't have Belinda's financial support."

"I saw you down by the river last night. Why were you there?"

She looked down at Emerson, and I thought that she wasn't going to answer. Finally, she said, "I was trying to work up the courage to go and talk to Lacey. I wasn't going to ask her for money," she added quickly. "But after you came by the other day, I realized that she and Michelle are the only family I have in the world now. I should try to make up with them. It's what our mother would have wanted. She would never want us to be so divided like we are. It would break her heart."

"Have you spoken to Lacey or Michelle?"

"No. Last night was going to be my first time, but I chickened out." She wouldn't meet my eyes.

"Did you notice anything unusual while you were by the Riverwalk?" I asked.

"Other than you standing there in the cold?" she asked. "No."

"Did you see anyone else there?"

She shook her head. "Only you."

"Did you see me fall in the river?"

She looked up from the cat on her lap. "You fell into the river? How?" She appeared so genuinely shocked by my statement, I knew that she couldn't be lying.

"Someone pushed me," I said.

"Why would —"

The front door of the studio burst open.

Adele jumped to her feet holding Emerson to her chest. I jumped up too but moved much slower.

Chief David Rainwater and Officer Wheaton stood in the middle of the room. Wheaton had handcuffs in his hands at the ready.

"Adele Perkins, we would like you to come with us to the police station," Rainwater said.

Adele shook her head. "No way."

"If you don't come, you will be arrested." Rainwater's amber eyes were narrowed.

She handed Emerson to me and then held out her wrists. "I'd like to see you try."

Rainwater nodded at his officer. Wheaton didn't hesitate and jumped at the chance to throw handcuffs on someone. He walked over to Adele and slapped cuffs on her wrist. He read her her rights. "You are under arrest for the murder of Belinda Perkins."

Adele pulled her wrists away, but Wheaton was stronger than her and held them fast. "I didn't kill anyone! Violet, tell them I didn't kill anyone!"

I stepped forward. "David —"

Rainwater held up his hand. "Wheaton, take Miss Perkins to the station. I will be following shortly."

Wheaton glared at me before he led Adele out of her studio.

I threw up my hands. "What is going on? Why are you arresting Adele?" Everything had happened so fast that my head was spinning.

"What are you doing here?" Rainwater asked.

"The boo—" I stopped myself because I had almost said that the books had told me to visit Adele that morning. "What are you doing here? How can you arrest Adele for Belinda's murder?"

"We have strong reasons to believe that she is guilty." He pressed his lips into a thin line.

"What are those reasons?" I asked.

He didn't answer.

"But she said that she left the book signing before Belinda died. She couldn't have done it then, and you see how small she is. How could she stab Belinda in the back like that? It doesn't make any sense at all."

Rainwater looked down at me. "She lied, Violet. More people do that than you know."

"But . . ."

"I have a witness," Rainwater cut me off.

"Who?" I asked.

"The mayor."

CHAPTER THIRTY-THREE

I walked home from Adele's studio in a daze with Emerson in my arms. Could Adele really have been the killer? I didn't know why it upset me so much. A little part of me wondered if it was because I wasn't the one who had figured it out. Maybe I had lost my knack for interpreting the shop's essence's clues? That was a scary thought, and it could be dangerous too. If I interpreted what the essence told me incorrectly, I shouldn't be trying to understand it all.

Then again, the essence had told me to go to Adele's studio, and then she had been arrested. Was it telling me that she was the killer too? I thought of all the clues from *Little Women* that the shop had given me. There was the passage about wanting to do something splendid before "I go to my castle in the sky." Jo March had said that she wanted to accomplish something great before she died. I had thought that was about Belinda because of her drive and ambition. It could be, but it could be about the killer too. Perhaps Belinda was keeping someone from reaching their castle. This made me think of Adele. She felt like Belinda had held her back by withholding money from her.

There was the passage about the "many Beths" who suffered in silence. I still believed that was the shop telling me to help Lacey. There was the passage about the white-hot anger in some people that was difficult to quench. I chewed on that one for a moment. Could it be that whoever had killed Belinda had been holding a grudge against her for a long time? I took a breath. Okay, two of the book riddles were solved, or as solved as I could foresee them being.

Regarding the final passage, I had no idea what the shop's essence was telling me. I recited it aloud as I walked, thinking that hearing it would somehow make it clearer. "Unfortunately, we don't have windows in our breasts, and cannot see what goes on in the minds of our friends; better for us that we cannot as a general thing, but now and then it would be such a comfort, such a saving of time and temper."

I walked by the houses in the bird neighborhood that were all fringed with snow and ice. With the exception of a few Cape Cods like Adele's studio, most of the homes in the neighborhood were French inspired, with wrought-iron gates and small balconies that overlooked the street.

My cell phone rang, and I removed it from my coat pocket. Lacey's name was on my screen.

"Violet, I have to go to the police station right now," Lacey said in a panicked voice in my ear.

"You've heard about Adele's arrest?"

"How did you know about it?" she asked.

I took a breath. "I was there at her studio when Wheaton and Chief Rainwater took her in."

"Why would you be at my sister's studio?" Lacey asked.

"I saw her at the river last night before I was pushed in."

"She would never push you in the river," Lacey said, aghast at the very idea.

"I never said I thought she did, but she might have seen something since she was there."

"Why was she there?" Lacey asked.

I stopped in the middle of the sidewalk and shifted Emerson in my arms. The cat didn't fight me. Now that he had gotten out for a little bit of wintertime adventure, he seemed to have forgiven me for penning him in the last couple of days. "She was working up the courage to talk to you," I said.

"She was?" There were tears in Lacey's voice. "She was going to come and see me?"

"Yes," I said.

"That makes me so happy." She took a shuddered breath. "We have to help her. Adele wouldn't have anything to do with it. She's only a child. How could the police chief think such a think about her?"

"Lacey, she's not a child. She's nineteen, and . . ."

"And what?" Lacey wanted to know.

I took a breath. "And she has a motive." I went on to tell her about Adele's studio.

"I cannot believe that you are taking the police's side on this."

"I'm not taking any side. I'm only telling you what I know before you go to the station. You should know what you're facing."

"Do you think that she killed Belinda?"

"I don't know," I said honestly. "I don't think so." I sounded even less convincing when I said that.

Emerson jumped out of my arms and ran down the street in the direction of Charming Books. I didn't have time to chase the cat at the moment. I knew that he knew the way home.

"Well, I know that she didn't," Lacey said in a choked voice. "And I need you to prove it. Please, Violet." She ended the call with a sob.

I stared at my phone for a second. Wondering how I could prove Adele's innocence and wondering if I should. *Little Women* had led me to Adele, and she had been arrested. Maybe that was the way it was supposed to be.

I had to be sure, and the only way to be sure in this case was to go to the last place on earth I wanted to go: the mayor's office.

I ended the call with Lacey, making no promises but telling her I would see what I could do. Then I texted my grandmother as I cut down a side street that would get me to the village hall a little bit faster. I told my grandmother what had happened the best that I could in the text message and said I would be back at the shop within the hour. I hoped that the last part was true.

The village hall was a giant building for a community of Cascade Springs' size. Twenty-some stone steps led up to the front door, which opened into an enormous rotunda where village events were held, including the bicentennial ball last summer.

Unlike city halls in big cities, there were no security lines or metal detectors. The villagers of Cascade Springs were a very trusting bunch. A trust that I thought they needed to reevaluate with the number of murders that occurred in the village.

I had been in the village town hall a number of times, but I had never visited the mayor's office. However, Nathan's office was easy enough to find because there was a directory on the wall telling me to go to the second floor. To my left, there was a set of marble stairs.

I walked up them, and my boots squeaked on the marble. Antique doors lined the right side of the second floor. To my left was an iron railing that overlooked rotunda below. It was a beautiful view of the room that I had never seen before. I could see the giant compass pattern shaped out of marble on the floor and the different hues in the marble columns.

A large part of me was hoping that Nathan wasn't there. It was possible he wouldn't be, since there was so much turmoil over at his family's winery right now. They might need him there. *They* being his mother.

The mayor's office was the third door to my left. I put my hand on the door handle, but it was locked. "Can I help you?" a disembodied voice asked.

I jumped and then I noticed an intercom

on the wall next to the doorframe. The red light was blinking. I pressed the button. "Hello, I would like to meet with the mayor if he's in." I let go of the button.

"Do you have an appointment?" the voice asked.

"No, but you can tell him that Violet Waverly is here to see him."

"Please wait."

I rocked back on my heels and waited. The minutes ticked by, and I considered pressing the button again to ask the voice if she had forgotten about me.

Before I could make up my mind, the door swung inward and a thin elderly woman with a pinched nose and glasses hanging from a chain around her neck stood on the other side with a sweater wrapped around her shoulders.

"I'm Bertie. I'm the mayor's secretary." She looked me up and down. "I thought you would look different."

"Different how?" I asked as sweetly as I could with my teeth being on edge.

She sniffed. "If the mayor has been holding a torch for you all this time, I expected something more."

It was one of those times when no response was the best option.

"You might as well come in. He wants to

see you even though I discouraged him since he has a full schedule today. He is the mayor, and I have to follow his orders." She said this last part grudgingly.

I stepped into the outer office. In front of me was Bertie's desk, which was perfectly neat. There wasn't a paper clip out of place. It was nothing like the office that my grandmother and I kept back in Charming Books, where everything was all helter-skelter. Judging by the desks, Grandma Daisy and Bertie would never be friends.

I wandered over to the giant map of Cascade Springs on the wall. It included Charming Books and all the other places I loved. I reached up as if to touch it.

"Don't touch that!" Bertie snapped. "It's an antique. The oils in your hands will destroy it."

I shoved my hand into the pocket of my coat like I had been burnt.

She gave me a beady look, which reminded me of Faulkner, and walked behind her perfect desk. She lifted her phone. "Mr. Morton, Violet Waverly is here to see you." There was a pause. "Very good." She hung up the phone and smiled at me. "The mayor is just finishing up with his last meeting and will see you now." She narrowed her eyes at me. "Make it short. He has a meeting with the electric company within the hour."

I thanked her, and just before I reached the inner office door, it opened. I jumped back.

Grant Morton stood on the other side of the door holding the knob. "You need to listen to me more often, brother. I'm the one who knows what to do when it comes to business." Grant turned and marched right into me.

"Umph," I said.

Grant squeezed my upper arms. "Violet, I'm surprised to see you here." Still holding me by the arms, he glanced back at his brother. "I didn't know you two lovebirds were back together. Meeting for an early lunch?"

I scowled at Grant. "We're not."

Grant was still holding on to me.

"You can let me go now," I said through gritted teeth.

He gave my arms another squeeze. "I know better than to touch my brother's lady."

I glared at him. I wasn't anyone's lady.

"Grant, go back to the vineyard," Nathan said in an authorial tone. "And tell Mom and Dad what I decided."

"No, thank you. I think it's a terrible idea, and I won't have any part in it. You have their phone numbers. Just because I'm a year younger than you doesn't me that you can order me around. I don't work for you, Nathan."

Nathan pressed his lips together.

"Violet," Grant said. "Lovely to see you as always. Give Sadie my regards."

Fat chance.

"Grant," Nathan said. "We can talk about the rest of this when I get back to the winery tonight."

Grant raised his eyebrows. "You're coming to the old homestead, Mr. Mayor? To what do we owe this visit?"

"Mother asked me to come over for dinner. She said that she wanted us all to discuss some business now that this mess with Belinda has been cleared up."

Grant tensed ever so slightly, but I saw it. "I don't know why they want you involved. I'm the one who is there every day. I can handle the business."

"I'll be the one in charge when they're gone," Nathan said. "It's what our parents want."

"We'll see about that, big brother." He stomped out of the room, nearly knocking me over as he went.

Nathan gave me an apologetic smile after Grant stomped through the outer office door. "I'm sorry that you had to see that, and I'm sorry too that Grant brought up Sadie. I know it's a sore spot between the two of you. Come inside."

I stepped through the doorway, and before he closed it, Nathan said, "Please hold my calls, Bertie."

"Whatever you want, Mr. Mayor." By her tone, Bertie thought holding his calls was a terrible idea.

"Where did you find the dragon?" I asked as I scanned the room. It was very masculine, as I had expected it to be. Sadly, in its long history, Cascade Springs had never had a female mayor.

"Bertie?"

I nodded.

He laughed. "She came with the job. She's been the mayor's secretary for forty years. Not a single mayor has had the nerve to fire her, myself included." He smiled, showing off his perfectly straight and white teeth. "Why don't you take a seat? I'm surprised that you stopped by."

I sat in an armchair in front of a marble fireplace. Nathan took the other chair. The fire was crackling nicely.

"I just came from Adele Perkins' studio," I said, cutting to the chase. "While I was there, Chief Rainwater and one of his officers came and arrested her."

"Oh." He leaned back in his chair and frowned. "I guess I knew that this wasn't a social call, as much as I might wish it to be."

I ignored his comment and went on. "Rainwater said that you were the witness who saw Adele kill Belinda."

Nathan scowled. "The police chief has no right to give up his sources like that. I will have him reprimanded."

I held out my hand. "Please don't. I wasn't going to let it go. He shouldn't get in trouble for telling me this."

"It's unprofessional," Nathan said.

"Please. Do it as a favor to me." The last thing I wanted was for Rainwater to get into trouble because of me.

He frowned.

"Did you see Adele kill her?"

"No," Nathan said. "But I saw her follow Belinda out into the vineyard. A few minutes later you found her dead."

"There could have been someone else out there waiting for Belinda."

"Like who? No one knew she was going to go outside. The only reason that she stomped away was the embarrassing scene with Lacey."

He had a point.

"Maybe someone was already out there and took it as an opportunity."

He shook his head. "You're stretching. The police told me Adele had motive. Her sister was cutting her off after supporting her art. She would have to give up her painting and her studio and get a real job just like everyone else. I would say that that would be a motive to kill for someone who had been coddled her whole life."

"Lacey thinks Adele is innocent."

"Lacey is her sister. Of course she wants to believe that, no matter how strained their relationship is. No one wants to believe that their sibling is capable of terrible things. I don't want to believe anything bad about Grant, but I know my brother is no saint. I have accepted that about him."

"I thought Grant is doing better since leaving the water company."

He wouldn't meet my eyes for a moment. "He is. I just think Lacey shouldn't look at Adele with rose-colored glasses. Her sister was the one who was trying to frame her."

"What do you mean?"

"Violet, she had the letter in her hand when I saw her follow Belinda outside."

"How do you know it was the same letter?"

"The envelope was pink. What are the

odds that it was another pink envelope when that was found with Belinda's body?"

He had a point. Adele had means, motive, and opportunity. I had also seen how volatile Adele could be. How she had destroyed that beautiful painting, and the screaming. It didn't look good for Lacey's youngest sister.

"Look, I know you want to help your friend and I admire your loyalty. You have always been loyal. It's one of you best qualities."

I stopped myself from making a smart comment on his lack of loyalty.

"My brother was here earlier because we rescheduled the frozen grape cutting for tomorrow night. We're inviting everyone back. The grapes need to get off the vines while the temperatures are right, and we need the help to do it. I would love it if you came out."

I stared at him. "You're kidding, right? You know that your mother wouldn't want me there. She told me never to go back to Morton Vineyards."

He frowned. "It doesn't matter what my mother wants. It's my business too, and I'm inviting you." He leaned forward and braced his elbows on his knees. "Do you remember what fun we had when we did that together when we were kids?" He looked me in the eye. "Do you remember our first kiss?"

"Nathan, stop." I held up my hand. "All that is over," I said, feeling happy that I could say that and really mean it. The old feelings were over. All of them.

He stood up. "I miss you, Violet. Not just because I loved you, but I miss you as my friend. Let's start over and just be friends again like when we were young. No pressure of anything else. I won't ask anything more from you."

Being friends sounded nice, but Nathan had spent his career running for office and talking people into what he wanted them to do. There was a reason he was the youngest mayor in the history of Cascade Springs.

"It's important to me that you come. It's an event for the entire village, and it wouldn't be right if you weren't there. Bring Grandma Daisy and Sadie too. Whoever you want."

"I'm not bringing Sadie." There was no question about that.

"Then Grandma Daisy. She loves to gather grapes."

I stood up too. "I'll talk it over with her."

"Thank you, Violet."

I nodded, feeling strangely like I had been tricked in some way, but I didn't know exactly how.

Nathan opened the door and held it for me. Bertie was on the other side with her arms folded across her chest and scowling. "Mr. Mayor, your meeting with the electric company is here. They arrived early," she said, sounding annoyed. "Clearly, no one pays attention to my schedules anymore. They are in the conference room."

"Thank you, Bertie," Nathan said, looking sheepish.

Bertie criticized Nathan for ignoring his calendar for a few minutes more, but I wasn't listening. All I could think about was that everyone in the Cascade Springs wine industry would most likely be at the grape cutting the next night, and if I really believed Adele was innocent or wanted to believe she was innocent, this might be my one chance to do it.

I walked to the outer door and came to a decision. Turning back to Nathan, I said, "Okay. I'll be there. I'll be at the grape cutting."

Nathan grinned. Perhaps he thought I had agreed to attend for reasons other than the murder. I was about to correct him, but instead I fled.

CHAPTER THIRTY-FOUR

As far as stupid decisions I had made in my life, going to Nathan's grape harvesting wasn't even in the top ten. Even so, it remained a stupid idea, and I kicked myself for agreeing to go all the way back to Charming Books.

Le Crepe Jolie was right next door to the village hall. As I reached the sidewalk in front of the town hall, I hesitated. I didn't know if I should go there and tell Lacey what I'd learned. Before I could make my decision, Joel Redding hobbled out of the café on a set of crutches. His guitar case was nowhere to be seen. I guessed it was too hard to manage with a bum ankle.

He scowled at me. "You again."

I frowned. "I was just thinking the same about you. What are you doing in the café?"

"I was just telling Lacey Dupont the good news that she was off the hook as far as the murder goes. She is no longer in danger of being blamed for the crime."

"What did she say?"

"Nothing. She wasn't there."

"She's at the police station with her sister," I said. "I don't think she would have taken your announcement as good news."

"Well, I solved the case, so I will just be leaving this village."

I scowled at him, "You didn't solve the case. I know Nathan was the one who told the police about Adele's possible involvement."

He frowned. "You seem to be well informed about what is going on."

"This is my village. I can't say that I'm sorry to see you leave it."

He smiled a slow smile. "I'm leaving for now, but I have every reason to believe I will be back. There is something about this village that intrigues me. There is something about you that intrigues me."

My mouth felt dry.

"Best of luck to you on your next trip to the natural springs. I hope the weather improves for you so that you don't have to break the ice again with a stone."

He turned and shuffled on his crutches down the sidewalk.

Part of me wanted to follow him and ask him what he meant by that, but a larger part of me didn't want to know. I prayed that he would forget about Cascade Springs, Charming Books, and most of all, me.

Knowing that Lacey wasn't at the café, I shook my head as I walked back to the bookshop. Emerson met me at the door and meowed. I removed my coat, hung it on the coat tree, and picked up the cat. Faulkner didn't so much as fluff his wings when I walked into the room.

Grandma Daisy was ringing a customer out at the sales counter.

"It's time to get back to the work of being a bookseller and put all this supersleuth stuff behind me," I told the cat.

I had to trust that if Adele had been unlawfully arrested, Chief Rainwater would get to the bottom of it. As my grandmother had told me many times, he was a good cop.

Emerson meowed as if in agreement.

Feeling the cat and I were in sync for once, I set him down on the arm of one of the sofas and began picking up the stray books that people had browsed through throughout the day. To my astonishment, every book morphed into a copy of *Little Women.* That was how I knew the police had gotten it wrong and arrested the wrong person for the crime. Adele was innocent.

I sat on the couch with my copies of *Little*

Women and read.

"Violet!" Sadie cried, and ran into Charming Books. As she flew through the front door, it banged against the wall. Faulkner was on his perch and cawed in protest. The big black bird circled the shop, crying, "Off with her head! Off with her head!"

Sadie didn't even seem to notice the stir that she had caused with the bird. "Violet! I need to talk to you right now!"

I blinked at her. I had been immersed in the world of the March sisters. It was dark outside. I had no idea how much time had passed. How long had I been reading? "I'm right here," I said. I was having trouble pulling myself out of the story. There were so many good bits of wisdom to be found in the novel, but I didn't know what any of them had to do with Belinda's murder. In many ways, I felt more confused than ever by the murder.

"There you are, Violet! Didn't you hear me come in?" She was shaking with nervous energy.

"Yes." I closed the volume of *Little Women* and set it on the stack in the middle of the coffee table in front of the sofa. "What's wrong? Are you hurt? You look like you are about to burst."

"That's because I *am* about to burst. Oh,

Violet, I don't know when I have ever been this happy. I needed something happy right now."

"What is it?" I couldn't stand the suspense any longer.

"Look!" She waved her phone in my face. "Look!"

"What am I looking at? I can't see the screen when you are waving the phone back and forth like it's a flag in a Memorial Day parade."

She froze. "Sorry. Look!" She put the phone in my hand.

I read the screen. It was an email addressed to Sadie. "Dear Ms. Cunningham, I am delighted to inform you that I would like to offer you representation to sell your novels. I would like to set up a call with you as soon as possible. I have several editors in New York who are presently looking for a voice just like yours. Please email me back at your earlier convenience."

"Oh my gosh!" I said as the enormity of the email hit me. "You got an offer of representation."

She jumped up and down over and over again. "Yes! I got an offer! From an agent! A real literary agent!" She flopped on the couch next to me. "I think I'm going to die!"

"Don't do that!" I cried. "Not before

you're published. Sadie, this is wonderful news. Have you spoken to the agent yet?"

"Yes, I emailed her back right away, and she called me almost immediately. She told me everything that she liked about the book. She's sending me some notes over to revise before we submit, but she said that I should be on submission in New York by the end of the month." She flopped back onto the couch. "I can't believe this is happening."

"How did you find her?" I asked.

"It is Simon's agent who signed me. He wrote a lovely referral. I mean, he's only read the first ten chapters of my novel, but he said I had an 'endearing voice.' An endearing voice, can you believe that? Have you ever heard anything as sweet as that? I can't believe he would say that about my writing, and he's such a great writer. That piece that he read at the last Red Inkers meeting brought me to tears. I told him so after the meeting, and that's when he asked if he could read my book. I was a little scared at first, since I write romance. I didn't know what he would think of it when he's such a gifted poet, but he said he stayed up all night and read all the chapters that I sent him. It was his idea to write a referral to his agent. I didn't think anything would come of it, but it has!"

I smiled. Sadie was a talented writer, and I could see why Simon would want to read all her work, but I thought it was interest in Sadie that had gotten him to stay up all night and read it more than anything else.

She sat up straight. "I hope the others won't be upset that I have an agent and they don't. Maybe I should pass and wait until the others are ready to submit as well. We can all do it together as a group."

"No." I plopped next to her on the couch and linked my arm with hers. "No, Sadie, for far too long you have put other people's needs above yours. Yes, Simon might have written the referral, but you wrote the book. Agents get referrals every day. It's your writing that caught the agent's eye."

"I might get published," she whispered. "It's hard to even fathom such a dream come true."

"There is no *if* about it, Sadie. You will get published. I'm so happy for and proud of you."

She leaned over and gave me a huge hug. "Violet, what's your greatest dream? What is it that you want most in the world? I have wanted this dream for so long. I can't believe that it might actually come true."

I stared at her for a moment. "I suppose it's finishing my PhD. I've been working at it for so long now that it feels less like a dream and more like work," I admitted.

"Is there anything else that you want?"

I glanced at the birch tree. I had another dream hidden in the most secret place in my heart, but I knew the fate of the Waverly women and knew that it couldn't possibly come true. So why say it and have my heart be broken yet again?

CHAPTER THIRTY-FIVE

The next day I taught my classes at the community college, and in every spare moment I had, I read *Little Women.* I kept hoping that something about the book would make the present situation clear to me, that it would lead me to the killer if Adele really was innocent. I believed that she was, but I couldn't prove it.

After my second class, I scrolled through my contacts for Simon Chase's phone number. I had all the Red Inkers' numbers in my phone in case there was some reason that the meeting had to be moved or postponed because of another event at the shop.

I found Simon's number and called.

"Goldman and Goldman Insurance, this is Simon Chase. How may I help you?"

I was taken aback because the voice on the line sounded so confident and self-assured. It didn't sound anything like the timid Simon Chase who had stumbled into

Charming Books.

"Hi, Simon, this is Violet Waverly from Charming Books."

"Violet," he said, clearly surprised that I was calling him at work. "How are you? Can I do anything for you?"

"You already have for Sadie. I wanted to call you and tell you thank you for writing the referral for her. She is beyond thrilled."

"I was happy to do it," he said, sounding more relaxed again. "She is a great writer and deserves a chance."

"I couldn't agree more." I paused. "That wasn't the only reason that I called."

"Oh, what other reason do you have?"

"It's about Belinda Perkins."

"Like I told you before, I can't tell you anything about any of my clients."

"I know, but say hypothetically . . ."

He didn't say anything in response.

"Say hypothetically someone other than the person who opened the life insurance policy out on Belinda was charged with the murder. Would the person who purchased the policy still get the money?"

There was a long moment of quiet, and I didn't think he would answer my question. Just when I was about to ask my question in another way, he said, "Yes. If the person who bought the policy had nothing to do with the wrongful death, that person would still get their money."

"Thank you." I said I would see him at the next Red Inkers meeting, and I ended the call.

Sebastian would come out on top from Belinda's death after all. I frowned. That didn't sit well with me.

After classes, I headed to Charming Books. My grandmother met me at the door. "Violet, I'm so glad you are here. I have to run out to the store. We're all out of sugar, and I have to make a cake for the Red Inkers meeting tomorrow. Did you hear Sadie's news?"

I smiled. "Yep."

She clapped her hands. "I can't believe we will have a published author right across the street from us. We will have to throw her launch party here and do it up right."

I grinned at my grandmother. "I know Sadie would like that just as soon as the book sells."

"Oh, it will sell. I've read it, and it's wonderful. If there is one thing that I know, it's books."

"I think you're right." I grinned from ear to ear.

"I'll be quick," she said, and with that she was out the door. I watched her hurry down the sidewalk in the direction of the small market in Cascade Springs. She passed Lacey Dupont as she went.

I waited for Lacey as she walked up to the Charming Books gate and came through it. In her hand she held a white bakery box that I was sure was full of all kinds of Adrien's delectable treats. I hadn't eaten anything since an orange at breakfast, so my mouth watered at the sight of the box.

· Sadie reached the front door of the shop and held the box out to me. "A peace offering."

I gladly took the box and asked, "A peace offering for what?"

"To say I'm sorry. I'm sorry how I treated you yesterday when Adele was arrested."

"Lacey, there is no need to apologize. You had every reason to be upset."

"Still, I feel horrible to have been taking it out on you when you were only trying to help."

I smiled. "How is Adele?"

"She all right. She's out on bail. Adrien is such a dear that he fronted the money to get her out."

Not for the first time, I thought what a perfect husband Adrien was. He was handsome, he could cook, and he could bail you out of jail in a pinch.

"Did you have any luck finding out who really killed Belinda?" she asked.

The books came to mind. "I'm afraid not."

She fiddled with the silver barrette in her hair. "I was afraid of that. Rainwater was very kind and told me about everything that was stacked against Adele. He said that we were lucky to get her out on bail at all. Do you want to know the worst part?"

"What is it?" I asked.

"Part of me is happy this happened. Not that Adele was arrested and certainly not that Belinda was murdered. I'm happy that some good might come out of this because Adele called me for help, Violet. It was the first time she has reached out to me in two years. We talked, and I think if we work together at it, we can rebuild our broken family. Maybe even Michelle can be close to us again. I'm hopeful for the very first time."

"I want that for you too, Lacey."

She pursed her lips. "I heard that the Mortons were going to have their grape cutting tonight." She frowned. "It's just like them to go on like nothing happened."

"I know," I said. "Nathan invited me to go."

"Will you?"

"Something doesn't sit well with me about

that place." I frowned. "I just don't think everything with the murder is resolved. I know the Mortons, the police, and maybe the rest of the village would like to believe that, so life can go back to normal."

"You think Adele is innocent, don't you?" she asked.

"I do, but not of everything. There's something you should know."

"What?" She chewed on her lower lip.

"Adele was out in the vineyard that night. Nathan saw her follow Belinda into the vineyard."

"That doesn't mean she killed anyone."

"Of course it doesn't, but I do think the two of them met."

"Why?"

"Because Adele had your letter with her. The same letter that was found with Belinda's body."

"What are you saying?"

"The police think Adele murdered Belinda and tried to frame you."

She shook her head. "I don't believe it. I can't believe it."

"I don't believe she killed Belinda either, but it is some very strong evidence. You can see why the police arrested her. So, you asked if I was going to the grape cutting, and my answer is yes. Maybe by going I can find some answers."

She hugged me. "Thank you, Violet. This might be the only way to bring my family back together."

No pressure, I thought.

CHAPTER THIRTY-SIX

"So, is this a sting?" Grandma Daisy asked as I thoroughly searched the car for any sign of Emerson. I wasn't going to have another stowaway situation with the little tuxedo cat.

I pulled my head out from under the front passenger's seat. "A sting?" I straightened up and climbed into the car.

"Well, yes," my grandmother said. "We're going to the grape cutting to snoop, are we not? I think that's what the coppers call a sting."

"The coppers? Does Chief Rainwater know that you call the police coppers?"

She thought about this for a moment. "Not that I know of, but I doubt he'd be surprised." She shut the passenger side door.

As I walked around to my side of the car, I shook my head and wondered how smart it was to bring Grandma Daisy as my backup on this mission to clear Adele's name. Unfortunately, she was the best that I had.

As we drove to Morton Vineyards, I coached my grandmother. "Please don't be too obvious. Mrs. Morton will be less than thrilled when she sees that we're there. The less attention that we draw to ourselves, the better. Don't make it look like we're up to something."

"Violet, we are always up to something."

She had a point.

Just like on the night of the book signing, there was a long line of cars in the Mortons' driveway waiting to park. Cutting the frozen grapes at Morton vineyards at midnight was a big event for the village. Even with what had happened earlier in the week, the villagers had still come out.

Grandma Daisy shook her head. "It's amazing that all these people can come back here like nothing happened, like Belinda hadn't been murdered here."

"We're here too," I said as the car inched up the driveway.

"True. But we're on a sting."

"Right," I said with resignation.

Grandma Daisy and I weren't the help this evening, so we went through the front door with all the other guests. Nathan and his parents were at the front door and greeted guests as they entered the tasting room.

Mrs. Morton's eye narrowed as we stepped through the door. "What are you doing here?"

"Mother," Nathan said in measured tones. "Violet and Grandma Daisy are my friends, and I invited them."

Mrs. Morton scowled at her son. "When will you finally be able to forget the Waverlys?"

"Camille," Grandma Daisy said with fake friendliness. "It's always so nice to see you. You always give us the warmest welcome."

I stopped myself from rolling my eyes. Grandma Daisy was laying it on a little thick.

Mrs. Morton's jaw twitched.

Mr. Morton held out his hand to my grandmother. "We appreciate all the help we can get with bringing in the grapes tonight. Isn't that right, Camille?"

"Yes, dear," she said through clenched teeth. Her tone clearly said, "We'll talk about this later."

Nathan smiled as if everything was perfectly fine. It must have been a trick that he had mastered as mayor. Nathan really was a good politician. "You arrived right on time. We're going to do a little introduction about cutting the grapes, and then we will go out. It's almost midnight now. With this many people, we should have all the grapes brought in by two."

Grandma Daisy looped her arm through mine as we walked around the room. "See any suspicious characters?"

I removed my arm from her grasp. "Grandma, let's not draw too much attention to the fact we are scoping everyone out."

"Good point," she said. "We should split up to cover more ground." She disappeared into the crowd before I could argue.

That wasn't going to be a problem. Grandma Daisy loose at Morton Vineyards thinking she was part of an undercover op. That wasn't going to be any problem at all.

I had almost started to go after her when another person caught my eye. Wine critic Jake Zule stood in the corner of the room with a pen and notebook in his hand.

I walked over to him. "Are you writing a piece on the Mortons?"

Jake jumped and dropped his pen.

I picked up the pen and handed it to him. "Sorry if I scared you."

He forced a laugh. "I was just concentrating too hard. I want to capture every detail about this for my article. I have never been a part of a frozen grape harvest before, and I think that it will add a lot to my piece to have firsthand experience."

"Is this the same article that you were working on when you visited Charming Books?"

"No, I already turned that one in. The editor was so pleased with it. He asked what else I had, and I suggested a feature on the frozen grape harvest. So here I am. If you will excuse me," he said. "I see someone I need to speak to." He walked away before I could say another word.

"I wish I could say I was surprised to see you here, but then we'd both know I'd be lying," Rainwater said.

I spun around and found the police chief standing against the wall in civilian clothes. There was humor in his amber eyes.

The butterflies kicked up in my stomach. "I'm not that surprised that you're here either." I smiled, so happy to see him.

"I already spoke to Daisy. She mentioned something about a sting that was going down. Should I be worried about that?" He pushed himself off the wall.

I shook my head. "I wouldn't be. It takes too much energy to worry about things out of your control, and no one can control my grandmother."

He laughed. "Why are you here tonight? Why do I think it's for the same reason that I am?"

"Nathan invited Grandma Daisy and me, yes, but I think we are both here for the same reason because of the murder. Do you think something will happen tonight?" I asked.

"I'm here to make sure nothing happens."

"Me too."

He grinned. "Rarely does nothing happen when you and Daisy are around, which makes me extra glad that I came."

"We really appreciate you all coming out to cut the last of the grapes!" Grant said, interrupting us. The younger of the Morton sons stood on a chair in the middle of the room. "It's been a rough week for our family, but we are so grateful to have so many friends and family to help with gathering the grapes. Together we will make short work of it. There is a table just behind me with knives and clippers. You can use either. Let's have some fun!"

The audience clapped. I searched the faces for Nathan but didn't see him. I turned to say something to Rainwater, but the police chief was gone.

I frowned and followed the line of the people picking up tools to cut grapes. When

I reached the table, I selected a pair of clippers instead of the curved knife. I couldn't use it after seeing one sticking out of Belinda's back.

Grant smiled at me. "Clippers. Good choice."

I nodded and stepped away from the table so the next person could make their selection. My goal for the night was to avoid Grant as much as possible.

I filed out of the winery with the other grape harvesters. I still didn't know where my grandmother was. The longer I was separated from her, the more worried I became. I wasn't sure how far Grandma Daisy was going to take the sting idea.

I stood in a row of grapes. There was a plastic bin every few feet to put the grapes into, and strings of bare bulb lights hung over each row so we could see what we were doing. I started to cut and put my grapes into the container.

I worked for a few minutes until the woman next to me groaned, and I looked at her.

She smiled. "My clippers broke. They must be an old pair. I need to go back for another."

"Here, take mine. I'll go find another pair." I handed her the clippers.

"Are you sure?"

I nodded.

She thanked me, and I walked back to the big house. As I did, I passed Grant and Jake Zule standing close together. This was the second time I had seen the two men talking. The last time had been at the winemakers' guild meeting. I ducked behind the next row of grapes and listened.

"You told me that this feature would be about my vineyard, and now you are telling me it's not," Grant said.

"I'm sorry. I just checked my email and my editor wants a broader piece about ice wine in general. He doesn't want it to be about any one place. I will still paint Morton Vineyards in a favorable light, but it will be a very small mention."

"That's not going to work. You promised me a story about my vineyard, highlighting what I do for it. Not my parents, not my brother." Grant's voice was hard.

"That's not what the editor wants. I have to write what he wants and be honest."

"Was taking the money that I gave you for a good review honest?"

I shivered as I remembered another passage from *Little Women* that I had read. The passage I'd thought Emerson had accidentally pointed to when he knocked the book off the bookcase. " 'Money is a needful and precious thing, — and, when well used, a noble thing, — but I never want you to think it is the first or only prize to strive for.' "

The murder was about money. That had been right all this time.

Jake said something I couldn't hear.

"I'm not taking the money back," Grant said. "That's my ticket to control you. I'm sure your editor would love to hear about you taking bribes."

"You wouldn't do that," Jake said. "You would be ruined."

"No, I wouldn't. I'm a Morton. I can get away with anything."

I shivered.

"I can't do as you ask," Jake said in a strained voice. "I'm sorry."

There was a scuffling sound, and I almost got up to see what was happening.

"Let go of me!" Jake said.

A moment later, Jake ran by my row of grapes back to the main house. I shivered as I crouched there in the cold. I had to find Rainwater and tell him what I'd learned. If Grant was willing to bribe Jake, what else would he do for a good review? Would he take it as far as murder? In that moment, all the clues that the books had been pointing me to solidified. I thought about the quotes the shop's essence had made me read, the ones about doing "something splendid before I go into my castle, something heroic or wonderful that won't be forgotten after I'm dead." All that time I had thought that had been about Belinda, but I had been wrong. The shop wasn't directing me to Belinda the victim, but to Grant the killer. Grant had always lived in Nathan's shadow, and he had wanted to do something great to prove himself. He had tried the fraud scam last summer, and when that didn't work, he had thrown himself into the vineyard, setting up the national retail deal. Even so, his parents had deferred to Nathan on decisions about the vineyard. That had to have made Grant angry, angry enough to kill.

A strong hand wrapped around my upper arm, yanking me up from the ground, and another hand covered my mouth. "Let's go for a walk, Violet," Grant whispered in my ear.

CHAPTER THIRTY-SEVEN

I gagged at Grant's hand over my mouth. It tasted like salt. He forced me to walk into the deepest part of the vineyard, away from the ice wine grapes to the summer vines where no one would be.

"Settle down, Violet," Grant whispered in my ear. I could feel his hot breath on my neck.

I felt the point of a knife in my back. I knew it was the same sort of knife that had killed Belinda.

"I'm going to move my hand from your mouth, but if you scream, I will cut you, and if you try to run away, I also have a gun. I will shoot you in the back. Understand?"

I nodded.

"Good girl." Grant removed his hand.

My mouth was dry. "Grant, you can't kill me. There are all these people here. You will never get away with it."

He laughed. "I've killed before in a crowd and wasn't caught."

My blood ran cold. I had been right; he had killed Belinda. I had to get away from him, but the knife was still pressed against my back. I didn't take the time to think or be afraid. I donkey-kicked him in the shin as hard as I could.

Grant yowled in pain and loosened his grip enough for me to wrench my body away from him. As I ran away, he sliced at me and cut a hole in the back of my coat.

"You can't get away," he yelled after me.

Yes, I could. I knew I could. Grant knew the vineyard, but what he maybe didn't remember was that I knew it too. Not much had changed at Morton Vineyards since I was a teenager, and I was going to use that to my advantage. I thought that I could run through the vineyard and around to the big house.

The soles of my boots slipped on the icy ground. Even in snow boots, I couldn't get any traction. I realized that it was fear that was holding me back. The shocking part was that it was fear of a man I had known all my life. I had grown up with Grant Morton. When we were younger, I had even considered him a friend. I had never thought that one day he would try to kill me. He was

Nathan's younger brother. A boy I had played hide-and-seek with as a child. A man I was playing a dangerous game of hide-and-seek with now.

I had to run along the long rows of vines. I couldn't break though the rows. There was netting over all the vines and frozen grapes to keep the wildlife from eating them before they could be harvested for ice wine.

I came around the side of the last row before I could see the house. Grant had pulled me so far away from it. The lights of the winery were so inviting. I ran so fast, I didn't realize that someone was in front of me until I collided with him.

Nathan grabbed me by both of my arms. "Violet, what's going on? Why are you running?"

Grant ran up behind us. He was panting.

"Nathan, we have to find Rainwater. Grant killed Belinda and tried to kill me too."

Grant laughed. "She's crazy. Are you going to believe her or your own brother?"

"Did you kill Belinda, Grant?" Nathan asked in a low voice.

"So what if I did? I did the world a favor. She was a horrible woman," Grant snapped.

My breath caught. I couldn't believe that he'd confessed.

"How could you?" Nathan asked. "Did you even think about the winery or our parents?"

I blinked. Why were the winery and their parents the most important things to consider when taking a woman's life? I would have thought that a woman's life would be the only consideration. I tried to get away from Nathan, but he held me fast.

"Nathan, please let me go," I said.

He ignored me. "How could you, Grant? You've ruined everything that our family has built."

"I did it for you, for our family. I heard what she was going to write about the family wine. It was a horrible review! It would ruin us just as we were about to sign that big retail deal and go nationwide. A poor word from Belinda Perkins would have ruined everything. I — we — had been working too long and too hard to let this ruin us. She called our ice wine barely tolerable over sweetened grape juice. After everything that Mom had done to bring her back to the village and set up that book signing for her. I couldn't let her ruin us."

"Grant, you can't kill someone if they are going to write a bad review," Nathan said in a low voice.

"I did it for the family."

"You did it to save your deal."

Grant's face clouded over. "That deal is what is going to keep the vineyard afloat. You are no help at all while you spend all your time playing mayor, and when you're not doing that, you're chasing after Violet." He laughed. "Don't you see, big brother, she didn't pick you. Everyone knows it's Rainwater she wants."

Nathan looked stricken by his brother's words.

Nathan wouldn't let go of me. Why wouldn't he let go? "Nathan, let me go," I said.

He held me tighter and glared at his brother. "Violet and I are meant to be together. Everything works out for our family in the end, or it would have if you hadn't ruined everything."

"I haven't ruined it yet. We can pretend none of this happened, can't we Nathan, just like my other schemes over the years?"

"I'm tired of cleaning up your messes," Nathan snapped.

"But you will still do it, won't you? A Morton can't be embarrassed. Isn't that what we have been trained to believe?"

I had had it. I couldn't listen to this anymore. I kicked Nathan in the shin just like I had his brother and wrenched my body away from him. "I'm calling the police." I turned to run away from them back to the safety of the winery, to my grandmother and to Rainwater.

"Wait!" Nathan cried. "Don't call the police just yet. We have to decide what to do."

I turned back around and stared at Nathan. "Decide what to do? We know what we have to do. Grant killed Belinda. We have to tell the police. Adele Perkins has been wrongfully accused."

"Nathan," Grant said in a soothing voice. "You don't want to do that. You know what this would do to our parents. Do you want to be the one that puts them through this?"

"Nathan isn't putting them through anything," I snapped. "It's you."

"I saved the winery!" he shouted loud enough that I hoped someone cutting grapes nearby would hear. "I saved the entire family. They should be thanking me for what I did, not the other way around."

It was in that moment that I realized Grant was delusional. There wasn't anything that anyone could say that would convince him that he wasn't within his rights to kill someone else for family honor and family business, but Nathan, Nathan should know better. I looked at the man who was the boy

403

that I had once loved. Nathan's face was pale, and his eyes darted in all directions as if they couldn't focus on one point.

"Nathan, you can't seriously be thinking of letting him go," I whispered.

"It will kill our parents if he goes to prison. It's better if he just leaves. Will you leave, Grant?"

"Sure, big brother, whatever you want."

"What about Adele?" I asked. "He framed her. She's in jail because of Grant right now, and she didn't do anything wrong."

"If your beloved Chief Rainwater is any good, he will figure out that she was framed and let her go," Grant said. "Either way, by the time he figures it out, I will be long gone."

I remembered being arrested and being accused of a murder I had never committed. It had been the most terrifying and humiliating experience of my life. I very well imagined what Adele was going through, and she had done nothing to deserve that. It had happened to me because of the Mortons, and it was happening to her because of the same family. I couldn't allow it.

"Violet, just let him go," Nathan said in a hollow voice. "He can start a new life somewhere else."

I stared at Nathan. I supposed that for all

those years, I had blamed Nathan's parents for his betrayal twelve years ago more than I had blamed Nathan. I had always believed that any big decision as to how to deal with the bad press after Colleen's tragic death had come from the elder Mortons. When I returned to the village last summer, Nathan had asked me to forgive him, and I had because, again, I had thought most of the hurt was because of his parents. Maybe it had been then, but at this moment when Adele Perkins was accused and Grant Morton was the one who had killed Belinda, it wasn't the elder Mortons creating the cover-up. This moment, when Nathan wanted to let his brother go and allow another person go to prison for the crime, was Nathan all grown up, standing on his own two feet and making the wrong choice.

"I can't do that," I said quietly. I wasn't even sure that he could hear me. I turned to go. "You've disappointed me, Nathan."

Grant laughed. "The problem with you, Violet, and people like you, you think when push comes to shove, people will do the right thing, but that just isn't true. When push comes to shove, people will look out for themselves. Nathan is doing what he has to do."

"Vi?" Nathan pleaded.

405

Against my better judgment, I turned back to look at him. I stared at his dark-brown eyes, eyes that I had once found comfort in during the darkest time in my life when my mother died. "I'm leaving, Nathan, and I'm going to find Rainwater. That's all there is to it."

I turned and walked away, and there was a crack in the still air. Just as the sound came, I felt myself thrown to the ground. Nathan landed on top of me.

I groaned and pushed Nathan away. It was then that I realized that he had been shot. Grant had not been lying about the gun.

Grant dropped the gun on the frozen ground and removed his winter coat, balled it up, and pressed down hard on the bullet wound in Nathan's side.

"Nathan! Nathan! I'm so sorry. You can't die." Grant pressed his cheek against Nathan's chest. "Brother, I'm sorry. I'm so sorry."

Gently, I picked up the gun. Grant didn't seem to notice, and I didn't bring it to his attention. My hands shook as I put the gun in the pocket of my coat, praying that the safety was on. I removed my phone from the opposite pocket and made the call that I should have made the moment the book's clues came to light in my mind.

As I made my call to Rainwater, I saw Grant cry over his brother. Theirs had always been an intense rivalry. Their parents had pitted them in competition against each other their entire lives. At least I knew now that the Morton boys, despite everything, loved each other, and that was something I hadn't known before.

EPILOGUE

A January thaw was a welcome relief at the end of the month. It was a brief respite from what had been a grueling winter so far. For me, the temperature hadn't been as hard as dealing with my own past and of course the murder. I needed time to breathe and think. Two things I rarely allowed myself to do.

As I opened the front door to Charming Books that morning, it seemed the entire village had a case of spring fever. Villagers were out walking their dogs and calling to neighbors. We all knew that winter wasn't done with us yet, and we were enjoying this momentary break. And this chance to gossip. There was plenty to gossip about. Grant Morton was in prison. Nathan was in the hospital recovering from a bullet wound. He had also resigned from the office of mayor, saying that he wanted to spend more time with his family and help with their business. Even after everything that had happened, Nathan's loyalty was to his parents.

I thought of a quote the shop's essence had showed me from *Little Women.* "Some people seemed to get all sunshine, and some all shadow . . ." I had mistakenly thought that since *Little Women* was a novel about four sisters, the quotes had been about the four Perkins sisters, but I had been wrong all along. The shop's essence hadn't wanted me to focus on four sisters but on two brothers. Nathan was the brother always in the sunshine and Grant was the brother always in shadow.

I hoped for Nathan's sake that he could put their lives back together, but it would be without me. I had spent too much time worrying over Nathan and being hurt by the Mortons. I'd let it go.

Emerson wove around my feet and walked out onto the front porch. He leaped onto the railing and walked back and forth across it like a tiger prowling his cage.

I thought it was best if everyone in Charming Books got a little fresh air. I went back into the shop and retrieved Faulkner's perch. He cawed angrily when I moved it outside.

I shook my head at him. "You need to get out more. It'll be good for you."

He flapped his wings and a moment later flew through the shop's open front door and landed on the perch I had brought outside. He fluffed his wings. He was twice the size he normally was. He buried his beak under his right wing. I shook my head. "You know, if Grandma Daisy hadn't adopted you when you were a little chick, you would be living out here all the time, including the coldest part of winter."

Faulkner removed his beak from under his wing. "I'm freezing!" He ducked his beak back down into his wing.

I squinted at him. Not for the first time, I thought that maybe the crow understood what I was saying to him. I had the same suspicions of Emerson. They certainly were peculiar animals, the pair of them.

"I'm impressed that you can get Faulkner to do anything," Lacey said as she and Adrien came up the walk to the shop. Adrien carried a huge bakery box, big enough for a full sheet cake.

I walked down into the yard. Grass peeked out from under the snow now. "It's not often you both come for a visit," I said.

"We decided to take a few hours off to spend together. Danielle can handle the café for a little while," she said.

"You look happy, Lacey."

"I am. Adele, Michelle, and I are having dinner together tonight. I feel like we can mend what is broken. Thanks to you."

I shook my head. "No thanks to me."

Lacey shook her head as if we were agreeing to disagree on this point. Adrien handed me the box. It was very heavy. "What's in here?"

"I have all of your and Daisy's favorites in there," Adrien said.

"We will love them. We will also have to exercise more if we are going to eat them all. Good thing the best way to get around the village is by foot."

Lacey grabbed her husband's large hand in her much smaller one. "Let's go, honey. Our time away from the café will be brief, and we have to make the most of it."

I waved to them as they left.

Grandma Daisy came down the sidewalk with a spring in her step. "It's good to see all of you outside getting some fresh air," she called to them as she opened the gate.

I stood on the porch and waited for her. I cocked my head. When she climbed up the steps, I asked, "Why are you so chipper?"

"You may know that there is an opening at the mayor's office." She grinned from ear to ear.

"I do," I said slowly.

"Well, with you taking over being Caretaker here and doing so much around the shop, I need something else to do. I can't float around the shop and idly dust all day."

"Oh-kay."

"So, I have thrown my hat in the ring to run for mayor."

"You what?" I yelped.

"And I'm running uncontested, so you are looking at the next mayor of Cascade Springs!" Her eyes twinkled.

"Her honor," Faulkner squawked, and Emerson put his paws on my grandmother's leg.

She scratched the tuxie between the ears. "Won't David be thrilled to work with me?"

"He will," I said with a laugh. "And he's already thrilled about something else."

"What?" she asked.

I smiled as Chief David Rainwater's departmental SUV pulled up in front of Charming Books. The police chief climbed out of the car and smiled at me as he walked toward the bookshop.

"You made the right choice, my dear, just like I knew you would." Grandma Daisy hugged me. "I see new beginnings on the horizon for us both."

ACKNOWLEDGMENTS

A very special thank you to my readers. Without you, *Murders and Metaphors* would never have happened. Your love for the Magical Bookshop Mystery series was so clear that it was able to continue in a new home. Violet, Rainwater, Grandma Daisy, Emerson, Faulkner, and I will be forever grateful to you for that.

Also, a very special thank you goes out to Crooked Lane Books — especially my editor, Anne Brewer — for giving Violet and the Magical Bookshop that new home.

As always, none of my novels would be possible without my superstar agent Nicole Resciniti. Nicole knew I loved these stories the most and fought to find them a new home. Thank you, my friend.

I also thank my family — Andy, Nicole, Isabella, and Andrew — for their love and support. And to my friends David and Mariellyn, thank you for listening to me work out all the plot points for this complicated story.

This novel owes a great debt to Louisa May Alcott. In researching her life and *Little Woman* for *Murders and Metaphors,* I was blown away by the visionary individual and writer she was. She lived and wrote on her own terms, but always put her family first. She was an incredible woman and writer and has my utmost respect.

Finally, to my Heavenly Father, thank you for letting me live my dream. There is nothing quite as magical to me as story. Thank you for letting me tell them time and again.

ABOUT THE AUTHOR

Amanda Flower, a *USA Today* bestselling and Agatha Award–winning mystery author, started her writing career in elementary school when she read a story she wrote to her sixth-grade class and had the class in stitches with her description of being stuck on the top of a Ferris wheel. She knew at that moment she'd found her calling of making people laugh with her words. She also writes mysteries as *USA Today* bestselling author Isabella Alan. In addition to being an author, Amanda is a librarian in Northeast Ohio. This is her third Magical Bookshop mystery.

The employees of Thorndike Press hope you have enjoyed this Large Print book. All our Thorndike, Wheeler, and Kennebec Large Print titles are designed for easy reading, and all our books are made to last. Other Thorndike Press Large Print books are available at your library, through selected bookstores, or directly from us.

For information about titles, please call:
  (800) 223-1244

or visit our website at:
  gale.com/thorndike

To share your comments, please write:
  Publisher
  Thorndike Press
  10 Water St., Suite 310
  Waterville, ME 04901